Flora's Glory

Also by VANESSA HANNAM

A Rose in Winter
Division Belle
Change of Key
The Hostage Prince

Flora's Glory

VANESSA HANNAM

To my dear friends
Heather and Dominic
from

Vanessa with love
(Nos Late)! xxx !

QUARTET BOOKS

First published in 2012 by
Quartet Books Limited
A member of the Namara Group
27 Goodge Street, London W1T 2LD

A catalogue record for this book
is available from the British Library

ISBN   978 0 70437283 2

Typeset by Antony Gray
Printed and bound in Great Britain by
T J International Ltd, Padstow, Cornwall

In memory of Shirley Eskapa.

Acknowledgements

With deepest thanks to a wonderful and sensitive agent and editor Elspeth Sinclair whose friendship and support turn dreams into reality and to Nicola Beauman for bringing me to her, and to Naim Attallah who makes things happen, together with his incredible team at Quartet.

But as any writer knows, an understanding family is essential and mine have been and always are my greatest inspiration. And special appreciation to my husband John Hannam.

Nothing can happen to any man that nature has not fitted him to endure.

MARCUS AURELIUS

PROLOGUE

St James's Palace, June 10th, 1688

To be seen, or not to be seen, posed no dilemma for Sarah Cooke. As a lowly servant she was not seen or even heard. She felt rising anger as she looked at the young, beautiful Queen of England, exposed, in the agony of giving birth, to the prying eyes of no less than thirty men, all members of the so-called Privy Council, and at least twenty-two of the court ladies who were just there for the spectacle, their expressions suggesting that it was nothing more than a cheap entertainment. Even that number did not include the more lowly midwives' assistants, pages, priests and assorted servants.

Sarah ruminated that no village woman would be expected to expose herself at such an intimate time. Even the farmyard animals she had tended as a child would seek and receive seclusion. Dogs and cats crept away to secret corners to produce their young.

Sarah was just another anonymous pair of hands who must pour the hot water into the porcelain bowl to cleanse Her Majesty in her most private place; she must be there when the baby emerged to hold the linen receiving blanket and take the after birth when the midwife had inspected it and parade it around the room on a silver tray to prove the authenticity of the delivery. Later she would have the more pleasurable task of assisting with the restoration of order; only then could the Queen's modesty be regained.

Sarah felt overcome by nausea as she imagined the indignity to which this elegant, fastidious woman was forced to submit herself and she vowed that if the day ever came when she herself became a mother even her husband would not see that private place which Eve revealed in all her wickedness: God's punishment had been to condemn all women to the travail of birth.

But for the moment that was a long way off, and sadly the poor young Queen was not among friends. She had already been criticised for choosing to have her baby at St James's Palace instead of the unhygienic and poky apartments at Whitehall where workman were still in residence in clouds of dust and noise. It was the Queen's choice and the first signs of the impending birth had precipitated the journey across the Park in her sedan chair the previous night, but the move had left the Queen chilled and anxious. Angry and hostile demonstrators could now be heard protesting at the King's arrest of the Protestant bishops. But at least the poor Queen had one true friend. Mrs Dawson was the Protestant bedchamber woman who had been present at the birth of all the King's children. She had been in church when she heard of the Queen's arrival at St James and hurried to the scene. She had found the Queen cold and disorientated, attended by Pellegrino Turini, her only Italian servant, and an anxious midwife Judith Wilkes who appeared to be unable to take command.

Mrs Dawson immediately took charge of the situation, snapping her fingers at the maidservants and demanding that the bed be properly aired and that Her Majesty be made comfortable and, prophetically, sending for a warming pan. Sarah had received the instruction and in turn commanded one of the hefty pages to get the pan at once. At first he had refused, saying it was not his job, and received a smart cuff on the ear from Pellegrino. The boy had returned just as the Queen's pains began to take hold of her.

The heat from the burning coals was so intense that Sarah had to give instructions to let them cool, after which she wrapped the pan in a woollen cloth and the Queen gratefully welcomed the comforting warmth between the agonies of her pains. Now two hours had passed and the Queen began to cry out. The throng of gaping jostling people pressed forward and Sarah and the other attendants were nearly pushed into the bed.

'Stand back,' commanded Judith the midwife as she began to do what was necessary to help the Queen.

'We must have air. Has none of you any decency?' added Mrs Dawson. Sarah resolutely stood her ground, ready to perform her duties, her heart beating furiously. Unbeknownst to her, Sarah was being closely observed by one of the gentleman officials, Lord Thomas Amalie. He had reluctantly complied with the order to attend the birth, as a Catholic with a reputation for a more compromising view than the divisive didacticism of most of James's advisors and henchmen. He would be a voice of authority and reason. Lord Thomas had realistically concluded that the contentious issue of the next Catholic heir to the throne was rife with controversy; he felt desperately sorry for the young Queen, knowing full well that spurious rumours were being circulated about the authenticity of her pregnancy. He refused to join the prying eyes of the attendant throng but instead watched the face of the young servant most carefully.

He watched as the young woman methodically went about her duties. She was obviously devoted to the young Queen and concern was etched on her face at her mistress's sufferings as she cried out, 'Oh you kill me; let me die.' Lord Thomas knew that such emotion could not be feigned and as the Queen cried out in her travail he saw a tear drop onto the bib of the girl's starched apron. He reflected that the girl was only a few years older than his own beloved daughter who would have been appalled by the event.

Suddenly, after what to him had seemed an interminable time, which he later learned was only two hours, the birth was imminent and the girl leaned forward with the blanket on which the screaming infant was roughly held aloft for all to see. The cry went round, 'A boy. God save the Prince of Wales.' Was it just his imagination or did the cry lack the customary joy at the birth of the King's son, Lord Thomas wondered.

Within minutes the midwife produced the afterbirth and after examining it carefully put it on the silver platter, handing it to Sarah whose job it was to parade it round the room for inspection.

Lord Thomas felt rather ill as he caught a fleeting glance of the bloody mass, unaware how closely he would be questioned about it in the future.

The girl remained calm and dignified, contrasting strongly with the gawping throng, and Lord Thomas decided to make enquiries about her when all the fuss was over. He had been most impressed by her. She was, he thought, a rare find and as the court was notoriously quixotic with servants, her future was by no means assured. Such a girl would be an excellent servant and might well be looking for employment if things developed as Lord Thomas feared they might.

The aging King's face was wreathed in smiles; the long-awaited heir to the throne had arrived, hopefully not to follow the previous boy who had gone to an early grave. Lord Thomas had to admire the King. He had sat patiently beside his young wife throughout the birth, holding her hand and murmuring words of encouragement. But he feared the joy would be short lived as the Protestant network of agitators was gathering momentum.

Sarah handed the silver platter to an attendant who removed it to a small dressing area behind the Queen's chamber. She returned at once to the midwife's side with ice-cold water brought to the door by a page and poured it into a large copper bowl filled with fresh rose petals; the child was unceremoniously plunged in the water, protesting wildly. The midwife took the opportunity, as was customary, to rub his gums with oil of cloves, and the clean receiving blanket was held ready to dry him before he was bound in neatly rolled finest swathing bands.

Sarah watched as his eager young limbs were tightly restrained and the bands wound round until he resembled a large chrysalis. His little cheeks puffed with indignation, he let out a further strangled shriek and just for a moment Sarah thought she saw fear in his bright unseeing eyes. She gulped a tear as she contrasted him with the bonnie baby brother her mother had delivered the previous year. She had last seen him lying on a rug, naked and nut brown from the sun, his sturdy limbs kicking merrily as he waited for his mother's breast. She had not seen him these nine months but he would now be a sturdy lad about to take his first steps whereas the King's baby son would only be unwound after many months. His legs would be weak and floppy, his skin white and peeling and his buttocks red and raw like meat from the excrement in which he would lie for hours on end as the royal nursemaids were notoriously slatternly, with little maternal supervision, and the grand lady in charge of the royal nursery was much too fine to trouble herself with a dirty bottom. She vowed that the next babe she held would not have such a life. She would be the one who would by whatever means give him what God and nature intended. She observed not for the first time that the gentry were not as God intended people to be and were in her opinion the authors of all their own misery. She rather hoped that the baby born to the Queen would not have the poisoned chalice of Kingship. Her feelings were confirmed as she looked at the strain on the old King's face. She saw anger, sorrow, bitterness and resentment, all rolled into a tangled web.

Part One

CHAPTER ONE

Catherine's Court, Suffolk, November 6th, 1688

'Love may break your heart, but a garden is constant,' said the man to the young girl. 'Like this garden, it may sleep but it is full of promises to be fulfilled. Look about you, listen to it,' he continued. 'You can almost hear the faint stirrings in the earth. Hope lives in a garden, my dear, constant rebirth and re-generation; spring will come, never fear.'

Lord Thomas Amalie held his daughter's slight body close to him in the winter cold. It was about to get dark and the sharp winter sun, whose rays had been uncluttered by summer foliage, hovered behind a low bank of violet cloud.

Flora knew the metaphor well; in her sixteen years, she had heard it often and yet it never failed to give hope and encourage-ment. She had inherited her father's love of gardens, his obsession with the botanical mysteries of creating new blooms, radiant in their beauty even though some of them, like her namesake, the tulip Flora's Glory, were the product of a tinkering with the natural order of things, a fact which to her gave their creation a mysterious secret life of its own.

'Yes, Father,' Flora agreed. 'We have the garden; we will always have the garden.' She smiled up at him, her fur-edged hood slipping to reveal her bright blue-grey eyes and pale complexion, her pointed chin and tilted nose which were the epitome of the conceived idea of beauty. It was her mouth, full and voluptuous, which strayed from this idea of perfection, and yet to Lord Thomas it was as with the tulips and plants he loved, the imperfections with their mark of uniqueness, their ultimate stamp of wondrous creation which both moved and bound him. And so it was with his daughter.

Catherine's Court stood in a winding valley on the turn of a river in the county of Suffolk. The house, built by Thomas's parents, bore more than a little of the Dutch influence. Thomas's mother Beatrice had been a wealthy Dutch woman from a staunch Calvinist family whom his father had met when in exile with the future Charles II. Lord Thomas's family were by tradition Catholic, but their loyalty to the Protestant Charles had necessitated discretion in the practice of their faith and the young couple had fallen in love. The couple had made a small fortune during the tulip craze and decided to return to England with the restoration of the new King Charles II. Thanks to the new King, who exercised a wise and pragmatic religious tolerance, Thomas was not obliged to distance himself from the family's long Catholic history. Thus it was with the restoration they had settled in England and built Catherine's Court with Beatrice's considerable fortune. They created the garden together in the Dutch style, much influenced by Beatrice's royal connections in her native Holland.

Thomas had perpetuated and strengthened the friendships established by his parents and particularly with William of Orange, Charles's cousin, now married to the King's sister Mary. When William came to visit his royal cousins in England, the sometimes frosty reception given to the young Protestant Prince was often alleviated by a visit to Catherine's Court to see the garden and discuss the plants, a passion Thomas shared with the young and taciturn Prince.

*   *   *

Father and daughter were both in a state of bereavement. Lord Thomas's wife had died the previous year, leaving two children, Ralph, aged fourteen and away at school, and their beloved Flora. Although Flora mourned her mother, she at least had the consolation of her betrothal to Roderick, her childhood sweetheart. The marriage of his daughter was also some consolation to Lord Thomas; two families with adjoining lands would be joined and Roderick would be a good and loving husband, of that he was sure. Nonetheless there was something which continued to trouble Lord Thomas. Despite the fact that both his wife and daughter had more than proved themselves equal to any man in intelligence and intellect, the law disagreed and a woman upon her marriage would surrender her wealth and legal obligations to her husband to do with as he pleased. In the light of this, Flora's choice of husband was a matter which greatly preoccupied her father, especially as Roderick's father had negotiated a very large jointure from Lord Thomas which would mean selling off some assets. This was a puzzle that weighed heavily with Lord Thomas. Whatever he left to his beloved daughter would go to her husband and there had been many cases of late where husbands had dissipated whole fortunes in a generation. Lord Thomas had discovered a way to avoid this and was in the process of arranging it. He had discovered a method by which he could nominate two trustees who would manage the estates for Flora and Ralph, until Ralph came of age, when he would inherit Catherine's Court and the estates and Flora would have the dower house and the extraordinary garden, one of the greatest in the land.

But there were many things which demanded Lord Thomas's attention at the moment, the matter of inheritance being just one. Lately he had frequently been called away from his family and the estate to London where the Catholic King James II together with his beautiful young wife Mary Modena nervously celebrated the birth of a male heir. Seeing the aging King James with his young Queen, the same age as one of his daughters, had filled Lord Thomas with disgust, and confirmed him in the view that he would not marry again. He had loved one woman and that was enough. He felt so desperately sorry for the young Queen who had been deprived of the kind of love Flora felt for Roderick or as he had felt for his own wife, falling in love with her the first moment he saw her in the haphazard court of the exiled Charles II.

'We must go inside, Daughter,' he said, suddenly feeling distracted. He was a man of instincts and something told him that all was not well. The purple clouds had become dark and an ominous chill wind had got up.

'Yes, Father, but where are the girls?' asked Flora, referring to her two devoted dogs. They were a mix of greyhound and whippet, mother and daughter, one sleek black and the other white and grey. She called their names, Diana and Hera, and the pair came bounding towards them, their strange lolloping gate performed in an audible unison as they came across the long grass parterre.

As father and daughter entered the house Lord Thomas felt the wave of pleasure he always felt as the aura of the house enfolded him. His mother had brought with her an elegant symmetry in the design of the house, with large arched windows and a roundel staircase from which all the rooms balanced perfectly.

The steward had lit a fire in the hallway and another in the salon, whose merry flames were reflected in the ornate polished wood of the priceless Biedermeier furniture brought by his parents from Holland. There was a heady perfume from large bouquets of summer blooms grown in Lord Thomas's glass-house, a fashion for cut flowers again brought from Holland. The two dogs confidently preceded father and daughter, their claws clacking on the highly polished flagged floors in the hallway then becoming silent as their feet alighted on thick Aubusson rugs in the salon. Without a semblance of apology they jumped onto a richly upholstered seat. Jack the steward came at once, casting a disapproving look at the recumbent dogs, while Thomas ignored it.

Jack melded into the comfortable room, serving tea, a new fashion from London. He was hoping, as turned out to be the case, that his Lordship would talk to the Lady Flora and reveal the truth about the disturbing and sensational rumours that had begun to filter through.

'There is news from Devon,' Lord Thomas commenced at last

when Flora had seated herself between Diana and Hera. Jack's ears pricked up. 'The Prince of Orange has arrived on the coast with his two hundred and twenty-five vessels and seven thousand men all intact.'

The steward's hands shook and the little china handled forks rattled on the porcelain saucers on the silver sweetmeats tray prepared by Meg the cook. Jack knew the significance of this at once. He said a prayer of thanks that his master had been wise enough to publicly nail his flag to the right mast. He had signed the 'Test Act' and by so doing saved his position as Lord Lieutenant and protected his estate and possibly his head from what many saw as the inevitable consequence of continuing to proclaim the Catholic faith. And now, the Dutch Prince so confident of his reception expected a nation to welcome him and the King's cousin Mary to relieve them of the Catholic threat! Jack became even quieter as his master elaborated on the news, he did not want to miss a word of it, and would rush to the servant's hall as soon as he could with this sensational development.

'Oh Father,' exclaimed Flora doubtfully. 'The last time we heard the wind was not in his favour, it seems unreal. I never thought it would come to this.'

'We must all keep calm, my dear,' said Lord Thomas firmly. 'This was inevitable, and by all accounts not a drop of blood has been spilt.'

'But surely this means a war between us all,' said Flora unsteadily.

'Not at all,' said Lord Thomas with a tolerant smile. 'The country could never go down such a road again.'

'How can you be so sure, Father, why can't we leave things as they are?' shot Flora angrily as she thought of the stories of fathers set against sons and families torn apart by this thing called religion.

'Sometimes men cannot see the writing on the wall,' replied Lord Thomas. 'His Majesty could have avoided this if he had learned to compromise,' he went on thoughtfully. 'You are right but at the day of judgement it will be man's actions which will speak for him, not the semantics of a man-made creed of faith. But I do believe that God sometimes takes a hand in the affairs of men,' he added darkly.

'So, Father, do we see the hand of God in this?' asked Flora.

'We do,' said Lord Thomas without hesitation. 'You may have noticed the wind has shifted to the west. I always know it, because the temperature falls. The Prince was able to land at Brixham two days ago having avoided the King's fleet mistakenly lying in wait for him at Portsmouth.'

'Well, if ever there was a sign there could be none clearer, it seems fate has joined forces with the Almighty,' said Flora.

An almost imperceptible smile played on Lord Thomas's lips as he looked indulgently at his clever daughter. 'Yes,' he agreed, 'it is being called the Protestant wind and will always be remembered. These are momentous times. Yes, it was surely an act of God which has spared much bloodshed.'

He stroked the head of the two dogs now resting their chins on his knees and wondered if this might indeed be that unprecedented thing, a bloodless revolution. He thought as he looked into the cool sharp gaze of the animals how the human condition had much to learn from the simple requirements which comprised their happiness as opposed to human beings who had so many unrealistic expectations from each other, most of which could not be realised.

'So, Jack?' said Lord Thomas quizzically, without turning his head. Master and servant often spoke of these things and Lord Thomas valued the simple straightforward views put to him by the man who in his opinion reflected the grass-roots voice of the ordinary man and woman, a collective view which the King had ignored at his peril.

Jack knew this was an invitation to speak. 'It means, My Lord,' he said slowly, 'that His Majesty the King and his young wife and baby can no longer sleep peacefully in their beds.' Lord Thomas listened carefully, nodding his head in agreement, encouraging the man to continue. 'We all felt as much,' Jack persevered. 'It was when the news came in October these three weeks ago that the Prince of Orange had said goodbye to what we common folk call Holland but fancy people call the States General. Yes, any man could see he would not stop until he had the English throne.'

Lord Thomas began to pace the room. 'You are right, man,' he said in his loud voice reserved for anger and revelation. 'Those complacent fools who advise the King said that the Prince would never dare to invade in the winter; that is where the man shows guile.'

'He must be a brave man, I will say that for him,' said Jack sagely.

Lord Thomas stood very still in front of the window. 'As to the Queen,' he said with a slight break in his voice, 'poor girl, you need not worry about her safety. She has already fled and gone to France with the child.' He stopped abruptly, indicating that he had imparted enough information to the servants' hall.

'Well, that at least is a mercy,' chipped in Flora quietly as she contemplated the ignominious plight of the most beautiful and gentle Queen that England had ever known.

Jack absented himself from the room as quickly as possible and sped down the long passage to the kitchens where an eager throng awaited the latest news.

*   *   *

'So . . . ' he said unhurriedly to twelve pairs of eyes and ears before pausing for maximum effect. 'The Protestant Prince of Orange has arrived in England with an army as big as has ever been seen in history.'

There was an audible intake of breath and Meg the cook collapsed in the kitchen chair. 'Oh Lord save us, we shall all be murdered in our beds,' shrieked one of the scullery maids.

'Hush up, girl, nobody asked your opinion,' Meg warned fiercely.

'Now I don't want any commotion and carrying on,' said Jack in his best voice, knowing that keeping an atmosphere of unruffled tranquillity in the household was his primary duty. It was essential that his master should be able to make the right decisions about more important matters without the interference of weeping scullery maids pleading secret female complaints as they neglected their duties; he wasn't interested in what they thought; servants mustn't have opinions.

'You must all listen to me,' Jack went on as silence descended. 'His Lordship is a wise man; he could see the way things were going. The King has not learned that men must be allowed to worship as they please, and sad to say trying to make the whole country come to the Catholic way has done for him.'

Meg looked up while dabbing her brow with a cold wet cloth. 'I may be a simple woman,' she said fervently, 'but I believe in the Holy Virgin, but the likes of those Protestants, why, they hardly believe that our dear Lord came with the angels. It's just not seemly.' She stood up, throwing her apron to the floor.

'Hush up, woman, it's all words,' said Jack irritably. 'The Master and many powerful men like him have all had to turn against their Catholic roots. The Protestants put up the Test Act to flush out the Catholics so that they could no longer ride two horses, and allow the King to pack the Parliament with his carefully chosen supporters.'

'So the Master signed the thing,' said one of the boys, shaking his head with an air of bewilderment.

'He did, lad, and because he did, he can still keep office as Lord Lieutenant and the Prince will take the throne and welcome your master to his court and keep the comfortable roof we all enjoy,' said Jack with an air of finality. 'We will have no more talk of this,' he went on. 'The Master's decision is based on many things we poor folk do not understand.'

The servants stood in silence, relieved that the burden of conscience had been lifted from their shoulders and assumed for them by their master. Now they could get on with their lives, reassured by Jack's stern stewardship, with what they supposed was his innate sense of the order of things.

The calm did not last for long. There was the clattering of horses' hooves and turning of iron carriage wheels on the cobbled forecourt. Whoever the surprise visitor was did not stand on ceremony. The wheels skidded to a halt, the horses rearing in their shaft, as the driver pulled them to a halt from unseemly speed. Heavy footsteps pounded to the door and a loud banging echoed in the cavernous hall.

There was a flurry of alarm and anxious looks were exchanged. Jack picked up a lamp and hurried to attend the arrival, snapping his fingers at the two hall boys who threw off their dark green aprons and followed the steward, recalling the many occasions when Jack had rehearsed them in a defensive procedure should it be necessary. They eyed the wall above the large oak chest beside the door where cutlasses and pistols were discreetly concealed, the swift retrieval of which had been rehearsed a thousand times.

'Take me to Lord Thomas! Stand aside, you ruffians, I do not wish to dally in this house of traitors,' bellowed the intruder as Thomas opened the door, his hand on the knife he kept in his belt. The man pushed past Jack unceremoniously, sending him off his guard, at which the two boys wasted no time. In what seemed like an instant the pistols were ready and pointing in the man's direction.

'Well done, lads,' Jack said breathlessly. His eyes were focusing on the man as he held up the lamp in the darkened hall. 'The Lord be spared, it's none other than Squire Temperly, Mister Roderick's father,' he announced in amazement.

'You mean the father of Lady Flora's betrothed,' ventured the senior of the two lads.

'Who do you think, you sons of pigs?' screeched the Squire.

More light appeared revealing the figure of Lord Thomas. 'Why Sir, what has happened to cause such an ungentlemanly arrival?' he asked testily.

'Happened, Sir?' spluttered the visitor. 'Is that what you call it? I call it a shameful betrayal of all we hold most precious and were we younger men I would ask for satisfaction . . . yes satisfaction; but to have the blood of such a man on my hands would be to be defiled, yes defiled,' shot back the Squire, seething with apoplectic fury.

'I shall not continue this except in the privacy of my library since I think you are unwell, Sir, and need to recover yourself,' said Lord Thomas with quiet authority, whilst steering the angry man by the shoulder. 'Jack, bring some refreshments for the Squire,' he added quietly.

'I will come with you to your study but I will not break bread in this house,' spat the Squire.

When the two men stood uneasily in the room, Lord Thomas had a moment to size up the state of the visitor. The man looked genuinely distraught and as yet Lord Thomas could not account for any of it.

'Now tell me what troubles you so deeply, man?' asked Lord Thomas with a forced smile.

'You . . . You, Sir, you have signed the Test Act,' replied the Squire, in a voice thick with emotion. 'You have denied the cornerstone of the Catholic faith, you have committed the grossest act of heresy. By doing so you have denied the transubstantiation of the holy sacrament.'

Lord Thomas regarded the incandescent face of his beloved daughter's future father-in-law with alarm and a vision flashed in front of his eyes: this would be Roderick in twenty years' time. Gone was the veneer of charming courtesy, there were no niceties, just cold indifference, here lurked a lack of reason or prudence. His imagination ran riot, and then he tried to calm himself with the thought that the boy would not necessarily be cut from the same cloth.

'I have a letter here,' the Squire said unpleasantly, thrusting a document at Lord Thomas who took it with a steady hand. 'Open it,' he boomed, his face becoming more bellicose by the minute.

'But Sir, the letter is addressed to my daughter,' replied Lord Thomas cautiously, turning the document around to examine it further.

'It is indeed,' barked the Squire with obvious lack of ceremony.

'I am not in the habit of reading my daughter's correspondence,' replied Lord Thomas evenly.

'Well, man, if we are to be so delicate, a theme not echoed in your betrayal of all decent gentlemen hold holy,' snarled the Squire, 'call the girl and let her open it herself.'

'No, Sir, I will do no such thing,' said Lord Thomas having quickly worked out what the contents would be. He had no intention of giving the Squire the satisfaction of seeing his daughter's face as she read the words. 'You will leave the letter and also my house, Sir,' he said abruptly. He was struggling to keep his temper under control, reminding himself of his time-honoured resolve to play his cards close to his chest, aware of the advantages of saying nothing when in doubt. And he was in doubt. Doubt as to the exact sentiments his daughter would find in the letter and in doubt as to his own judgement, which had welcomed Roderick into the family.

But a voice of caution piped up in the back of his head. It told him to wait before jumping to conclusions.

He called for Jack who came at once; Lord Thomas knew his quick-thinking servant would have been close by, sensing trouble. 'Show the Squire to the door and send for Miss Flora,' said Lord Thomas calmly.

The Squire made as if to go and then turned with an after-thought. 'Tell me,' he said in a worryingly reasonable tone, as if the answer to the question he was about to ask might in some way alleviate his fury, 'I have been told that you have taken the Anglican Communion; that at least I do not believe of you. In the name of decency, assure me it is not true.'

'I have, Sir,' said Lord Thomas at once, 'and it tasted as before, like a rather indifferent port.'

The Squire became effulgent; he reached spontaneously for his sword and in a flash Jack was at his side, large and purposeful. 'The door, my Lord,' he said loudly. The Squire flounced from the room and Lord Thomas had the curious sensation that none of it really mattered, except, of course, his daughter's happiness and his mind was already considering how the matter should be handled.

Flora was not far away. The arrival of her future father-in-law at such an hour and the muffled strains of his raised voice through the thick oak door had alarmed her, to say the least, and her mind raced. She thought at once that something must have happened to her beloved Roderick. But then why should the man be so angry? She entered the door to see her father standing by the fireplace holding the letter.

'My dear, sit down and read this. It is addressed to you,' he said ominously. 'The Squire wanted me to read it, but I refused. I do not know for certain what is in it, but I must warn you that I think you will not be pleased by what you read.'

Lord Thomas put a steadying hand on his daughter's shoulder and gently led her to a chair and handed her a knife with which to cut the ornate red seal. He was impressed by the steady hand with which she opened the stiff parchment. He observed her head moving very slightly while she read the contents, betraying not a glimmer of emotion.

'Here, Father, read it,' she said eventually.

It was from Roderick. The message was clear, but the words were not his, at least, so thought Lord Thomas. They could not be from the boy's heart. The betrothal was at an end; Lord Thomas had committed a folly which had put his daughter beyond any hopes of a suitable Catholic union. There was no gentlemanly attempt to dress the news with any regret, no mention of the love that had bound these two young people.

The father looked at his daughter, expecting girlish tears, anger, anything but the still resolute composure. She did not turn to him.

'We will not speak of this again, Father,' she said unhurriedly with downcast eyes. She stood up and Lord Thomas extended an arm. 'No, Father,' meeting him with a fierce gaze, 'this is too great a matter for tears, or even words. What I might say now would not fully express the strangeness of what I feel. I will say only this; it is a mistake, Father, to give your whole soul to another human being. You might think that such a gift were in tender loving hands, but in truth only God knows the soul you have trusted, and God must leave you to be the guardian of your own destiny. It seems I was wrong in my gift of trust and God has saved me. I thank Him.'

Flora had seen her father's grief when her mother died, and before that his distress at the death of two of their babies in infancy. She did not want to give him more sadness; this was her journey, perhaps the first step to becoming a self-sufficient woman. She would weep alone. She realised she had not known Roderick at all. He was not his own man as she had thought, but a weak mouthpiece of his father and a polemic which he did not even believe in. Tears would be wasted on such a man. She would thank God later for her deliverance.

CHAPTER TWO

Ignatius Kettle's School for Boys, Norwich, November 1688

It was very cold and after a fitful few hours of sleep, the dull thud of consciousness awakened Ralph Amalie and fear flapped its wings and dragged him back to the dull reality of the miserable days and nights which were his life at the school. Little Ralph, as his dearest departed mother used to call him, although at just fourteen he was not little anymore, sat up, trying not to wake the two other occupants of the narrow board with a straw mattress which called itself a bed. Of course when his parents had seen around the school they had been shown a cosy dormitory with luxurious duck-down coverlets and pitchers of water and fresh cakes of castile soap and fresh cotton towels.

Even after a year Ralph still experienced an overwhelming wave of nausea each morning, but he managed to get to the bucket in the corner of the freezing, barely furnished room and retched as quietly as he could. The constant nervous nausea was not as much through hunger although it gnawed at all the boys like an angry dog, especially at night, but through trepidation as to how the day would be. He hadn't at first noticed that his nightshirt was sopping wet and smelled of urine. Benedict, a much younger boy and one of Ralph's two bedmates, had wet himself again. Ralph hurried back to shake the boy awake.

'Ben, it's happened again,' he whispered. The other boy, Charlie, woke and felt the bed with his hand.

'Oh God, please help me. I am so sorry,' wept poor Benedict; he was only ten and had more or less been forgotten by his father who had married again upon his mother's death and produced a new brood of children for which Benedict was a mere inconvenience.

'Quick, the bell hasn't gone and it's hardly light. Get the mattress from the coffin bed and change them round,' hissed Ralph.

'I daren't go near it,' said Benedict in a petrified voice.

'Me neither,' said the third boy.

Ralph thought about the fate that awaited the wretched Benedict if he were discovered and without hesitation pulled the stinking mattress to the corner of the room, to the bed where two days previously a boy had died in the night; quietly and without protest the lad had succumbed muttering to what in his delirium he described as the gentle angel who came to claim him. Ralph and his two friends, for that is what they were, united in their concern for one less able to withstand the consistent beatings and lack of nourishment.

Ralph managed to get the mattress to the bed and then the two other boys helped him complete the task. Despite his brave determination Ralph felt a catch in his throat as he thought of the pathetic lonely boy who had breathed his last in the corner bed, but being of a singular nature he overcame his emotions and blocked off the thoughts. The task was completed just as footsteps could be heard approaching the door.

'Look out. Here comes Steaming Kettle!' warned Charlie.

'So what is this?' boomed the brooding black clad figure of Ignatius Kettle. 'Boys with the stink of concealment. I know it when I see it. Such diligence! Already up and dressing and eager to start your Ovid. It is most unusual. Stand forward Master Amalie, for you are the boy who needs flogging into submission, and if there is something to hide the sin will lie with you.'

Ralph stood forward, observing the hated figure of their tormentor. The man was tall but did not at first appear so as he constantly stooped, leaning forward with narrowed eyes and a hooked nose from which a droplet of moisture always hung, lengthening until it dropped, usually as ill luck would have it, in some poor boy's food. Indeed, his large fulsome mouth also appeared in a continuous coating of spittle, which would increase lasciviously during the beatings. Imagining what would surely follow, Kettle had begun to utter little grunts, as if in anticipation of something delightful.

'Sir,' replied Ralph at once, 'as Crito the sage said, "If you have eyes to see then see."' Ignatius Kettle exploded, his face hardening. 'What insolence, is that any answer? And I see you other boys are sniggering, lift your shirts and I will teach you all to cheek your superior.'

With that, Ignatius produced the birch he kept behind his back and ran it between his fingers. The boys obediently bared their buttocks and lower backs. The first thwacks struck with unusual force even by Ignatius's standards. Ralph and Charlie remained silent but Benedict began to sob and soon there was a faint odour and Ralph realised that Ben had messed himself.

Something snapped inside Ralph's head that he could bear no longer. It was not his own pain but that of the lesser robust Benedict that had tipped him from submission to a frenzied animal fury. It happened suddenly and he was not afraid of Ignatius; after all he was more than a match for the man now they were no longer boys. They would no longer be bullied into this strange inexplicable submission. He turned, hauling up his breeches, and lunged at the man, catching him in a tackle around the knees. Taken by surprise, Ignatius lost his balance and fell to the ground with a crash, hitting his head on the floor with a thud. For a moment he lay motionless. The boys' eyes met decisively and they were astride him, Ralph seizing the rod from the man's hands.

'Sit on him,' Ralph shouted, 'and I will show him how it feels.' Charlie continued as best he could. To Ralph's surprise Ignatius had not uttered a sound.

The boys regarded the recumbent figure of the hated Ignatius with horror; at least it became so as one thought struck them simultaneously. They had killed Ignatius Kettle. They regarded the body with revulsion and a silence descended, relieved only by approaching footsteps. The large shadow of Mrs Kettle stood in the doorway; she carried with her a powerful smell, a mixture of camphor and stale clothing, suggesting a brief glimpse into what the boys all felt was a repulsive private life. What her husband lacked in bulk she had in folds that seemed to ripple when she moved. The unfashionable and incongruous colours of her only two gowns accentuated the size of her powerful frame. Today it was the red one, and it melded with the thin stream of blood that stained the floor round her husband's head.

She let out a scream, so blood curdling that other footsteps followed quickly. For a reason that he never quite understood, Ralph ingeniously invented what became the accepted version of truth.

'Mr Kettle fell,' he explained quickly. 'He hit his head.'

There was a short silence before Mrs Kettle sunk to the floor in a mound of fetid skirts and cradled the head of her departed husband.

With a mixture of dismay and relief Ralph saw that Ignatius was not dead at all. With a gasp the man opened his eyes and gazed into those of his wife.

'Where am I?' he asked weakly. 'Why am I on the floor, wife, and why is everyone here staring at me in that impertinent way?'

The boys stood transfixed as it became clear the Ignatius had no memory whatsoever of the attack, and, indeed, could not remember why he had been with the boys in the first place. Ralph's heart had been pounding with terror but now his mood verged on euphoria as he realised he had invented an explanation which appeared plausible to everyone.

*   *   *

Later that morning the draconian regime of the school had returned to normal except for the soiled bandage which Ignatius wore on his head and a slight faltering in his voice as he took the class through Ovid's *The Legendry Origins of Athens*.

'You, Mister Purchase,' said Ignatius suddenly, slamming down his volume on his ink-stained desk. 'Step forward.'

There was a sigh from the other ten boys, and Ralph felt, as they did, a mixture of relief that for once it was not him who would receive admonishment.

'Repeat the last sentence,' barked Ignatius.

'I have forgotten, Sir,' the boy replied in a whisper.

'What did you say, boy?' boomed Ignatius, his eyes dilating with excitement.

'Forgotten,' said the boy almost inaudibly.

'Well, boy, I will teach you to forget your Ovid; put your hands on the desk.'

The birch came down on his swollen, chilblained knuckles. It whistled through the air not once but six times and blood started to ooze. The boy made no sound. So inured were they to the regime of beatings that the event caused little or no comment. How many times had Ralph heard the phrase 'spare the rod, spoil the child'? It was part of an ethos, but coming so soon after the events of earlier he was forming a resolve in his mind. He would not submit to this just because it was what was expected. He would write to his father; he would smuggle the letter out for he knew Ignatius intercepted letters home; he would tell his father everything, suggest that he had a tutor at home. Anyway, he thought, after his mother's death his father had need of companionship, especially as Flora, his beloved sister, would soon be married.

The more he thought, the more determined he became. As the dreary day wore on with a lesson in the Hebrew Psalter followed by Genesis and then the lesson in Greek, Ralph formed a plan, he made a decision He would write to his father, announcing his return and, using the few coins he had saved for such an occasion, he would travel back to his home.

Events sometimes have a will of their own and this, as it happened, was one such occasion. Later that evening, when the boys were sitting at their evening studies, construing a chapter of *Tully's Offices*, Ralph was summoned to his schoolmaster's presence. His heart sank. Alone with the vicious fury of Ignatius he would not be able to fight him off. The man had probably regained his memory of the attack in the morning and Ralph's thoughts took him to the ignominious fate of perpetrators of crimes of violence and the disgrace he would bring to his family. With these thoughts racing he went to the dreaded study.

'Mrs Kettle has packed your things, Mr Amalie,' said Ignatius in a low sepulchral tone. Ralph's mind raced. Had something happened to his family? He felt sick. 'You are to be collected at dawn and taken back to your father, Lord Amalie. I will have no Protestant traitor's blood in my establishment,' Ignatius continued contemptuously.

'Traitor, Sir?' piped Ralph indignantly. 'Do you speak of my father?' he demanded. 'If you do he will surely demand satisfaction.'

Ignatius looked at the boy, surprised by his bravery. Despite the severity of his teaching methods, he had an almost sentimental attachment to the finished product. He liked to send polished brains into the world, armed with superior knowledge and intellect. Ralph was one of his best boys. He knew the child had a better aptitude than most; it had been his spirit that had had to be addressed, it had needed to be moulded into submission. As far as Ignatius knew, there was only one way to do that. Fear must rule and with it came unquestioning obedience. Of course over the years hysterical mothers had come to the school and berated him, but his technique of sending for the boy and conducting the little lad in his Latin verse, his knowledge of geography, his Greek, his knowledge of Homer's *Odyssey*, was compacted and perfect. The boy would begin to take a pride in the amazement on his mother's face and the smug 'I told you so' glances the father would give to the complaining woman.

But now Ignatius sensed rebellion in the air; the boy stood defiantly before him, his face screwed in puzzlement, and Ignatius reluctantly conceded that he owed him an explanation.

'Your father,' he began, 'his Lordship, has seen fit to sign a document which puts him outside the only true faith.' He went on slowly as if the very words pained him. 'We keep you away from the mendacious world of politics, boy, but now I must tell you what catastrophe has occurred, for it is that which will bring about bloodshed and treason.'

'What is it, Sir, this thing you speak of?' asked Ralph fearfully.

'The Protestant wind has brought the usurper Prince of Orange to our shores and that wind was fanned by men such as your father, his Lordship. I can say no more.' There was a silence and then of course Ignatius did have more to say. The matter was too disgraceful in his eyes to be left there. Meanwhile Ralph was having feelings of redemptive joy. He would be home, he had escaped disgrace; Ignatius Kettle had no recollection of the earlier event. The voice of Ignatius intruded on the reverie.

'Your father has nailed his flag to the Protestant mast,' he said with menacing deliberation. 'You and your family will never be received by decent men here on earth or in the Kingdom of Heaven until your father recants. But I hope I have taught you the powers of reasoning. Think on this, boy, you do not have to be cut from the same cloth'

Ralph stood very still. There was a brief silence and then he responded in the clear tone that Ignatius had taught him. *'Ite nunc fortes uber celsa magni dulci exempla via* [Oh strong be heart, go where the road of ancient honour climbs]. That,' he finished, 'describes my father.'

Suddenly in the room there were two men, not a man and a boy. Ignatius gazed with pleasure at Ralph. He could not but admire the steady unflinching look of the wide-set blue eyes, and the distinctive nose which had begun to suggest courage, bravery and honesty. Ralph was tall for his age and very thin, a fact not unconnected with the appalling food provided by the cheese-paring Mrs Kettle. Despite this, his hair was thick and dark, bristling with health. He had a wilful determination undaunted by his year at the school. He unnerved the old man especially when he accentuated a point with a thrust of his chin. Ignatius saw before him the man the boy would become and realised that even if events had not taken matters forward beyond his control he could not have contained the boy any longer.

For the old man there had been many goodbyes but he seldom allowed himself to become fond of a boy. But there was something different about this goodbye. He felt an emotion he had not felt for all his adult life, a thing which he had suppressed since his early childhood when his mother had died. It was a kind of love completely alien to him. This feeling suffused his entire body, there was nothing lustful about it, not the sort of feelings he had once or twice observed in a young male teacher who takes an unhealthy interest in a young boy, and he had seen one or two of them. There was a poignant sadness about it, tinged with regret; he knew that this was a boy with a future, a destiny, which he had, in his own way, helped to forge. He was proud of the boy who stood before him. He had been no more, in his eyes, than firm, he had given the boy the desire to learn, the discipline to apply himself; he knew that the composite attributes for success were a mixture of many things and this boy had them all. Ralph had borne the death of his mother stoically, without letting his heart freeze up like a walnut as his own had done. He had still protected those younger and less able to survive the slings and arrows of life. Ignatius had been at first irritated by Ralph's protective feelings towards boys like Benedict. He knew that he had beaten Ralph at least twice for misdemeanours for which were not his but for which he had taken the punishment to save a friend. For his own part he had administered the punishment just the same, because of a niggling irritation at Ralph's superior sense of selfless loyalty.

How nice it would have been, thought Ignatius dangerously, to remain part of the boy's journey, to share in the pride of laurels to be won. He reflected that he had no sons of his own and no friends to speak of. Then there was Mrs Kettle whom he had long ago stopped seeing at all. His mind raced for an illogical moment; perhaps if the woman had produced a child of her own, she might have tempered Ignatius's regime? But never once had she cautioned him to kindness. But then that was not the way, a good Master must not be liked; he must be feared, reasoned Ignatius. But just for a second he allowed himself to enter a room in his mind where he had never ventured before. He wanted to send this boy on his journey with some little acknowledgement of Ignatius's humanity.

Divested of the role of pupil, Ralph also saw something different in the dusty room, as if he saw it for the first time. He saw the piles of volumes stacked on the floor and randomly on shelves that dipped in the middle with the weight of the books, the fly-blown, thickly leaded windowpanes behind Ignatius's head, the dreaded desk and the worn patch of carpet where boys had stood waiting for the beatings to come. Above all there was the smell of faded leather and ink, of fusty clothing and damp logs that never seemed to glow as fires should. At that moment Ignatius made the unusual gesture of coming from behind his desk and taking the long fire iron from by the grate and stoking the smouldering flames vigorously. They sprang to life and almost at once the room was full of light and warmth. The desk no longer stood between them and Ignatius stretched out a hand. He thought the boy would not take it but he did, with a manly dignity that further impressed the old man.

'It grieves me to part with you, boy,' Ignatius said gruffly. 'Your father will be proud of you. You have a fine brain. Remember what Hippocrates said: "Men ought to know that from the brain alone arise our pleasure, joys, laughter and jests as well as our sorrow, pains, griefs and tears."'

There was a pause. Ralph was thinking, trying to remember, and then he found the words. It was a year since Ignatius had drummed into them the words of the great sage and how dull they had seemed at the time, but something in his head brought them back to him in a brilliant flash.

'"Through it in particular",' he began, '"we think, see, hear and distinguish the ugly from the beautiful and the bad from the good."'

'That we do, my boy,' said Ignatius. He felt a catch in his throat, and wanted Ralph to leave quickly before he betrayed his emotions. That would be a step too far on a journey he could not risk.

The boy smiled at him just briefly, but enough to light a candle in the old man's heart. Then he was gone and the fire dimmed again and Ignatius slumped in his chair. He fumbled for a rag in his pocket and dabbed his eyes. He did not know why he cried, but he did so until Mrs Kettle came barging though the door, dragging a weeping Benedict by the hand. Some minor crime was described as she pushed the trembling child towards the desk.

'Mr Kettle will deal with you now,' she shrieked.

'Leave us, wife,' said Ignatius wearily.

He did not beat the boy, but rather set him to some improving words. When the child had gone he sat quietly until he fell into a deep sleep. His dreams were troubled and confused, something involving young Ralph, but when he awoke he could not remember them. He felt in a mad way that he had experienced some kind of epiphany.

CHAPTER THREE

Catherine's Court, November 1688

Flora was working in the stillery. Lord Thomas had been standing quietly watching her for some time. He felt a profound pleasure as he did so. In the turmoil of political and personal events that continually battered his family, a definition that included all his faithful retainers, his daughter's diligent application to the household's domestic calendar was the one constant thing he clung onto. Since her mother's death Flora had had to take up the role of chatelaine of the big house; today she stood surrounded by preserves laid out in perfect order on thick slate shelves. Although winter had not yet come with the vengeance it brought from the North Sea, the cold in the north-facing room already hurt him as he breathed. He had been troubled lately by a persistent cough; he could see his daughter's own breath vaporising on the cold air. Her slight frame was bundled up in a voluminous sheepskin coat, over a spotless white apron. On her slim hands she wore mittens, knitted by the maids, who themselves were permitted them in the winter since Flora had wisely pointed out that girls with bleeding, chilblained hands were not hygienic.

As she moved from shelf to shelf inspecting the bottles of summer fruits, meats soaking in brine and vegetables carefully laid out under thick sacking covers to stop them taking the light, he saw her lift the cover revealing the first tender white shoots of chicory peeping through the rich loamy soil. He reflected that such was the life of a good man, looking for the light which continually eluded him. His daughter's small feet made no sound as she darted about like a busy moth in an improvised pair of the sheepskin floor polishing boots used by the male servants for the wooden floors in the parlour.

Life in the big house could be very lonely for a girl with no siblings, which is why she had been sent away to her aunt for most of her education. Since her return following her mother's death, he had been amazed by the harmony that existed between his daughter and the many servants who kept the big old house in sparkling order; in fact he had to admit things had never been as good as they were now in that respect. There was a little bit of him which was almost relieved that she would not after all be leaving to marry Roderick, and now he had news of another return and indeed a new arrival at the house.

Flora heard him coughing and turned in consternation, hurrying across the stone floor. 'Father,' she said anxiously, 'that cough of yours concerns me. I will make some of mother's onion and sugar potion, the one where we leave the onion on a bed of thick sugar. The juice will sooth you and kill the infection which is causing the trouble.'

'Thank you, Flora,' said Lord Thomas gratefully, his words muffled in his kerchief, which he had pressed to his mouth, quickly replacing it in his pocket before she saw the dark red stain.

'So, dear Father,' said Flora, taking his arm, enjoying the comforting feel of the coarsely woven wool jacket he wore when going about his duties on the estate. She noticed with alarm that she could feel his bones through the fabric and on closer inspection she saw that he had lost weight; his breeches hung loosely about his legs, the waist secured with a frayed silk cravat.

'You should not be here in the cold,' she said solicitously.

'Wherever you are it feels warm to me, my dearest daughter,' he replied with what Flora detected as unusual feeling. Her heart missed a beat; there was something palpably vulnerable about her father on this cold November morning. She saw that without him her world would collapse, he was the foundation upon which her entire happiness depended. She felt a shiver of anxiety and she caught her breath in the frosty air; she and her father were as one person, her worries were his, they were underwritten by his firm sensible approach to life. Even the latest setback with her broken engagement seemed somehow resolved without the painful necessity of discussion, but he was her rock; no other man could occupy the place her father had in her heart. But sometimes recently in a sickening moment she went fleetingly to a place in her consciousness where she seldom ventured, a lonely wilderness without him beside her. Of course the day would come when he would no longer be there, but he had always been so strong, determined and effective that it had always seemed a long way off. But now, just for a second, she thought about the day when she would not smell the country air and wood smoke on his old woollen jackets or see his warm smile of pleasure when she interrupted him in his study.

She alone was allowed to go there unannounced and he would drop the task in hand and talk to her about the most unexpected things, his theories on the great universe, the configuration of the stars, the work of his hero the great Galileo who nearly lost his life for the heresy of his discovery that the world was not flat like an enormous plate, but a sphere and constantly moving around the sun. She knew that it was her father's way, to bury himself in these things and local affairs during times like these. In some innately intuitive way he knew he was powerless to intervene. Here, so far from court, things went on comparatively normally whilst she knew that events in London were gathering a terrifying momentum. There had been many comings and goings with more than the usual number of messengers and her father had been especially preoccupied.

'Will you come to my study, my dear?' her father asked. 'While you were so busy in your freezing domain,' he said shivering, 'we have a visitor, Lionel Wellbeloved. He is such a support to me, he has been so closely involved in our family affairs; his know-ledge of the law is always invaluable, and he has saved us from any pitfalls. He has come from London and I want you to be with me when he tells us what dire things have been going on; he looks very grim I must say, so I fear the worst.'

Flora was always pleased to see Lionel Wellbeloved and she had a premonition that the time would come when his wise counsel would be more useful than ever. 'Of course Father, I will come at once, but go on ahead of me; I must make myself respectable for Mr Wellbeloved,' she said busily. 'Jack,' she called as she threw down her apron. She knew the man was not far away as she had heard him berating one of the pages for some misdemeanour. He came looking anxious and pulling on his best jacket.

'Take the best ale and some cold venison and Meg's fresh bread for our important visitor and make sure the boys bank up the fires in his lordship's study,' she cried as she made for her chamber where she had a fresh gown.

*   *   *

'Miss Flora, you look so like your mother, God rest her soul,' said Lionel Wellbeloved, smiling benignly as she came through the door in a grey velvet gown with dark ermine collar and cuffs, with one of her mother's woven shawls over her shoulders. The room was warm; the two men got up from their chairs by the fire. The big oak table was strewn with papers, some of the scrolls still unfolded. Normally Flora would have sat her father's feet on a small stool, but today her father was most insistent that the three of them adjourn formally to the table.

Flora sat between her father and Lionel; although she knew he was the same age as her father, he could have been a decade younger and his ruddy complexion exuded rude health. He divided his time between what were obviously important duties in the city, although Flora often wondered quite what they were. He had a large estate about twelve miles away and a wife who did not circulate in society but stayed at home running the large house and a flotilla of children whose numbers seemed to increase on a regular basis without comment, as if such events were merely to be expected. He was the kind of man who people trust, the result of an unnervingly perceptive gaze from dark blue eyes, one of which had a slight fleck of brown in the iris. The fleck had always fascinated Flora and Ralph ever since they were small children and she often wondered if Lionel had

43

become so used to people looking long and hard at him explained why everyone turned to him in times of trouble. It had always been said in the family, 'We will ask Lionel, he will know,' and so it proved today.

'I shall tell you the latest news from London,' said Lionel when they had sat down and Jack had filled three silver tankards with ale.

'Please proceed at once, I can hardly imagine what brings you all the way here,' said Lord Thomas.

'The King has flown,' Lionel told them coolly as if it were not surprising.

They both gasped. 'What do you mean, "flown"?' blurted Flora.

'We all suspected he would; the man has no stomach for a fight except on an actual battle field, the slings and arrows of Kingship are quite beyond him,' said Lord Thomas sagely.

'Agreed, my dear friend,' said Lionel. 'But the manner of his departure was shockingly ignominious. He stole away in the night with diamond buckles sewn in his waistcoat like a common criminal. To make matters worse, he threw the great seal of office into the Thames from the craft which was to convey him to a ship to make his escape to France.'

'I can hardly believe what you are saying,' Lord Thomas exploded.

'Surely by doing such a thing, he has lost all respect. What on earth possessed him?' ventured Flora.

'He did so in the belief that without the great seal Parliament could not sit in what he thought would be a temporary absence while he gathered support in France,' Lionel explained.

Lord Thomas was, unusually for him, at a loss for words. The whole affair made him weary of the human condition and he slowly shook his head in despair.

'It seems incredible when you think of the power he has thrown away,' said Flora.

'It gets worse, I am afraid,' said Lionel. 'The rabble in London went on an orgy of destruction. The wretched King was apprehended, and returned to London in the most pitiable circumstances. The man showed no courage, and appears to have lost his senses.'

'From what you say the man seems to be incapable of rational thought,' said Lord Thomas grimly. 'One thing is sure: he has lost all credibility by his flight.'

Flora's mind raced as she thought of all the people who would be affected by the King's facile behaviour. 'And what news of the poor Queen and her baby?' she asked fearfully.

'It is fair to say the die was cast when he sent the young Queen to France with the Prince of Wales,' Lionel explained. 'She should have stayed as she was advised to do. Things would have sorted themselves out; we would all have protected her.'

There was silence in the room whilst Flora and her father thought about the news and Lord Thomas sought his daughter's hand and held it briefly; he could see she was genuinely perturbed by the awful thought of what might follow these momentous developments. 'And now the now the poor woman is a prisoner of the French King on whose mercy she was obliged to throw herself,' he said slowly. 'How the French must laugh at us as they scoop up our discarded kings and queens,' he added ironically.

Flora felt her heart racing, 'Oh how I pity that poor girl,' she cried emotionally. 'I tell you both this, it would be better to stay an old maid than to put yourself in the clutches of men to lose control of who you are, to forfeit the right to decide what you can do with your own body . . . it will never happen to me, I swear it.'

The two men regarded Flora admiringly; it was seldom that a woman expressed herself so frankly. Lord Thomas caught Lionel's eye, who smiled back at him indulgently. In view of his failing health he had appointed Lionel a guardian of his children's affairs. They had of late been considering this very issue and it was because of this that Flora was now included in the exchange of information in the clandestine man's world of Lord Thomas's study.

45

'I commend you, daughter, for your compassion towards that poor young woman,' said Lord Thomas warmly. 'I very much hope that you will never be in such a position. Unfortunately it is the fate given to people in such high places. They may be lucky in some respects but they do not have the luxury of the freedoms we all strive for and sometimes take for granted.'

'I can assure you, Father, I take nothing for granted,' shot Flora. 'But the King assumes that somehow he will be looked out for although he has abdicated the responsibilities of Kingship. He does not deserve the crown! I want to know more about William. What is he like, Mr Wellbeloved? Please tell us.'

Fired up by her youthful curiosity Lionel remarked that Flora was a very beautiful young woman and that she also had a sparkling, unjaded intelligence and he wondered if that beauty would be a gift or an affliction. One thing he was quite sure of was that she was destined for more than a quiet life in the country such as was the future for his own comfortably plain little daughters.

'He is a clever man. He has cunning and he stalks his prey: he knows exactly when to move. He plays life like a game of chess. He knew exactly how to do as little as possible and wait for other people to reveal their vulnerability.'

'But what about loyalty? James is his father-in-law.' asked Flora.

'He feels no particular loyalty to James,' answered Lionel. 'Those Stewarts created many hostages to fortune. Charles and James were very patronising to him when he came to visit the court as a young man. They mocked him for his small stature and reserved character. Despite everything, he is of a sensitive nature and I do not believe he will forgive them. In a way you might call this a kind of revenge.'

'All right then,' said Flora. 'But what I do not understand is how a daughter could betray her father as Mary has done, and by all accounts the sister Anne is just as bad. Surely the Crown will sit uneasily upon Mary's head? I pray that I could never be so traitorous to my own father whatever the circumstances.'

'Well, dare I say it, it is all about love in the end and not the lack of it,' concluded Lionel. 'Both daughters were separated from their father when they were young, to be brought up as Protestants; then Mary was traded to William, a man she initially found repugnant and sent to Holland, a strange place which she hated. But she is a woman of great character and after a while she looked for more in life than a deceptive outward appearance and fell in love with her strange, unprepossessing, clever husband and his country. She will do nothing without him and it is together they will take the Crown, and I do believe her sense of destiny is greater than her father's.'

Flora sighed and reached for her father's comforting hand and he gave her an encouraging smile. 'It is so strange,' she said pensively. 'We can feel so isolated from these astonishing events, as if they don't concern us at all.'

'It is because the country suffered so much during the time of that monster Cromwell,' said Lord Thomas. 'Now we all feel that events will take their course and none of it is worth dying for.'

'Father, that is shocking,' gasped Flora pulling away from him.

'Yes, I just feel that,' Lord Thomas responded bluntly, 'life invests itself with the inevitable. But it does not absolve me from my duty to the country I love and the family I have the honour to protect. That means protecting them from the folly of those who do not care for an individual life. But I, my dear daughter, would not send a single young man to fight for James, and that is how so many of the country's finest men feel.'

'You are right, my dear friend,' agreed Lionel. 'And you are not alone. There are men like Lord Feversham, the head of the army. He has seen fit to disband them armed but without pay, as clear a remit for a man to follow his own will as ever I saw. No, my dear,' he said looking directly at Flora, 'the city is not the place to be at the moment. We will wait quietly on our estates until things have taken their irrevocable course, and now I must take my leave of you and get back to my home. I have been away too long. I must get back to what really matters and that is friends and family, those things dearest to us all.'

Lord Thomas looked affectionately at his daughter and felt strangely calm despite the tumultuous events in the country. Lionel got up and leant for his hat, from which he was never parted. He patted it into order and gave it a brush with his hand. 'I am on my way now,' he said, fixing father and daughter with his compelling odd eyes. The speckled iris seemed to dilate as he spoke to them both. 'I leave with this thought,' he said quietly. 'In a matter of months the King's flight will be all but forgotten as William steps into his shoes with seamless competence. We have reason to be optimistic.'

'God be with you, my dear friend,' said Lord Thomas as Lionel departed. The man embraced his old friend and, turning to Flora, took her hand with unexpected aplomb and raised it to his lips for a mere whisper of contact and gave her a formal bow.

Flora felt a peculiar metamorphosis, a flash in time whereby that one gesture she left her childlike state behind her. It was both liberating and testing.

'Flora, let us sit down again. I have some important family developments I must share with you,' interrupted her father's voice. 'Young Ralph is coming home! He will be with us before nightfall.'

Flora's first reaction was of joy. She jumped up from her chair and hugged her father, and then she drew back in alarm.

'Oh Father, has he done something wrong?' she asked apprehensively.

'No, it is I who has been the cause of this by declaring myself in the matter of the Test Act. This act of pragmatism seems to have had the most far-reaching effect on our family,' Lord Thomas admitted.

'I don't understand,' said Flora frowning.

'Well, my dear, it seems that he who pays the piper calls the tune. Ignatius Kettle's establishment depends quite heavily on support from some big Catholic families who will not have the child of a dissenter in their midst. The fact is that had I been willing to match their generosity our friend Mr Kettle would gladly have overlooked their religious sensitivities. This of course is an illustration of Mr Kettle's lack of sound judgement, since the days of Catholic supremacy are numbered and their coffers will soon run dry. But I did not feel inclined to underwrite my son's education with a man who can be bought with a few coins; so Ralph is on his way home.'

This news was imparted with Lord Thomas's customary accuracy, but Flora detected an underlying look of concern in her father's face.

'Although the circumstances make me furious, I cannot wait to have Ralph back where he belongs,' said Flora. She was remembering her deep sadness when he had bravely set off for the school he already hated after their mother's death and it struck her how so much of their lives was an implicit resignation to the way things were done, without asking the reason why.

'And now to the next thing,' Lord Thomas continued briskly, a trick he had when he wanted to fly something past someone without them having time to think on it.

'But father . . . ' Flora attempted to interrupt.

He held up his hand and persevered. 'I am sure you remember my telling you about the young girl who was in attendance when our young Queen gave birth to the Prince of Wales, God help the poor souls. Well, as I thought, when the Queen had to flee for her life she could not take her faithful servant and the girl has no wish to serve the wife of the Prince of Orange, our new Queen Mary, and in any case has not been asked. As I told you, I was much impressed by the girl's bearing and I told her to get in touch with me if she found herself looking for employment.'

'Oh, I can see what is coming, we are to have a new servant,' said Flora with a twinkle of amusement. She was used to her father's tendency to pick up waifs and strays. The house was already full of many of her father's finds. She had to admit each one would have laid down their very life for their employer and benefactor. She did remember her father's account of the girl, and, with her marriage plans abandoned and her brother returning, she could think of a role which might suit such a person.

'Well yes, my dear, how well you know me. Her name is Sarah Cooke and she will be arriving tomorrow. I suggest she brings her skills to you as a fitting servant for a young lady with an establishment to run, and, besides, there is something else I must speak to you about,' said Lord Thomas. 'But first let us go to the kitchens and share all our news.'

Lord Thomas put his arm about Flora's shoulders encouragingly and followed him to the kitchens.

The warmth from the enormous open hearth welcomed them into a hubbub of activity. Each corner of the cavernous room was busy: piles of early winter vegetables were being prepared on a vast slate slab, a boy was stringing together onions, another was deftly peeling leeks. The game boy sat in another corner skinning a hare, and through a door in the far corner wafted the thick, faintly sour smell of cheese. The dairymaids could be heard singing as they churned the butter on thick black marble shelves supported by painted carved cows legs. The room was unusually busy as the tinker had come unexpectedly to line the rows of copper pans with tin to prevent the poisoning that would come with prolonged boiling.

'And you, you ruffian,' Meg the cook could be heard exploding, 'due on the first of November in time for the Yuletide boiling and there you are nearly three weeks late and what will happen to all my winter puddings, I ask you?'

'You are lucky to get me at all,' answered the man. 'Folk who know better these days are boiling puddings separately so as not to mix up the flavours and that means more pots so I am in demand, Mistress Meg, and there is no call for complaining. So how about a tankard of sack for a poor honest man?' continued the man cheekily, catching Meg about her ample bottom.

Jack called the room to silence, embarrassed that His Lordship should be witness to the familiar banter that went on in the servants' quarters and all twelve of the kitchen servants stood awkwardly, wiping their hands on their aprons. At first there was an atmosphere of apprehension. These were strange times and they had been deserted by their King, whose health they had prayed for each day in the manor chapel.

'Young Master Ralph is coming home today, and we, his family,' Lord Thomas announced, spreading his arms expansively and using the collective term which referred to blood relations and servants alike, 'will make a fitting occasion for the return of our young master . Your mistress will stay and make a plan with you and no expense spared.'

There was a flutter of approval; any opportunity for a change in the regular domestic life of the household was a bonus. For the servants, the last such event had been to celebrate the betrothal of Miss Flora, and they had all been given new shoe leathers for the occasion.

As Lord Thomas left the room to Flora, he heard an excited cacophony of voices as they gathered round their young mistress to talk about the evening. It was not long before Lord Thomas's thoughts were interrupted by the dreadful screams of the best pig and the shrill laughter of the kitchen maids. He went to his study and sat a while before he fell into an afternoon slumber beside the fire. He dreamed of his wife, they were together as a family and all was well with the world. He awoke with a start. The room was dark except for the embers of the fire and it was a few moments in that no man's land between dreaming and waking that he felt his wife with him still, as if she were in the room; 'I wish you were here, my dearest wife,' he said softly, 'I need you, but it will not be long.'

CHAPTER FOUR

Catherine's Court, December 1688

The return home had been a turning point for Ralph; everything seemed the same and yet he knew that things were subtly different. His father seemed preoccupied, as if he had temporarily absented himself from the present. There was something about him which suggested he was weary with the challenges of running the estate and his duties as Lord Lieutenant. More and more fell upon the shoulders of his sister Flora who Ralph noticed going in and out of his father's study with lists and papers. She began to see many of his father's visitors and took delivery of the pamphlets that regularly came from London.

Ralph was pleased that the new servant Sarah was a person far above the normal village girl. She had taken a great deal of the running of the house from Flora's shoulders and had skilfully negotiated the hierarchal jealousies she might have encountered with the other servants.

After a few days Lord Thomas summoned brother and sister to his study for what he described as a 'family meeting'. Ralph had been so thrilled with the liberation his homecoming had given him that he had been, to say the least, neglectful of his personal hygiene. It was Sarah who took matters into her own hands.

'Now, Master Ralph,' she announced on the day of the meeting, 'you are never going to your father's study looking like that. It's off to the scullery where I will clean you down like the young rogue you are.'

There was no room for argument. Although Ralph suggested a bowl of water in his chamber would do the trick, Sarah was having none of it. Soon the boy was in front of the roaring fire, looking doubtfully at a huge copper tub full of steaming water. There was a table beside it set out with cakes of soap and brushes. Knowing that his protests would fall on deaf ears and wanting to look his best for his father, he knew he had to get into the water quickly, sitting down to hide his modesty from Sarah and a young page who was resentfully fetching the hot water from the kitchens below.

Sarah had been raised in a tough farming family and she had been witness many things, not least cruelty to poor defenceless animals, for which she had a total aversion. But children were generally regarded as a treasured blessing and cruelty to them would be a thing so abhorrent that the community would oft take matters into their own hands if they got wind of it. As the boy lent forward in the water Sarah let out an involuntary cry.

'Lord have mercy, what has happened to your back, Master Ralph?' she gasped, crossing herself.

'It's nothing, Sarah,' he said quickly.

'Nothing, it's not nothing,' said Sarah. 'You have been beaten, boy, and by the look of it not for the first time. I had cousin who was beaten in the navy, and it was nothing so bad as this. Who did it to you?' she persisted.

'Look, Sarah, this happens at schools, all the boys are beaten,' said Ralph firmly. 'You must swear not to tell my sister or my father; they have enough to worry about, and anyway my father says I will be taught at home from now on.'

'But, Master Ralph, the wounds are festering. There is yellow pus coming out of them. You could die if we do not treat them, you should have shown them to somebody, is that why you have not washed yourself?' she asked gently.

'Listen, before I let you put something on them, promise not to tell anyone,' Ralph said, turning to meet Sarah's steady, not taking no for an answer gaze.

'If this secrecy is to spare your family, Master Ralph, I will hold my tongue, but only on condition that you let me dress these wounds every day. If there is any talk of your going back to that place, I swear to God I will tell your father.'

'That is a promise, Sarah, and if you and I are friends it must not be broken,' said Ralph.

'Do you know, Master Ralph, it amazes me when I see how the gentry, with all their God-given gifts of a warm bed and full stomach, can create such wickedness when there is no need of it. My folk had a rod on their back from the moment they were born; they had no need to make one. Just to have a healthy family reared to fear the good Lord and thank him for a meal on the table and a healthy pig for the winter was enough and we value what we have got.'

'That's how we are taught to be men, I suppose,' said Ralph ruefully.

'I saw such evil with my poor Queen, the way she was treated and had to flee for her life with her little babe. Your father, God bless him, was the only decent man or woman in the room where that poor mite was born. I saw his Lordship again when he was called to London to testify about the birth of that poor baby, Francis they called the child. We were in the room together when everyone was questioned. They said the child was smuggled in a warming pan. Your father spoke like the true gentleman he is. "You should all be fearful of the day when you come before God who knows the truth, as do you all. Francis Stewart is the true son of the King," he said and then he went on, "Is there not a man with common sense among you? I saw the birth to my shame, for it was not decent, the Queen suffered as you will all suffer for your lies at the Day of Judgement." And then he turned to me, Master Ralph, and he said, for I will always remember it, "You have told God's truth, girl, and you get no reward for it, and I suspect you turned down a princely sum when you would not lie. If things do not go well for you, come to my family." And he gave me a piece of paper with this house on it.'

'It was a good day for us then,' quipped Ralph.

Sarah would not be deflected from her story and went on regardless. 'There was no point in staying at Whitehall when the Queen fled, the rooms were filthy. People came and went as they pleased and did what they liked. I caught a gentleman relieving himself on the Queen's bed. It made me weep. Nobody paid or fed us anymore. The Queen's things were left in a shocking state for anyone to see, even her petticoats. I tried to take care of it but nobody noticed, and that is how I am here. It was your father who stretched out a hand to me when I was abandoned like all the Queen's servants. "From now on," he said to me when I came here, "we are your family." And that is how it will be, young Ralph, so when it is right for them I will do what is right and I will care for all of you including your sister who is as fine a girl as I ever did see.'

While Ralph was ruminating on the story, thinking yet again what a modest man his father was and realising just how many people were bound to him through profound gratitude and loyalty, Sarah took the ewer of hot water the page had just brought and poured it down his back. He stifled a cry of pain as it flushed through the runnels of infected flesh. Sarah called to the page. He came running as Ralph lent forward gasping.

'Now, boy,' she said to the nervous lad, 'you will hold your tongue about what we are to do with your young master here, you will not speak of these wounds to anyone and if you do I will see you are sent away.'

The boy agreed, feeling slightly sick, as he saw the wheals on Ralph's back.

'Now, boy, I am going to the steward's room to get some neat brandy and you will stay here while I go and keep the water in the tub warm.'

In a short time she was back with an old sheet and a flagon of brandy and a jar of maggots. The story she had told the steward had not been believed but Ned already trusted the girl and knew well enough that in a big household some things tended to go with a nod and a wink. One thing was sure; the girl was no drinker and deserved the praise that Lord Amalie had given her.

Sarah tore the linen into strips and folded one for Ralph to put in his mouth to bite on knowing the pain would be excruciating when she poured the brandy on it.

The boy stoically muffled his cries as she gently patted the area; the damage was too deep for a paste and still oozing bloods so she applied some clean linen and bound his chest with clean strips.

'Now, boy, we will tidy you up and then you will be fit for your father, but when your meeting is over you will retire to your bed and I will bring the maggots to you. They are the only way to clean the wounds, you will lie on your stomach for the night and I will sit with you and when they are gorged I will put on more of them. By the morning the place will be clean of pus and dead flesh and I will apply the aloe paste and we will have you healed in a few days. God knows what would have become of you if we hadn't got to this in time,' she finished, putting her hands on hips to make the point, sure Ralph would do as he was told for once.

*   *   *

The day had been lit with a feeble winter sun and darkness had come suddenly, and Lord Thomas's study assumed a different feel. The heavily book-lined walls closed in, Jack had put up the thick wooden shutters, and a bright fire blazed in the huge fireplace. Hera and Diana had already found their usual position and gazed blinking into the flames as if transported to some halcyon grove. There were moments when Lord Thomas envied them their well-ordered, comfortable lives. He reflected that the human condition brings with it a predisposition to worry. This was just such a moment. His two beloved children were soon to arrive to eat supper by the fire. It was the first evening they would have spent together since the big celebration supper for Ralph's return and there were some serious matters which he needed to discuss. Never before had he felt the heavy mantle of responsibility as he did now, because he knew in his heart that the day would come when he would no longer be able to protect them and control their lives and this was the hardest thing he had ever had to bear.

The door opened and Jack came in carrying a tray. 'Shall I

wait until Miss Flora and Master Ralph come before I set the meal?' he asked.

'Yes, set the tray down and bring us some ale and elderflower water now, Jack. You are a good and faithful servant,' he said reflectively.

'No more than you deserve, your Lordship,' said the man quietly, bowing as he left the room.

He did not have time to shut the door before Ralph and Flora came in. Lord Thomas did a quiet appraisal of his two children. Ralph had sprung up so that he was now the same height as his sister, he had a faint down on his upper lip and when he greeted his father there was a small break in his voice; and then there was Flora whose beauty never failed to strike him, reminding him of her mother. They made a charming duo, she so feminine and his son already showing the signs of the man he would become. That at least, he thought, was consoling, and he reflected that life was an endless series of challenges, and that no sooner had one been surmounted than another presented itself. What he was about to discuss with them would be a test of all the boy's maturity and of his daughter's strength and intelligence; he had no doubt about the latter but he knew that this would not be enough in a world dominated by men.

'Let us gather round the fire,' he said, drawing them both in his arms. And there for a moment in the warm still room they were a family enjoying a fleeting moment of complete happiness.

'My dearest children,' Lord Thomas began slowly. They both sat forward in their tall wing-back chairs, watching their father's face as if anticipating some news that would go ill with them. 'There are things we must talk about, plans to be made, for we have to run our lives rather than letting them run us,' he began.

'Father, you look so serious,' Flora interrupted anxiously. 'Do you have some bad news?'

'Not exactly,' replied Lord Thomas. 'The fact is, dear children, I am not well. I have the coughing sickness and the condition is not improving. We all know the sickness comes and goes but we must be prepared. The time will come when I must take my leave of you and join your dearest mother, which is God's gift to me; you see there is not a day has passed when I have not missed her.'

'No, Father . . . no,' cried Flora, throwing herself to the ground and hugging his knees.

She began to cry quietly and Ralph felt his eyes prickling and tears beginning to trickle down his face. The sight of his sister's shoulders heaving and the noble face of his father in the flickering firelight consumed him with a dark black grief. He realised that he had returned home full of hope and confidence that this was a new beginning, after all the sorrow of his mother's death and the ghastly ordeal of his schooling, but it was all to be taken from them with their father's last breath.

'Be brave, my daughter. I have some time left and we will make good use of it,' said Lord Thomas, caressing her thick chestnut hair.

'Father, what are we to do without you, we will be orphans,' Ralph stammered bravely.

Lord Thomas had resolved to keep the situation as un-emotional as possible since he knew his children would need cool heads to deal with the world with which he had begun to feel increasingly weary. 'Come here, my boy,' he said sensibly, 'sit on the footstool at my feet as you used to do and we will make a plan, for it is you, Ralph, who will be the man of the family then. It is you who will have to watch out for your sister and care for this great inheritance for your own children.'

'I will, Father, I swear I will,' said Ralph, although he felt as if his heart would break into a thousand pieces. Whatever happened he was grateful to Ignatius Kettle who at least had taught him courage and self-control.

'The first thing I must do is explain to you both how things are,' said Lord Thomas. 'As you know this estate and the home farm will be yours, Ralph. Flora will have the dower house and the priceless garden which has in it the rarest tulips which helped make our fortune in the world and which have been of great interest to our new King. But, Ralph, you are not of age and will not be for four years. I will have to appoint a guardian, who will obviously be Flora.'

At mention of this Flora reacted violently there was much she wanted to say. 'But, Father . . . ' she tried to interrupt.

Lord Thomas silenced her with a gesture and continued in an even voice. 'As you know, children, Flora will be able to manage your affairs. But any fortune a woman may have goes to her husband upon her marriage for him to do with as he pleases, and many a great fortune has been debauched because of this iniquitous law.'

'If I were Flora I would remain unmarried,' said Ralph perspicaciously.

'No, clearly this cannot be the case,' said Lord Thomas with a short laugh, which lightened the atmosphere. 'No, Ralph, your sister must marry,' he continued in a business-like fashion, 'she must be given a jointure and things must be done in a proper manner, so that I will leave this world a happy man in the knowledge that all will be well with my children.'

The room suddenly took on an ugly hue as Flora leapt to her feet, protesting violently.

'Father, do you mean I am to be sacrificed to a man of your choosing like one of your cattle?' she raged. 'I do not choose to marry and in any case where do you suppose I can find a husband in so short a time . . . frankly I would rather stay an old maid and protect Ralph. I care not for the male sex after what has just happened, with the exception of you, dearest father and of course Ralph.' Flora's cheeks were blazing and her small bosoms heaving. She was in a state of fury such as her father did not think her capable and he was both pleased and alarmed to see it.

'You did not give me a chance to finish,' said Lord Thomas. 'As you know, Lionel Wellbeloved is at court in the Chancellor's office. I have consulted him and I have protected Flora's property. There is a way; I have nominated him and a colleague as trustees for Flora. She will have a life interest, any heirs she may have will be the ultimate beneficiaries, no husband can take it from her, and if she should die without children it will go to you, Ralph.'

'How clever you are, Father,' said Ralph. 'I know of another reason why these things are so important. If people do not sort these things out the Crown is the freeholder of every bit of land in England and it will take it back. I learned that with Mr Kettle when we did Roman Law.'

'I am impressed with you, Ralph, but let us not forget the matter of a husband for you, Flora,' said Lord Thomas. 'I have a plan, Flora, and I have already put it into motion. We shall go to London; you might find a suitor who offers more than the weakling to whom you lost your heart. Who is to say a more practical approach would not produce a happier result?'

'Flora, Father may have a point,' said Ralph bravely and again Flora began to object, getting up and pacing about the room.

'Calm yourself, I will strike a bargain with you, Flora,' said Lord Thomas. 'If you do not find a man who pleases you in time I will not bring my authority to bear and will say no more on it; but you will have to play your part and be the fine lady you must become. Will you do this for me?' He knew she would not refuse.

CHAPTER FIVE

The Palace of Whitehall, February 1689

It was February and the new King and Queen had taken the throne in a bloodless revolution. Of the many rumours rumoured circulating one claimed that even the sheets were not taken from Mary of Modena's bed when Mary her stepdaughter arrived at the Palace and went to bed at once, suffering from exhaustion. But now the hastily assembled court was in session and things had reverted to a semblance of normality, as instanced by the gathering of young bloods and courtiers on this winter evening. This was an affair the royal couple attended under sufferance, preferring each other's company in the peace of their own apartments.

'Who is the girl standing with the older man, talking to those abominable Churchills?' asked one of them, Lord Edwin Grantley.

'Oh my dear fellow, that is little Flora Amalie, and the man is her father Lord Thomas Amalie. He is very thick with John Churchill,' replied his friend, Frederick Buckley.

'Oh yes I know the man now you come to mention it. He is well suited to the company. He swung with the Protestant wind when it suited him, like the Churchills who still keep their options open like the slimy climbers they are,' said Edwin, casting another languorous look at Flora.

'I think that is a trifle censorious. After all, many people have done the same. Just because you kept your Protestant head down during the Catholic monarchy doesn't absolve you,' quipped Frederick Buckley smartly.

'Well, tell me about the girl, we are getting off the point,' said Edwin.

'The father has brought her to court to find a husband, I believe,' said Frederick laconically.

'Does she have fortune?' asked Edwin bluntly.

Frederick did not answer at once. A girl like this new arrival, both pretty and possibly rich, was a prize. With his first thought of himself, Frederick wondered how best he might seek an introduction to his own advantage. But his mind traversed the opportunities and decided that he might be better served through a more vicarious acquaintance; Edwin Grantley would be more useful to him if he were to be endowed with a fortune. 'She does,' he said. 'The family have Dutch connections; they made a deal of money with tulips when they were the fashion. They say the family estate is remarkable, and the father is a shrewd businessman.'

'Is he now?' pondered Edwin, paying even greater attention to the young beauty who was looking decidedly bored.

He took notice of her gown and knew at once that it came from one of the best court dressmakers; it was of the latest fashion with folds of pale blue velvet sewn with pearls pleated under the breast and flowing gracefully to the ground with a little train the girl had attached to her sleeve with a satin bow. The light from the hundreds of candles caught the stones in a fine necklace of sapphires and diamonds, showing off her long neck and thick chestnut hair curled with contrived artlessness in smooth swirls, one of which danced enticingly on the girl's small round breasts.

'Do a fellow a favour and present me,' Edwin said. 'You can't keep a jewel like that hidden for long and I would like the first bite of the cherry.'

Henry bridled delightedly at the thought. 'I will with pleasure, dear fellow, since I won a tidy packet from you last night and I expect funds will be running short,' Frederick answered with a slight sneer. 'But I warn you,' he went on, 'there will be no bite of that cherry if you intend to spit out the pip; the father guards her like the Holy Grail.'

As introductions were made Flora swept a low curtsey as she had been instructed; the young man who had approached so forcefully made no secret of his admiration and his eyes travelled her small body with hardly disguised intensity. She felt herself blushing and clicked open her fan to hide her face.

Truthfully, Flora was not enjoying herself. She had taken an instant dislike to Sarah Churchill who had for some reason taken it upon herself to be a kind of unofficial mentor to her. She hated the woman's over-gushing enthusiasm and found her constant references to the new Queen's sister Anne, a plain woman whom Lady Churchill seemed to have mesmerised, tiresome. Flora knew she had a fault: she spoke in haste and too frankly, and Sarah's propensity to dissemble, flatter and sparkle fascinated her, and a small part of her began to see that such insincerity was perhaps part of the emollient required to survive in this fast treacherous pool. She thought the woman was ill educated and unread. It was said that she could hardly write. But for all that Flora did have to admire the way at this moment she was bantering with the supremely handsome and confident young man who had approached.

Against her better nature she had to admit the young man had a beautiful godlike face. He was unusually tall and had a faultless roman profile and golden hair; in fact Flora thought he looked much as a Greek god might have looked. But there was something forbidding in the eyes, very bright blue, steely and cruel. Even so, his bright intelligence overruled any doubts she might have allowed as to his attractiveness.

Edwin made no bones about his interest in Flora and decided at once that the best line of approach would be to win over the father whilst mounting a subtle play for the daughter. Co-incidentally, he had recently come to the conclusion that he must marry and set his house in order. Flora Amalie was a fresh face at court. What's more, she could be wed and bedded in the country, out of harm's way, before she developed a taste for court life. The last thing he wanted was a wife who would cramp his style. Once a man had a wife in the country many a married beauty would find him a suitable bedfellow for the odd dalliance. Besides, he might even fall in love with the girl.

Now that, he thought silently, was a distinct possibility with this latest arrival, an opinion confirmed when the girl started to take an interest in his presence and joined in the dialogue he was having with Lord Thomas about the construction of Dutch ships. The girl seemed to know everything about the comparative build of English and Dutch vessels and even went into a complicated explanation of ship building in Ancient Athens. For a moment he forgot he was talking to a girl and offered her the same responses he would give to some important dignitary – that was until Sarah Churchill's unwelcome intervention.

'Now, my dear, enough of your country laddish ways,' she said with a coy conspiratorial look at Edwin. 'Young men look for more in an elegant young lady than a dull discussion about old bits of wood,' she continued with a slight laugh, in her high affected voice, unaware that she was the architect of a prophetic moment.

'Not this young man, my Lady,' said Edwin with a flourish. 'I find intelligence and education in a woman irresistible. After all, the court is full of empty-headed chameleons. Such women are lost to respectable posterity; how refreshing it is to find one who reads like a perfect book filled with knowledge and integrity.'

When he had finished there was an awkward silence and Edwin saw Frederick look pointedly at his buckled shoes as if the words were an embarrassment. But Edwin seized the moment and confidently took his advantage. He saw Lord Thomas look quickly at his daughter who met his gaze with an almost imperceptible smile, and then the father winked. Lady Churchill saw the exchange and was subtly disarmed; turning her back and shrugging her shoulders in petulant annoyance she walked away with a token curtsey.

Edwin was increasingly enchanted by the girl and particularly with the closeness to her father. They were clearly friends and the girl was used to talking about things other than fashion and frivolous gossip. 'May I show your daughter the view of the river from the gallery?' he asked Lord Thomas.

'By all means, if her maid accompanies her at a discreet distance,' Lord Thomas agreed, beckoning to Sarah who had been hovering in the shadows.

Before Edwin could take his new prize to the gallery, there was suddenly a buzz of excitement and word came that the King and Queen were about to make an appearance.

Having so recently arrived Lord Thomas had not had the opportunity to present his daughter; the whole process was very haphazard, unlike in the court of Charles or James, where such matters were carefully orchestrated with utmost attention to protocol. Now it was a different matter. Chances had to be seized and this was one for Lord Thomas. He had been given some minor appointments at court under the newly crowned King and Queen and was aware that his Protestant loyalties were under scrutiny, but so far he had had nothing but pleasant dialogue with William, who took a keen interest in the Amalies' famous Dutch Garden.

The crowd fell back in silence as the King and Queen approached and Flora had her first glance. William was a great disappointment to her, a small insignificant-looking man with a distinct stoop and a craggy, sickly face with a large, pronounced nose and rather small eyes. He was surrounded by a group of immensely tall men who drew even more attention to his diminutive height and stature. These, Flora was informed later, were his Dutch attendants. He exuded an air of discomfort and did not smile readily at the line of sycophantic courtiers. The Queen, on the other hand, was a handsome woman; she was at least a head taller than her husband, with a gracious kindly manner which charmed without effort and it was she to whom Flora was first presented. The King, upon seeing the introduction, joined them and fell into a casual relaxed discourse about the garden he was commissioning at Hampton Court, to be built in the Dutch style. Edwin watched the informal ease with which Lord Thomas and his daughter conducted themselves in the royal presence and was more enamoured than ever.

It was immediately clear to Flora that the King was a reticent person. He let his wife do the talking, and it was she who spoke warmly to Flora.

'And is this your first visit to the court?' she asked in a musical mellifluent voice, dipping her head a little as she was substantially taller. Flora felt at ease at once and had the impression that the Queen would be genuinely interested in the answer.

'Yes, Your Majesty,' Flora replied, fully intending to expand on the theme and then thinking anything she would say would sound stupid. At a loss as to how she should proceed she began to rack her brains for some intelligent comment but none came. The older woman, realising the girl might be tongue-tied at her first introduction to the royal personage, stepped in with the benevolent ease which Flora would grow to love and admire.

'Your father, Lord Thomas, is well acquainted with the court,' she said warmly. 'I remember him when I was young, and the King my husband has seen your beautiful garden in Suffolk. He came when he was staying with his cousin, the late King Charles.'

Flora looked at this gentle woman and found it almost impossible to believe that she had been party to the conspiracy that sent her own father James into exile with his wife and children. She asked herself how she could possibly have believed the absurd story that the Catholic heir was a changeling smuggled in under the noses of dozens of ghoulish onlookers. She knew that Mary and her sister Anne had both been separated from their father at an early age to be reared as strict Protestants and of course her own father had been forced to deny the Catholic faith, and he was a man of honour who must have recognised the deep abhorrence the country had for the Catholic Stewarts.

'I hope Your Majesty will pay us another visit one day,' said Flora bravely. The Queen nodded charmingly and moved on.

'That was well done, madam,' came a whispered voice rather too near Flora's ear to be seemly. She looked in surprise and saw it was Edwin. He had been watching the exchange.

'I think the Queen is a very lovely person,' said Flora. 'I hope she does come to our garden. My father has some new blooms which will be at their prime in about April.'

'So, where do you reside while you are in town?' asked Edwin.

'We have a small house in Paternoster Row; I have hardly been there but my father used it a lot when he was in service to King James,' replied Flora.

'I know the houses,' said Edwin thoughtfully. 'Did your family build it after the fire or did you buy it from someone?'

'My parents built it,' answered Flora. 'It is a beautiful house. After the fire they refurbished it with many new ideas, it has water closets and big windows and it's all built of stone.'

'We do have a lot to thank Charles for,' said Edwin. 'He had the vision to rebuild the city with a plan; people talk about London as it was before the fire, it was a haphazard dirty place. I was only three so I do not remember it.'

'That is what my father says,' said Flora. She was in fact making the quick calculation that Edwin was twenty-six and wondering why he was unmarried. 'It was a blessing in many ways,' she went on. 'I do believe that the dreadful pestilence that killed so many festered in all those old buildings. My mother used to say the fire was apocryphal.'

Edwin was not used to women who spoke as Flora did. He was both intrigued and a little wary, but he decided she was clearly her father's daughter and the man obviously had a sound business head on his shoulders. Everyone knew that buying up land devastated by the fire was a clever move. And the man would have struck a good deal because of its proximity to the great cathedral which was still being rebuilt from the plans of the great Christopher Wren. One day, when the building was finished, the Amalie fortune would be even greater.

'There is a drawback to the house,' said Flora as if reading his thoughts. 'I do not like the fact that Newgate prison is just around the corner. It is terrible to think of all those poor souls in there, sometimes awaiting the hangman just because they stole food for their child. If the wind is in the right direction you can smell the place.'

Edwin was sizing up his prey; the girl had a natural bloom about her. Obviously she was not a girl who would care for the life at court although with the new King and Queen things would be very different and a girl like Flora, with a mind of her own, would be more prized.

Lord Thomas had been aware of Edwin's interest in his daughter and saw that Flora was not averse to the attentions of this handsome blade. He decided to put a stop to the encounter for the moment and to make some enquiries about Lord Edwin Grantley. He had seen the man about the court and knew he came from a good Protestant family. He knew the father had died and the family estates were in Suffolk, but there was something a little too self-assured about the man, which concerned him.

'Come, my dear, we must circulate. I have people who want to see you, relations of your mother's who are from Holland, in the King's retinue,' said Lord Thomas, giving Edwin a token nod.

CHAPTER SIX

Paternoster Row, London, February 1689

'Where's the harm in it, Master Ralph?' asked Tom, the London steward.

'I should tell father, that's the harm in it,' replied Ralph.

'Look, there is nothing wrong in it. It's Monday and it's hanging day, the biggest one as well, twenty-four of them at Tyburn on the three-sided gibbet,' said Tom gleefully.

Tom was what Lord Thomas described as a 'good man'. He didn't know his precise age, but he had been rescued from sweep work as a lad by Lord Thomas's wife, who had refused to let the lad go up the narrow chimney whilst it was still warm. She had called for brushes and the sweep had come with the boy, who shivered with fear, his bony, undernourished limbs already suffering from burns.

'Wretched man,' she had cried. 'Leave the boy here and I will find a place for him.' She had done just that and the lad had grown into a trusted servant who today had charge of young Ralph on a day about town.

They could already hear the commotion as the crowd gathered outside the gates of the prison. There was much cheering and jollity as if it were a day of celebration; the throng was so dense that it spilled down the road outside the Amalie house, and the sun shone brightly on the winter morning.

'I don't understand,' asked Ralph falteringly. 'Why is everyone celebrating? It isn't as if the poor things have much to look forward to.'

'It's like this, Sir,' said Tom. 'They are going to their maker, and most probably they think nothing could be worse than the life they have had; and the crowd are not from the gentry, though there are plenty of them who will have paid good money to sit in the stands and watch the spectacle. No, these are the common people and they want it to be a good day for these folk. They will all come out dressed in their best; the relatives bring in all they can for the occasion. This is the day when they will show great courage, they will die bravely and folk will cheer them. You will see they will stop on the way and flowers will be thrown and the best sack for them to drink, so they are more or less insensible by the time they get to the place.'

'I can't imagine it,' said Ralph doubtfully.

'No, young Sir, you probably can't,' said Tom. 'The likes of you get their heads chopped at Tower Hill and no great send-off except jeering and insults, and that's no way to go. Our way, we make them feel they are somebody just for this one day and that's the way it is with the ordinary people. You see, the difference is that your people have always thought they were somebody all their lives until that axe comes down. And that must come very hard,' he said as an afterthought.

The decision as to whether or not to join the throng was, however, taken out of Ralph's hands; the crowd had become so dense and the momentum so forceful that turning back was impossible. Before he knew it, Ralph was in Warwick Lane and steadily moving with the throng to the infamous prison at Newgate. Although much had been made of the newly created building it still sat in a rank miasma of fetid human detritus. As they approached, a rousing cheer emanated from the crowd as the heavy iron gates were opened to reveal a cart containing the shackled figures of twenty-four condemned men and women. To Ralph they presented an astonishing sight, some of the men decked out in full morning dress, contrasting with their pallid prison skins; the women in a motley configuration of tatty white dresses, some of them reminiscent of a wedding garment. The girls, of which there were about four or five, held baskets of oranges and nosegays of fresh flowers, all that is except one. Ralph judged the girl to be about the same age as him. But on her sat no bloom of youth, her face was etched in dumb misery as some poor animal on its way to the slaughterhouse. She was painfully thin and a strange mixture of greyish rags clung to her body. As they got nearer Ralph pulled at Tom's sleeve.

'Look at that poor girl. She can only be my age. What can she possibly have done and why hasn't she got clothes and things like the rest? She is hardly decently covered.' asked Ralph.

'Older than you, Master Ralph, by at least five years. She has been starved all her life; it stunts the growth, you see, and she probably had no one to look out for her and was too weak to ask,' said Tom sadly.

The temperature had risen in spite of a light fall of snow the day before, and the combination of the dense mass of human bodies and the bright sunshine had already made Ralph hot. Without a moment's hesitation he pulled off the new velvet jacket his father had given him for his arrival in London and pushed through the throng. For some reason, as if sensing his approach, the poor girl turned and caught his eye. It was a moment he would remember all his life: her face told a tale of suffering and fear, and carried an expression which spoke of resignation to the terror that awaited her, also of abject loneliness and despair. It was a picture of the human condition which struck at the very core of Ralph's being. He thought of his own life, so surrounded by privilege and love. He had the warmth of the new coat, made of the finest cloth, the buttons of exquisite mother of pearl and French lace ruffs at the cuff. Under it he had a thick silk shirt and even without the coat he had more to cover him than the poor girl. He thought again of Ignatius Kettle and almost thanked God that he had at least experienced something of hardship.

He threw the coat while her look held his and she caught it and held the luscious fabric to her cheek and called out to him; he couldn't catch the words, but guessed it was a thank you. She struggled into the jacket and as if to match her newly found finery, someone threw her a bunch of flowers; they looked like hellebores and sprigs of bright red berries.

Ralph could not take his eyes from the girl. It was as if he had been bound in a tryst to go with her and be her guide, her supporter in her hour of need.

'Master Ralph! What in God's name do you think you are doing?' cried Tom, who had just caught up with him in time to see the whole spectacle.

'I had to,' said Ralph. 'The poor girl had nothing; I will not leave her. We will follow her right to the end; give her courage like the rest.'

'You are a fine young man, Master,' said Tom. 'A brave one too, when I think of Lord Thomas's anger when he finds you have no coat to go to court. Like as not I will lose my own shirt over the matter.'

'No you will not,' said Ralph. 'I will tell Father the truth, you had nothing to do with it. I won't desert her; how could I? Look, she still holds my gaze.'

Tom looked at the girl and sure enough she had fixed young Ralph with her gaze; her eyes seemed to plead with him and then they flashed for a minute to Tom's and he swallowed as he felt a catch in his throat. He was a man toughened by the vicissitudes of life but he had been saved by a kindness before his soul hardened, forever brutalised as had been so many of Tom's fellow men. If this act of kindness could save the girl's soul in her hour of need, so that she might find her redeemer in whom Tom, despite all, still believed; the young Master would have done something for a father to be proud of.

'The poor souls, but at least they have Jack Ketch to do the drop. He is the best, not like some who get it wrong: the cables do not hold and they all fall, only to be hanged all over again and that is not a pretty sight.'

Ralph felt sick and just for a moment he thought he did not have the stomach for this, but then he saw the girl still looking at him imploringly from the back of the cart. He waved at her and pushed forward. The cortege moved at a slow pace in the dense crowd, and Ralph and Tom kept up with a steady walking pace.

The journey took about two hours along the Old Bailey and then into Holborn and as they neared the dreaded place at

Tyburn Ralph heard more cheering crowds , but to his disgust the noise came from a group of finely dressed gentry sitting in elaborate stands garlanded with coloured ribbons. Orange sellers shouted their wares and vendors of all kinds were keeping them all well stocked with refreshments of every description and they looked as merry as if they had come to watch a performance at the King's theatre. On a nearby sward of grass several coffins lay with open lids.

The cart did not stop but proceeded to the infamous gallows, which were triangular in shape with three posts acting as supports. It came to a halt and the pathetic men and women were hustled without ceremony into another cart which went quickly under the gallows.

The portentous figure of Jack Ketch stood on a small platform, nodding graciously about him as if he were the great hero, paying particular attention to a row of houses nearby which Tom informed him were in a very grand location called Bryanston Square.

'You see, Master Ralph, they have little iron balconies where the residents have a good view.' In one they could see the Sheriff in his fine regalia. He made a sign to Jack Ketch who bowed in acknowledgement as if the proceedings were now declared open.

The condemned suddenly went quiet; the girl began to weep and Ralph tried to press forward. He suddenly had a desire to push through the crowd, to save the poor young girl in any way he could. Tom saw that his charge was in a frenzy of emotion and laid a restraining hand on his shoulder.

'There is nothing you can do, Master Ralph,' said Tom. 'I should not have let you come, it's best we start home and you try to put this out of your head. I thought I had the stomach for it but I don't, so let's go quickly.'

'No, I will not go now. I shall get through and keep watch on the girl,' insisted Ralph, who, despite himself, was stifling back tears of horror and disgust. He managed to push with more strength than he knew he had and called out to the girl. She was crying miserably and one of the other women, who was wearing a strange white cockade in her hair, tried to comfort her. A man shrieked at the woman, his voice blurred with drink. 'What use your cunny now, Fanny Coupling?'

The angry mob turned on him and he disappeared from view.

To his relief Ralph heard Tom's voice behind him. 'You see, that man betrayed his class and he will get a beating for that. Fanny Coupling is one of the greatest whores. There's many a man out there would take her for an honest woman if it weren't too late,' said Tom, shaking his head mournfully.

It happened so quickly that Ralph almost missed it. One moment the cart was standing still under the gallows, the next Jack Ketch and two assistants roughly put the nooses about the prisoners' heads and in what seemed like a second Ketch lifted a whip, frightening the horses who reared away, and the prisoners dropped, their feet desperately trying to find the ground.

'Oh, the Lord save us, the girl is still struggling she was too light,' said Tom, a note of hysteria in his voice. Several people had emerged from the crowd and ran to the gallows, pulling at the feet of the hanging prisoners, some still flailing wildly. They hung onto the feet, pulling them down, but no one was there to help the girl in her agonies. Tom pushed forward and as Ralph let out an agonised cry he pulled at her little feet and her body went limp.

To Ralph's never-ending shame he was violently sick. When he looked up, weeping relatives were taking down the bodies and gently laying them in the waiting coffins. There was none for the girl. 'Tom, what will happen to the poor girl?' asked Ralph brokenly.

'Don't worry; she will be given a burial. There is a gentleman who does it out of the kindness of the good heart he has. But I tell you, Master Ralph, I pray to the good Lord that I never see the like again. I saw it once when I was a lad but it was for a murdering robber who killed the driver of a coach and I was glad to see him go; but this is a shameful thing, since I know half of those poor souls had only stolen to feed their starving families. Let us go now to the church at St Paul's to pray for their souls.'

CHAPTER SEVEN

Paternoster Row, February 1689

'So my dear, the Commons has agreed that James by his ill-advised flight has in essence abdicated. I cannot understand the obdurate stupidity of a man so blinded by his own sense of rectitude. The Crown will be offered to William and Mary jointly, as she will not accept it on her own, and they will not accept the idea of a regency,' said Lord Thomas.

It was the end of January and the weather was so cold that the Thames had frozen over. Flora was pleased to be at home in the comparatively cosy London house where coal fires burned continually in all the grates. She had grown used to the pall of smoke that enveloped the city, synonymous with the murkiness of the constitutional events which occupied the Whig House of Lords and the predominantly Tory House of Commons. Her father attended all the debates, and was left in no doubt that the power would lie with William.

'Is it true that William has said he would not consider becoming what would be no more than a gentleman usher to Mary?' asked Flora.

'It is,' Lord Thomas confirmed. 'And he has said that he would accept Anne, Mary's sister, as heir should he have no children. I for one hope the matter will be resolved quickly, but the Tories have a deeply held conviction that the Monarchy is a sacred institution and I as a Whig see a more menacing picture. James has betrayed his country and now has a powerful French army at his back. The Catholic cause would be a tryst with the devil. No, he has lost the throne for the Stewarts; the curtain has risen on a new era.'

In truth, Lord Thomas had sought his daughter out on a

more personal matter than the traumatic events at court. As they had been talking he had been watching her closely. All the while she had been working on her sewing, her hands fluttering lightly as butterflies among the brightly coloured silks. His heart expanded in his chest: she reminded him so much of her mother; in his eyes her beauty was perfection as had been his wife's, but he thought of the many missed opportunities to tell Flora's mother how he felt. It had not just been her looks but also her bright stalwart character which gave such power to her loveliness. Perhaps it had been out of a kind of fear that should she have known how much he loved her and admired her she would become complacent about him. But many had been the moments when he had regretted the silence, long after she had left him for a better place. But now he felt at least he had a chance to repair what was left undone with his daughter, who gave so much joy by her very existence. His health had not deteriorated as he had feared but he knew the reprieve was only temporary, even though the remission had lulled his children's initial fears at the prospect of losing him.

There had been a comfortable silence; Flora looked up suddenly with her cool gaze. 'Father, you have been watching me. I know there is something on your mind,' she said affectionately.

'You know me so well,' replied Lord Thomas, putting a hand on her shoulder. 'There is something we need to speak about, and it is Edwin. I have noticed you watching him at court at every occasion.'

Flora stopped her work and lay it down in her lap with what he thought might be a slight gesture of irritation.

'He is going to ask you for my hand in marriage, Father,' she blurted. Everything had happened so fast. She burst into tears. 'I don't know what to do,' she cried.

'I guessed as much! He doesn't waste time, does he?' her father replied. 'Surely the first question you must ask yourself is, do you love the man?' he declared

'I don't know what love really is,' said Flora with a troubled look. She had loved Roderick, or so she had thought, and she had thought he loved her, but any such love had been proved worthless to her by his betrayal and her heart had hardened against such a commitment. She had decided to forget about love, to concentrate on more practical aspects to her choice of husband since, as she well knew, marry she must.

Lord Thomas had in fact suffered almost more than Flora herself when Roderick had shown such detestable lack of fibre. He could well understand how his daughter had now decided on a more pragmatic approach to her future. At first he had been encouraged in his enquiries about Edwin. He had known the man's father who had been a well-thought-of Parliament-arian. He had held a seat in Parliament until he had been ousted by King James's underhand methods of packing the house with Catholics but now the seat had been restored and, mysteriously, although Edwin had been offered the seat upon his father's recent death, it still remained vacant.

The absence of a decision upon the question worried Lord Thomas, but even more worrying to him was the fact that neither he nor Flora had so far visited Edwin in his country home where his widowed mother still managed the estates during her son's continuing absence, as he spent his time at court or in the company of the gaggle of feckless young men who gathered like limpets on the coat tails of London society.

Lord Thomas agreed the man had more than his fair share of charm and was certainly well off, he was impeccably connected and if he decided to take his father's seat in Parliament he would be a serious figure. But there was something in the man that worried Lord Thomas. He didn't know if it was a cunningly disguised weakness betrayed in his rather too generous mouth which spoke of a loucheness, or his verbal flippancy, which tended to trivialise everything, admittedly to the amusement of his young acolytes. He had seen Flora laughing with the others and that too had concerned him, for he knew his daughter was of a serious nature.

'I would like to make a suggestion,' said Lord Thomas.

'Tell me, please,' said Flora eagerly.

'I propose that before you encourage the young man to take the thing further we pay a visit to his family, for it is only when you see the lion in his lair that you will see the true nature of the man,' said Lord Thomas. 'You have to satisfy yourself that he is a man who will care for you and provide a future for you away from this place and, I am sad to say, away from all you love at home, for the tree cannot be replanted so to speak until it finds its roots in new soil. You will have to be sure that this man can be a father and husband, a man with whom you can grow old and one with whom your beautiful spirit may walk through life compatibly.'

CHAPTER EIGHT

Founder's Hall, Norfolk, March 1689

It was decided. Edwin greeted the suggestion with enthusiasm and a few days later there was Lady Grantly awaiting them in the doorway of the historic house.

'Oh my dear, I shall like this,' Lord Thomas murmured as the coach came to a halt in the cobbled forecourt.

'And I,' Flora added, squeezing his hand.

The house dated back to Elizabethan times and had been built with the fortune Edwin's ancestor had made when he joined one of the first expeditions to the East Indies. The plan had been ratified in September 1599 in Founder's Hall in the City of London, hence the name of the family home. The man had been an ordinary merchant and knew little of the sea, but he had learned quickly and commanded a fleet of vessels manned by experienced old sea dogs whose courage and ingenuity had been rewarded with huge fortunes and the establishment of the spice trade which had made England the glorious nation that Queen Elizabeth loved.

The house was constructed of mellow red brick with a plethora of leaded windows looking onto formal gravel walks and a maze of clipped yew hedges. Set into the façade above the windows were intricate scrolls and plaques depicting many of the ports and arms of the countries and islands to which the first Edwin Grantley had sailed with such skill and bravery. Roses of all varieties clung to the weathered walls, the first tiny green shoots waiting eagerly for the spring. The whole was both welcoming and had, whilst still being a statement of the wealth of its creator, a cosy, informal air, unlike the ordered symmetry of Catherine's Court to which Flora was accustomed.

'Welcome,' said Lady Grantley expansively, stretching out her arms, her long lace sleeves billowing in a ripple of breeze.

'Madam, it is a pleasure to travel on such a lovely day and your greeting is in keeping with all your son has led us to expect,' said Lord Thomas, giving her a courtly bow.

She gave him a smiling curtsey and turned to look at Flora whom her father was assisting in her descent from the rickety coach steps.

'And this, Lady Grantly, is my beloved daughter Flora,' said Lord Thomas proudly.

'I have heard so much of you, my dear; in fact Edwin has spoken of little else since he returned to plan your visit,' said Lady Grantley as Flora gave her a curtsey.

'Is Edwin here?' asked Flora after greeting her prospective mother-in-law politely. She looked round impatiently, disappointed at his absence.

'He was only a moment ago, but he is in such a dither, supervising all sorts of details for your entertainment. He will be here directly, I am sure,' Lady Grantley reassured her, taking her arm and leading her into the house.

They were immediately enveloped by the fragrant smell of burning apple wood and beeswax polish. The entrance hall floor was polished like glass and a substantial collection of armour lined the walls. On an ornate carved oak staircase, the light from many thick candles accentuated the warm feeling of domestic harmony. Flora and her father felt reassuringly at home.

'How lovely to have the candles lit so early,' Flora commented appreciatively.

'Yes, that is all Edwin's doing. He wanted everything to be perfect for here on the fens the light seems to fade in an instant and Edwin detests darkness.'

Something about Lady Grantley's remark set an alarm bell ringing in the back of Lord Thomas's mind, but he did his best to dismiss it, trying to think only of how charming Edwin's mother was.

There was no doubt that the charming Lady Grantley was,

like her son, prepared to take his Flora to her bosom; he could tell by her satisfied smile as she watched her. Lord Edwin liked a pretty woman and she had a bearing he had to admit was quite delightful. Despite her widow's black, which she wore with great elegance, a crisp white fichu of exquisite lace framed a youthful neck, upon which sat a very beautiful face; her hair was caught in a lace cap and he could not guess what colour it was, but her eyes were a deep blue, matching perfectly a pair of sapphire earrings, her only concession to colour.

'Come into the drawing room. Edwin will, I am sure, be with us shortly,' said Lady Grantley.

The sound quickly muffled in the panelled room hung with rich tapestries which Lady Grantley referred to as her 'Arrases'.

'How lovely the hangings are, Lady Grantley,' said Lord Thomas. 'Pray, what are the stories depicted?'

'Oh, thank you, Lord Thomas,' replied Lady Grantley. 'They are the history of Orlando and Artanasa, and of Troy. They are all worked with gold and silver threads on clove-coloured cloth, which is why the light from the candles makes them so beautiful, and they are all lined in thick velvet which keeps the room so warm, for I do so hate the cold. Upstairs in the sleeping chambers we have forest motifs and some most beautiful and elaborate designs of fruit and foliage.'

Flora's eye had begun to focus on the cosy, elaborate furnishings. It was a style to which she was again unaccustomed, since the rather more simple interiors of Catherine's Court were of the Dutch style. She had begun to feel very much at home in the house and her eye fell upon the many fine furnishings, cedar tables and chests, some of them draped with thick brightly coloured velvet cloths, and thick rugs covering the original Elizabethan floors. As she slowly absorbed the room, she caught sight of a harpsichord in the corner.

Lady Grantley followed Flora's gaze. 'Do you like the instrument, my dear?' she asked.

'I do, Madam, and I would dearly love to play on it later, if it would please you,' replied Flora.

'And that you shall,' came a strong male voice from the doorway.

'Edwin, at last; we could not think what had become of you,' said Lady Grantley, obviously relieved.

'Flora,' Edwin said smilingly, taking her hand and holding it to his lips in a way which made Flora blush.

Lady Grantley saw the greeting with pleasure. There were many reasons why the prospect of so charming a wife for her son might alleviate some of the many concerns she had about him.

She loved him very deeply and whilst the rest of the family, including his three married sisters, was exasperated by her apparent blindness to her beloved son's failings she was in reality only too well aware of them. She knew that Edwin was charming and intelligent but he had a weakness, and that was easily exploited by the company he kept. A wife could be the making of him, or so she thought.

For Lord Thomas's part, he was a perspicacious fellow and had read the young man well. For him, the meeting with the mother was of singular importance. If Flora were to marry him this would be her home, of which she would be mistress, and he made up his mind to explore what ideas Lady Grantley might have for her own future if this were to be the case.

Edwin continued in a long lingering look upon Flora's modestly lowered face, during which Lord Thomas met the indulgent smile of Lady Grantley. There was between them an indefinable and sudden understanding and he began to feel more at ease about his daughter's future. He liked Lady Grantley; she was a distinguished and charming woman and had obviously married and produced her family at a young age since she looked no more than forty. Such a woman would be a kindly mother-in-law and surely a steadying influence on Edwin who had probably begun to tire of sowing his wild oats.

'Lord Thomas, welcome to our home,' said Edwin warmly as he interrupted the reverie. 'I was in the kitchens when you arrived, organising the wines with the steward. I did not hear you as they are separated from the house by a long passage in the French style since we did away with most of the boiling cauldrons and installed new hearths for roasting.'

'You must forgive Edwin,' Lady Grantley interrupted quickly, nervous that their guests might not wish to be embroiled in a lengthy domestic discussion. 'My son gets enthused very easily. We had a fire here a few years ago. It started in the bake house and although sadly we lost a young maid, whose fault the fire was, our stewards acted quickly and the flames were doused swiftly. But Edwin has moved the kitchens and we now have only boys near the fires, since it is the skirts of these poor girls which are the problem.'

'How dreadful,' Flora exclaimed, although truthfully this came as no surprise, since these accidents were a common occurrence in busy kitchens where the welfare of lowly female servants was low on the list of priorities.

'Now let us talk of something more interesting,' said Lady Grantley as she offered them some cordial from tall silver cups. 'Why don't you retire to your chambers to prepare for our evening meal?' she asked after a brief conversation. 'The stewards showed your servants to your rooms, so everything should be ready for you.'

'Yes, Mama, and perhaps I should tell you that one of my sisters is joining us tonight with her husband, as they live quite nearby and are anxious to meet you,' said Edwin, addressing the information primarily to Flora, who acknowledged it with a curtsey as they left the room to mount the panelled staircase.

*   *   *

Sarah was waiting with everything in order when Flora arrived. A magnificent elaborately carved oak four-poster bed occupied nearly all the floor space. It was hung with heavily embroidered silk curtains, lined with contrasting coloured velvet. There were matching armchairs and footstools, a cabinet inlaid with mother of pearl with numerous tiny drawers in which Sarah had placed Flora's toiletries and a large table with an ornate lace cloth beside which was a long full-length mirror. As Flora caught sight of herself in the reflection, to her surprise she also saw the figure of Edwin. She turned at once.

'Ah, please forgive the intrusion but I saw you had left the door open and I came to tell your maid that there is hot water waiting below stairs and I omitted to ask the boy to bring it to the door.' He looked firmly at Sarah as she arched her brows in surprise since she would not normally have been expected to make such a visit below stairs, which was most definitely the job of a lowly boy servant. But Edwin winked at her and at once she knew it was a ruse to be alone with her young mistress.

Before Flora could express her discomfort at such a request of her beloved maid, Sarah dropped a curtsey and left the room, calculating that the interval would not allow time for any improper activities.

As soon as she had left, Edwin covered the distance between himself and Flora. Catching her around the waist, he held her closely and rapturously kissed her. He propelled her towards the bed and together they fell into the plump pillows. Flora's body responded to the warmth of the room and the pounding of her heart and although she wanted to submit to her desires, for there was no denying the attraction she felt for him, she determined to remain pure. At first, Edwin, aware of the melting responses on her mouth and the sensuousness of her breathing and the muffled moans with which she responded to his passionate incantations of desire, had other ideas. It would be so easy to overpower her and he had taken the precaution of slipping the bolt on the door after Sarah's departure, but with unexpected force Flora pushed him away, sitting up on the bed while he lay, somewhat abashed, looking up at her.

'Edwin,' she said slowly. 'I know little about these affairs, and I know you have been with many women and there can be few secrets of the female body that you do not know, but I will not share my own except in the marital bed.'

Edwin had, up until now, had a strangely ambivalent attitude to women; he was well aware of his own attractions for the opposite sex, and indeed the ready availability of women in the circles in which he raced had made him cynical about the concept of love. He had simply taken his life and milked it of all he could get out of it, with little or no thought of the future. He had left it to his mother to think about that. He had been under the misapprehension that she did not suspect the true nature of his life; but the arrival of Flora and her father, with the clear directive that she would be his wife if he asked her, and the joy he had seen in his mother when she met her, had opened his eyes to the hovering presence of Nemesis.

As he looked into Flora's eyes he saw the vehicle for his own salvation. All the years of social imprinting that he had inherited from his antecedents appeared in his subconscious with a chorus of disapproval. He would not spoil her. Rather, she would be his prize; she would save him from himself, that person that he dared not confront until now.

'You are not like the other women I have known,' he said gruffly. 'Let it be done well, dear Flora. I will ask your father tonight before we dine so that we may celebrate.' He hesitated, pulling her down on the bed again but this time with a very different purpose. 'I respect you, Flora. You are the first woman I have said that to.'

'Respect me!' she cut him short indignantly. 'You must love me, Edwin, I will settle for nothing less.'

'Love!' he said quickly. 'The word is tired for me, Flora. I have often used it when I did not mean it but wanted to assuage my desires; it is a word which women do not understand where men and their lusts are concerned; this word love opens the door to sin as if it were not a sin but an entitlement. What I feel for you is better than love, it is adoration. Love is part of that, but worthless without what I feel for you, which is so many things. You may laugh, but respect me too.'

She did laugh suddenly. 'Do you know, Edwin,' she said, lowering her voice seductively, 'what you have said has settled the matter; let us get about the business of our wedding with no more talk of meanings. These are semantics. It is in the business of living that we will find love.'

And so it was decided and later, when the family, Flora's new family, sat around the long refectory table which had served the Grantley family for two hundred years, there was great happiness. For Flora, because she had become enamoured of Edwin since she had seen him in his home and she had liked and chimed with Edwin's mother at first sight, realising how much she had missed her own. Marrying Edwin would give her back a mother and hopefully lead to her becoming one herself. Their eyes met across all the congratulatory chatter and she felt real joy and relief, as if she had been released from many things which had been hard to bear. She and Ralph would be part of a family if her father died, as she feared he would.

Lord Thomas was pleased because the doubts he had held about Edwin had evaporated in the warmth of the Grantley family. Edwin's mother was an exceptional woman. He thought wistfully how, if he had not known that his days were numbered, he might even have courted her himself.

Lady Grantley felt relief. This was the sort of fine young woman who would rein her son in, the son of whom she did not want to hear ill but about whom she had felt a deep mother's concern, yet chosen to focus on his better qualities, blaming the idiotic feckless company into which he had fallen for any bad behaviour. Perhaps now, she thought, he would want to be where he belonged – with this beautiful young woman.

But there was one person present who did not share this universal joy and that was Sarah. She came from a country family where men worked so that they could eat, and slept so that they could work; the gentry were different. With some exceptions, of which Lord Thomas was one, they slept to recover from the excesses they saw as their right; they ate and drank with no thought of who or what had given them the beneficence of their groaning table; and their sleep was not to restore weary overworked limbs, but to enjoy the sweet dreams of their abundance. She did not like Edwin, there was something discomfiting about him and the mother Lady Grantley saw it too. Sarah saw the intent way she watched her son as if suspecting there was a dark secret in his life. But with the denial of a mother's heart, Sarah suspected that Edwin's mother would do anything rather than discover an unwelcome truth about her handsome, amusing son.

Sarah knew it was not her place to alert her young mistress to these intangible concerns; no, she would watch and be there when and if, with her down to earth countrywoman's instinctive guile, she could advise and protect. It was not only Flora's interest that alarmed her. What about Master Ralph? How would he fit into all this? Sarah knew without being told that Lord Thomas had a sickness and would probably join his maker sooner than he would like, and what then, she wondered?

For the time being, however, an air of relief exuded from all members of this soon to be intertwined family. However, unbeknownst to them all Edwin had a personal battle to fight and he had seen the innocent Flora as his inadvertent rescuer.

CHAPTER NINE

Catherine's Court, April 1689

'A more beautiful bride could not be imagined,' said Lord Thomas, his heart bursting with pride. Flora had just descended the wide staircase in her gown. It was her mother's, carefully preserved with lavender and camphor. It was as bright and effulgent as the day Flora's mother had worn it. Sarah had repaired the hem of the train upon which one of the bridal attendants had stepped all those years ago; and some of the drop pearls that bordered the tightly fitting bodice had come loose and been replaced. They were now intertwined with ivory coloured ribbons tied in bows at Flora's petite waist. Lady Grantley had produced a family veil of intricate, gossamer-thin French lace secured by the Amalie tiara of diamonds and pearls.

There were four little flower girls with satin purses full of fresh rose petals to scatter in front of the couple on the triumphant parade. Ralph had been given an important role, master minding the seating for the two hundred guests. The estate workers and retainers were dressed in all manner of Sunday finery but there was not one of them who did not feel keenly the sense of loss that Lord Thomas would feel as he gave his beloved daughter to a man in the eyes of God. It was of course the simple country people who subtly empathised with situations like this. They did not send their children away to far off places or dispatch their small children to be cared for by others. Families stuck together and a bridal couple would oft as not live with the family even when the babes began to come.

All these things were wrenching at Lord Thomas's heartstrings as he walked up the nave of the local church. There was a lush silence, the strains of music from the players fading on the air.

Birds sang outside in the sunlit churchyard; Flora's train had been dropped to the floor and swished on the stone flags as she walked in tandem with the beating of her own heart.

Edwin looked around with an expression of awe. He fidgeted nervously with one of his lace cuffs. There was something ethereally beautiful about this girl to whom he was about to commit himself and for the first time in his life he was confronted with the feeling – unusual, for him – of responsibility. For a moment he almost felt like running away. But at the moment when Lord Thomas gave him his daughter's hand and her veil was lifted and she looked into his eyes with a simmering desire, albeit couched in suitable reserve, he took her gladly and lovingly, only riddled with doubts as to his own worthiness.

In her young girl's heart, and comforted by her liking of Edwin's family, Flora entertained only the prospect of romance and love and happiness. She thought of their wedding night, the first together, with a mixture of anxiety and excitement. They were to spend it in the suite of rooms previously occupied by her mother and depart for Edwin's home the following morning.

*　　*　　*

Her father had commissioned new hangings and the room was packed with spring flowers. Sarah had pulled back the fine linen sheets and early jasmine flowers had been scattered; the signs were auspicious and a warm glow surrounded the bride and groom. The door was finally closed and Flora was alone with her husband.

The bridal night was not as she had expected. Her surprise had, however, been tempered with a small measure of relief. She had had nobody to whom she had been able to confide her anxiety about this coming together in raw nakedness and she had never seen a man without clothes. Although Edwin had been discreet and retained his undershirt, the glimpse she had of him had unnerved her. Yet he seemed to have lost the urgency of previous advances.

'Stay awhile, Flora dearest,' he said, suddenly drawing back. 'I have a greater joy than the marriage bed to share with you.' He went from the bed to his dressing chamber and re-emerged carrying a densely embroidered carpet bag. He placed it on a table and slowly unlocked it with an expression of sublime, anticipatory joy. 'Lie back, my dearest wife, and I will share something with you, something which will take you to a place you hardly imagined.'

Flora's mind began to whirl, she felt the first tentacles of a cold fear tweaking at her heart; she sensed that something was not as it should be on this, her wedding night. What was Edwin talking about, what mysterious journey did he want to share with her? The answer was swift in coming as he pulled open the bag and produced a glass bottle. It was ornately engraved with a serpent-like motif and contained a dark liquid. He pulled off the stopper and placed the bottle to his lips. The liquid moved slowly as if it were thick and glutinous. He swallowed and a look of sublime joy crept over his face.

'Now you must drink, Flora,' he said in a dreamy low voice, his eyes half closed as if in a moment of ecstasy. 'You must share this with me or we cannot be husband and wife, you need to sup with the Gods as I do.'

Flora sensed danger; she knew at once this was a dark evil. She had heard of such things, gossip in which she had taken little interest since she could not imagine such atavistic things being part of anything in her life.

'What is it, Edwin?' she cried hysterically. 'It is bad, I know it is. I have heard tell of it, it comes from the East and it is made from poppies and it brings a man to death and ruin.'

'I have no need to explain to you, madam,' he responded angrily grabbing her night shift and forcing it open exposing her breasts. He seized one of her nipples in his fingers and twisted it until she shrieked with pain.

She recoiled and leapt off the bed, grabbing her new ermine cloak, a present from her father; luckily she had left it on a chair by the fire. She stood in the firelight defiantly, breathing hard as her face went white with fear.

Edwin sat up in the bed, his eyes blazing. 'You dare to defy me, madam,' he bellowed in a voice she had never heard before. 'You are my wife; you have vowed to obey me in all things. You will come to the bed this instant,' he went on chillingly. 'You will take off your clothes or by God I will rip them off your back and you will open your mouth and your prissy little legs and you will do as I say and that will not be the only thing you put into that pert little maiden mouth of yours.' In a flash he was off the bed and bearing down on her with a glazed expression. But she was too quick for him and darted under his outstretched arms. She was at the door within seconds and miraculously it opened before she got to it. There stood the calm composed figure of Sarah, carrying a pile of linen.

'Oh, my Lady,' said Sarah, using Flora's new married title, 'I am sorry to disturb you. I meant only to leave the clean linen at the door and the girl has come with more coals for the fire.' The calm normality in Sarah's voice diffused the situation as if by magic. Flora knew at once that Sarah had been looking out for her, indeed had luckily been listening at the door. Their eyes met and Sarah held her mistress's in a steady meaningful gaze which spoke volumes, leaving no doubt that she understood the urgency of the situation. Tears were pouring down Flora's cheeks and she started to tremble like a leaf. She had the stark realisation that her husband, the man to whom she was now legally bound, was possessed by some awful demonic force about which she had no understanding.

'My Lady,' Sarah went on in a low voice, 'shall I bring you some elderflower wine?' Sarah held her mistress in a steady gaze and let her eyes stray over her heaving shoulders, for by this time Flora could not control her tears, but she had the good sense to cry silently while her mind raced, knowing that Sarah, in her indomitable way, was thinking quickly.

'How curious,' came Edwin's slurred voice. 'A timely intervention, may the devil take you both.' He turned and walked towards the marble table where he had left the bottle. He picked it up and tipped it to his lips. 'You to hell and I to heaven,' he muttered incoherently. He turned and fell onto the bridal bed as if in a torpor; his head fell back and his eyes closed, his breathing becoming thick and laboured.

'He is gone, my Lady,' said Sarah.

'Gone,' Flora cried. 'Do you mean dead?'

'No, my poor lamb,' said Sarah. 'But he might as well be. I had my suspicions, the mood changes, all the symptoms; he is a slave to the stuff.'

'I don't understand,' wept Flora, 'he turned into an unrecognisable fiend.'

'Come; let us go from this room. Leave him to sleep it off. He will be out for many hours, no good to anyone. You had a lucky escape, they say one sip of the stuff and you make a pact with the devil you can never be free of.'

Sarah found Flora's robe and slippers and steered her, like a rudderless ship, from the room and quietly closed the door. She led her stumbling mistress to her own modest quarters, a small cosy room adjacent to Flora's old bedchamber.

'Get into my bed, the linen is clean and fresh and I will bank up the fire and fetch you a posset from below. Bolt the door when I go, and when I get back we will decide what is to be done,' said Sarah in a quiet, firm voice.

Flora lay shivering until Sarah's return, heralded by a discreet tapping on the door. She had been thinking while her faithful maid had been gone, that without doubt she had been saved from a disaster so abhorrent as to be almost unimaginable. Any barriers which might have existed between the two women no longer existed. They were two friends whose survival was interdependent.

She raised herself from her collapsed state at once and let Sarah in. 'What am I going to do?' she asked in a trembling voice.

'I do not know,' said Sarah frankly, 'but the time has come, Madam, when we must keep a cool head, and if I am to be of use to you I must be allowed to speak my mind, in privacy of course,' she added emphatically through pursed lips.

'I know,' said Flora, nodding. 'You have hinted at things, and I have not wanted to listen. I suspect you had an idea about the sort of things that were going on in Edwin's life.'

'Indeed I did,' Sarah agreed, leaning down to the glowing fire and plunging the poker in the flames to heat it, wishing it was Edwin's heart. She pulled it out and dropped it in the drink she had brought up to the room; the milk bubbled up with a soothing smell of rum and she handed it to her grateful mistress. Flora watched Sarah as her brow furrowed. She was obviously thinking carefully about what to do. Yet again, as on so many occasions, she was struck by Sarah's practical objective approach, the way she carried out her own home-spun recipe of 'when all is in chaos keep the small things in perfect order.' The warm drink was just another example of a practical way of giving them both time to think.

'You see, it is servants' talk,' said Sarah after a few minutes. 'There can be few secrets from the person who washes the linen and takes the morning drink to a master or mistress. Of course I knew all was not well with Lord Edwin, it was the mood changes, you see.'

'I had noticed them, he was so convincing at explaining them away and oh Sarah . . . How am I to tell Father?' Flora could not go on. She bent her head and sobbed pitifully, as if her heart would break.

'I know,' nodded Sarah. 'I fear for him because the sickness has begun to return, his man has seen it in his kerchiefs and on his pillows in the morning.'

'So how am I to explain this calamity? It will kill him!' asked Flora, wringing her hands in anguish.

'You do not have a choice,' said Sarah in her newly acquired role as advisor and friend.

'You must explain to me first,' said Flora. 'What is this thing and can Edwin stop it? Can he ever be normal?'

'It is made from poppies; men have made great fortunes from it. It comes from the East. The talk is that Lord Edwin's family built their wealth on it. They were traders, as you know.

But many a young blade has fallen under the evil spell of the stuff, the gentry dress it up by calling it laudanum but sailors call it opium. They brew it by making juice from the head of the flower into a sort of syrup and then a powder. I believe your husband does it because we backstairs have smelt the sweet sickly stink of it.'

'But it makes him into a devil, why would he do that, and does his mother know?' asked Flora.

'One taste of it and a man is a slave to it forever, or so they say. And now your future is a fragile thing. It is an iniquitous thing that a man can lord over a woman in this way,' said Sarah passionately, 'and the fact is that unless we can save him from this, he could debauch your entire fortune and young Master Ralph's, and bring us all to ruin.'

The reality of what had happened gradually begun to dawn on Flora. She felt young and defenceless, and had it not been for Sarah's resolute dispassionate resolve she could not imagine what she would have done.

Luckily Sarah was at her best when faced with a challenge. After all, most of her life had been a challenge; facing these things head on was the only way she had ever known. It was what separated her from the gentry who so often awoke wide-eyed and stupefied when disaster struck, unable to make rational decisions when unexpected events interrupted their quest for pleasure.

Of all the things that Flora had dealt with this was probably the worst, because it was completely alien to anything she could have imagined. But Sarah's strength empowered her and gradually she started to feel her utter bewilderment replaced by anger and determination and rational thought. She decided that she would run her life rather than let it run her.

'Thank you, Sarah,' she said suddenly, taking her servant's hand in her own. 'I see now it is not just my problem but one we all have to deal with together. I have Ralph to think of and of course all of us, the family as we know it. I won't let you down, Sarah, I swear it. Together we will triumph over this evil. I feel

94

sorry for Lord Edwin's mother; she is a good woman and she deserves more.'

Sarah pressed Flora's hand encouragingly and they talked calmly together about the course they should take, deciding that they would have to tell Lord Thomas in the morning.

'Don't you fear, Lady Flora,' said Sarah as the fire dimmed in the grate. 'I will look out for you, and we will find a way. I promised your father and he gave me a chance in life. Without him I would be nothing, I was never one to forget what he did for me.'

And so it was decided. The two women's eyes met. They were two women who would not be beaten into any kind of submission. Flora took Sarah's hands and, holding them, brought them close to her furiously beating heart and made a promise to her.

'I do not take you for granted, my dear friend. Your loyalty to me will be honoured both now and in the future; the friendship of women transcends anything that can be forged between a man and a woman. It's our best chance, Sarah.'

Flora slept in Sarah's bed as Sarah slumbered easily in an armchair by the fire. It did not bother her much, she was used to grabbing sleep when she could. She was used to being the eyes and ears of her mistress, it was how best she could protect her as she crept about in the servant's garb of anonymity: invisible but, when necessary, lethal.

Ralph found them when he came to Sarah's door in the morning. She had forgotten to slip the bolt and he peered into the room gingerly.

'Flora, what are you doing here?' he cried in astonishment. 'It was your wedding night, why are you not with your husband?'

Sarah went to the door, and put a hand on his shoulder. Her life was now set on a path irrevocably bound to these two young people, Flora and Ralph, and though in years she was not so much older than her mistress, she had a world of experience behind her on the battlefield of life. She had learned cunning without betrayal, strength without ruthlessness, and, above all, she knew that faith in her own spirit was something she could pass to these two soon to be orphaned young people. She made an important decision. She would instruct not consult; the situation needed clear-headed action.

'Come sit down, Mr Ralph,' she said kindly, fluffing up a cushion in a chair by the fire. 'You are a man now, soon you will be head of a family, you have responsibilities; you will have to be told the truth, how things are so that together we may do the right thing.'

Ralph took in the charged atmosphere in Sarah's humble chamber, and recognised that for the moment it was the command centre of an inexplicable drama.

'Tell me then,' he said in a steady, grown-up voice, a hand on each knee as he sat very still and upright.

It was Flora who told him everything, and Ralph's face did not change expression. If he had learnt anything at Ignatius Kettle's establishment, it was that life was hard; furthermore it was just when things seemed to be going well that danger lurked with a sly sneer.

He listened intently and eventually the two women waited for him to say something. He got up and looked out of the window. Dawn was breaking, mist rising from the still cold earth; he had had an awful vision that soon his father would be in this same cold earth, and then as if in answer the first rays of sun picked at the gossamer veil and lifted it swirling up into the sky. The morning would be set bright and fair with the promising haze of a May day; he felt hope.

'We will walk in the garden,' he said in a gruff surprisingly deep voice. 'It is our garden, and whatever we have to do, it will remain so. We will tell Father all of it; he needs to know. If we do not tell him, he will sense all is not well and he will not be able to help us overcome this, and some fresh air will clear our heads.'

*   *   *

In their mind's eye the beauty of the garden was curiously heightened by the poignancy of the situation. This should have been the morning when Flora walked arm in arm with her new husband, awash with love and as one with the happy birds

96

celebrating the spring. A fat blackbird sat proudly on a sprig, eyeing the landscape as his mate waited with their demanding brood. The smell of damp earth tinged with the scent of blossom filled the air as they went to the tulip garden. The waxy green buds were about to burst and moved delicately together in an eddy of breeze, giving them the appearance of a lake sparkling with glistening droplets of dew.

It was here that Lord Thomas saw them as he came for his early morning constitutional with the dogs. They had sat down together in a little shelter he had built for his wife; it was situated discreetly at the end of the formal tulip garden, protected by a high wall with espaliered fruit trees now heavy with delicate pink flowers. They were so deep in conversation that, at first, they did not appear to see him.

'And why are you three here?' he asked in a puzzled voice. He had not slept well, the coughing had returned, but until now he had at least dared to hope that his family was settled on a path which set his mind at rest.

'My Lord, something terrible has happened,' offered Sarah hastily, getting up at once and throwing him a low curtsey.

Observing the awkward silence between Flora and Ralph, Lord Thomas acknowledged her greeting with a nod and turned enquiringly to his daughter.

Flora looked down and gave an apologetic look, but neither could find the words.

'Come, my children, this silence does not bode well; for the love of God, will one of you tell me what is going on?' he barked impatiently.

'My Lord, perhaps, if you will permit, I could help my Lady to explain to your Lordship,' said Sarah with lowered eyes.

'No, Sir,' Ralph interrupted quickly. 'I will tell you, for it is not proper for my sister to have to speak of such things; I am here to protect her,' he went on manfully.

'Come, let us go inside where you can all tell me what the matter is,' said Lord Thomas, trying to keep the anxiety from his voice. But below the surface lay a deep well of fear.

'In a word, my poor sister is given to a villain,' said Ralph bravely when they had arrived in Lord Thomas's study where a young maid was laying the fire. Sarah had signed to the girl and she had hastily retreated without a word, cunningly effecting to clean the brass handles on the door opposite in the long passage, where she would hear a verbatim account of things she would pass on to the servants as soon as possible. Depending on the nature of the gossip the girl could expect at least an extra helping of pie and it wasn't long before she realised it might also be a tumbler of Jack's ale.

Lord Thomas flinched. 'What can you mean?' he replied indignantly, throwing Flora a sideways glance.

'Lord Edwin, my brother-in-law, has a secret he has cleverly hidden from us all,' Ralph persevered boldly, reinforcing his decision that he should be the spokesman.

'So isn't someone going to tell me what this is all about?' Lord Thomas snapped, his face beginning to colour with fury. 'Has the man laid a hand on you, Flora? By God, if he has he will regret it,' he bellowed.

'If you would like, Master Ralph, I will explain,' said Sarah, glancing in Ralph's direction.

Ralph nodded and Sarah began in a calm measured voice while her benefactor listened.

When she had finished a silence engulfed the room, interrupted by the steady, contented breathing of Diana and Hera who had taken their customary place by the hearth. Their long silky bodies miraculously curled into neat curved balls. Occasionally during the horrible narrative, they had lifted their disdainful heads, casting their bright beady eyes in the direction of their master, remaining poised still as statues.

As the tale unfolded, Flora thought, recounted in Sarah's simple language it seemed more unbelievable than ever. The whole affair appeared disconnected from reality; and she shuddered. She thought in a mad way how the family dogs, with their routines of food and walks and fireside naps, were a barometer of domestic life which had begun to run so perfectly at Catherine's Court and wished she had not ventured out of the cocoon of their lives into a world full of mendacity and danger Now it was all about to crumble like a pack of cards.

Lord Thomas's face had hardened; slowly he got to his feet and walked to the window, silently surveying the garden. Nobody spoke, Flora sat in abject misery. Still in silence Lord Thomas went to the bell-pull by the hearth and peeled it loudly. The sound echoed through the house like a clarion call and Jack the steward was at the door in seconds.

'Send for Lord Edwin,' Lord Thomas bellowed. 'No delays, man, and use the front stairs. Take the hall boy with you, he is a sturdy lad. Drag the man here if necessary,' he finished roughly.

'Yes, Sir, at once,' said Jack, turning in haste and leaving the door ajar, his feet crashing on the stone floor as he cried out for the hall boy. The footsteps could be heard mounting the wooden staircase and going down the gallery. Still nobody spoke; there was an implicit understanding and confidence that Lord Thomas, despite his failing health, would have his own way of dealing with the calamity.

They continued to sit awkwardly until a commotion could be heard which suggested Edwin's reluctant arrival. Muffled oaths of protest could be heard approaching and Flora's bleary-eyed husband was delivered unceremoniously into the room.

He slumped immediately into a chair and sat motionless, a tell-tale bruise on the side of his face. Jack nursed a fist menacingly, wishing he had done more to Edwin while he had the chance. Edwin closed his eyes, shutting out the powerful image of the family whom he had so abused and the unnerving image of Jack and the boy hovering by the door, ready for more like two fighting dogs.

'Jack, you may go now, but will you both wait outside the door and I will summon you,' said Lord Thomas in a level voice. The men shuffled from the room, Jack barely resisting the desire to administer one more cuff to the recumbent figure of the despicable of Lord Edwin.

Flora coolly regarded her young groom who only the day

before had been the object of her girlish hopes and dreams. She hardened her heart; she envisioned a carapace and wrapped it about her. As if in empathy, Sarah took Flora's cold hand and held it.

'What have you to say?' said Lord Thomas, loading the question with menacing simplicity.

'I am lost,' relied Edwin in a hoarse whisper.

'Lost, man, what do you mean lost?' trumpeted Lord Thomas indignantly. 'You are here in this room with your young bride and her family whom you have betrayed. We look for more from you by way of explanation.' Truthfully, although Lord Thomas appeared calm he had a very real desire to kill the man. It would be easy to do, a quiet accident while the man was in no condition to defend himself, but then he reasoned that he would be a murderer no better than the depraved figure of the man who had brought them all to this low place.

Edwin had no answer and began to weep. It was a sight both shocking and unbearable; no one in the room had ever seen a grown-up cry like a child.

'I simply do not understand,' said Lord Thomas with thinly disguised revulsion.

Sarah sniffed disdainfully. 'Would you like me to explain to his Lordship?' she asked the heaving figure.

'No Sarah,' shot Flora, suddenly finding her voice. 'Edwin, Sarah has already explained to me. You are addicted to this evil thing, the poppy juice, and you quite simply cannot do anything without it. I have seen the people you mix with when you are at court; I suppose they all do it and think nothing of it.'

'What is this? No words? Has the devil got your tongue as well as your sense of decency?' barked Lord Thomas. 'Pull yourself together, man. Sarah, send Jack to get him some water, and some ice from the ice house.'

Edwin slowly began to open his eyes and contemplate the awful abyss into which he had dragged his new family. He sat up in the chair, pulling his dishevelled clothes together and turned his once handsome face to his father-in-law.

'Opium teaches only one thing, which is that aside from physical suffering, there is nothing real,' he said brokenly. 'May God forgive me,' he said thickly, turning to Flora.

'God may do, but I will not,' Lord Thomas expostulated.

Jack came back with the water and ice wrapped in a cloth which he clapped unceremoniously to the man's head, handing him the drink, half of which he let spill to the floor.

Jack did not leave this time; there was something he wanted to say, not because he had any sympathy for Edwin but because he felt it would be helpful to Lord Thomas and his poor young daughter to know just what they were dealing with.

'Your Lordship, begging your pardon for my impertinence,' he said forcefully. 'I know something of the affliction which has come upon my lady's husband. As we are family and I am here to protect your Lordship, may I be permitted to speak?' he asked.

'Of course, Jack,' said Lord Thomas. 'Anything you can say to us which might help us to understand this disaster will be appreciated.'

'Lord Edwin is possessed by a terrible addiction to a thing which has a terrifying power and it makes no distinctions. It's ruined good and bad men alike, it's worse than strong liquor which has ruined enough men, God spare them,' he said crossing himself. 'Once a man had sampled it,' he explained, 'he is a slave to the devil and all his works.' Jack paused for a moment unsure as to whether he should proceed.

'Go on, man,' urged Lord Thomas.

'Sarah and I had our concerns,' Jack continued at once, 'but it was not our place to say. You see, I had a cousin who had come back from sea and brought the stuff with him and then, when he could not get any more, although he would have murdered his own mother for the getting of it, he suffered horribly. He shook like a man with the ague. His limbs seized up and he writhed in agony. His innards turned to water and he entered the depths of hell.'

'Oh my God,' said Flora despairingly.

'Well, come on, Jack, where is the man now? Does this tale have a satisfactory ending, what can we do?' asked Lord Thomas, glancing at Edwin contemptuously.

'He is normal now, my Lord,' said Jack. 'We are a strong family. He had two fine sons who locked him in his room where he had to suffer the punishment God gave him. It took many weeks to get him right and sometimes he screamed like a man on the rack and begged for death. But our prayers were answered and Josiah, for that is his name, is restored to his life and his family.'

Jack did not tell the family about a sailor he remembered who had come home from the East to his home village. The man had died a dreadful death, ravaged by the pox and the evil consumption of the potions which had led him to such a dark end.

'Jack,' said Lord Thomas unequivocally, 'take Lord Edwin to the room beside my own chamber, see that he is made comfortable, and post two men by the door. He is not to leave the chamber, and we his family will decide what is to be done. Ralph, you will go with them and make sure the windows are shuttered.'

Edwin could see even in his befuddled state that he had no choice but to do as he was bidden. Flora regarded him numbly, her feelings blunted and as for Sarah, she had made up her mind that her mistress's husband was a bad lot. Her feelings were mirrored by Lord Thomas, but he knew that now this man was contracted to his daughter, extricating her would be no simple matter.

When the door was closed and Lord Thomas was alone with Flora and the faithful Sarah, whom he knew would be an integral part of whatever plan was decided, he told them be seated.

'I must ask you this, Flora, and I am sorry to do this in front of Sarah, but we can have no secrets from her since the situation is as dire as can be. Are you still a maid?'

'Yes, Father,' replied Flora, blushing.

'Thank the good Lord,' said Lord Thomas with a sigh of relief. 'We can have the marriage annulled.'

Sarah gave a satisfied smile; she had known the master would have a solution. She turned to Flora, waiting for her agreement, but none came.

'No, Father,' Flora threw into the silence. 'If we can save Edwin, we must try. He is my husband whether I have lain with him or not. You must go and see Lady Grantley. His mother is a good woman; he is her son, she will be expecting a home full of love for him, our rooms prepared with garlands of flowers, my wedding linen on the bridal bed. I could not be so cruel as to decide to discard Edwin without explanation.'

It was at times like this that Lord Thomas thought that if your children are no better than you are then you have lived in vain; but nothing detracted from the knowledge that he had proved to be a bad judge of character, not only of Flora, for she had a determined look in her eye as if she would be mistress of her own destiny, but also of the two men who had sought his beloved daughter's hand.

'Very well, if that is your wish we will go to Lady Grantley together, but this is on the condition that Edwin stays here under lock and key until our return and gives you some assurance that he knows what is at stake here.'

'I will go to him and explain and I will not be alone,' said Flora, glancing at Sarah who gave her a reluctant nod of assent.

Lord Thomas looked at his daughter with her youthful confidence still undaunted by the slings and arrows of life. As she left the room he felt a rising anger that fate should have dealt his family such a blow.

CHAPTER TEN

Founder's Court, April 1689

'This must be bad news you bring me,' said Lady Grantley, her face very white. A chill wind had got up and whipped round the courtyard at the front of the house, which always stood in the shade. She could see by the faces of Lord Edwin and her new daughter-in-law that something had happened. She closed her eyes briefly as if to blot out a distressing vision, as if by not seeing, it might not be real. She forced a thin smile and pulled her bright silk shawl tightly round her shoulders. She had been looking forward to the arrival of the bridal couple and had only just had time to prepare everything, having returned from the happy wedding the previous day.

The sight of the Amalie coach sweeping up the drive had made her heart leap. She had seen Lord Thomas alight and hand down Flora; both of them looked so solemn and Flora's eyes were red rimmed. There was not a sign of Edwin. Her stomach turned over and she felt she might faint. Recently she had been the recipient of much bad news, but the wedding and the acquisition of a delightful daughter-in-law had, she hoped, turned things around.

'Madam, Lady Grantley,' said Lord Thomas, quickly putting a protective arm about her shoulders. 'Do not distress yourself . . .' Before he could go on she pulled away from him, her eyes frantic.

'It must be Edwin. Has something happened to him? You must tell me at once!' she cried hysterically.

'Edwin is safely at Catherine's Court,' said Lord Thomas truthfully.

The journey had taken four hours and the horses stood sweating while hastily packed overnight luggage was unloaded.

'The animals look exhausted,' said Lady Grantley, mildly relieved. With a concern typical of her kindly nature, her immediate concern was for the horses. 'Take them to the stables and let them be attended to,' she instructed the waiting steward, 'and let your men go to the kitchens for refreshment and to be shown some quarters for the night.' The steward eagerly acquiesced, knowing that whatever had befallen Lord Edwin would soon be graphically explained by the Amalie servants, few of whom had much respect for the young lordship.

When Lady Grantley had composed herself, and the three sat in finely carved chairs in the long window of the salon, the charged atmosphere gave way to a need for explanation. Sunlight shafted onto Flora's delicate features, and she adopted a composed smile which belied her true feelings because she felt desperately sorry for her mother-in-law, almost more so than she did for herself. Gently she took the woman's trembling hand. Lord Thomas felt increasingly resentful; he felt it was unbelievable that he could be with these two elegant women, about to discuss anything as sordid as Edwin's story.

'We will not mince matters, my Lady,' said Lord Thomas, and he proceeded to tell Edwin's mother the state of affairs without dissemble.

Her face did not change expression, retaining a cool composed exterior throughout the whole sorry saga. 'So much I did not understand,' she said flatly when he had finished. Both Lord Thomas and his daughter exchanged glances, puzzled at the sanguine way she had absorbed the news and both felt that the mother had known more of her son's weaknesses than they had realised.

'I thought it was the company at court, the late King . . . ' she started in a resigned voice. 'I mean Charles, of course. For all his brilliance, he had about him a degenerate court. You see, when he died, God rest him, we thought James would change everything, but he was weak and in a way it flourished as licentiously as before. In some respects it was worse because Charles was deceptively shrewd but his brother showed no such guile. Edwin had a good position; he had the support of that terrible couple, the Churchills. We thought he was doing so well, but I see now that his father was right when he wanted him to come home and run the estates. He persuaded us, of course, that great things were happening and that he would be a part of them. Oh, it is all so terribly sad,' she said, suddenly losing her composure and putting her hand to her forehead, tears beginning to well in her eyes.

'Madam, I feel very deeply for you,' said Lord Thomas with genuine compassion. 'But we came here with solutions, if there be any,' he said guardedly. 'And I must think of my poor daughter, she has to be protected. I feel sure you will see that until Edwin can be restored she cannot be a proper wife to him in the . . . ' he stuttered awkwardly, ' . . . in the biblical sense.'

'Please, Flora, do not think he is as bad as he must seem to you. Edwin was a fine person before he fell in with these people,' Lady Grantley responded quickly. 'But we will not accept Flora's jointure until my son's recovery is assured,' she added.

Flora had sat in a miserable silence up until now but she set her wide gaze on her mother-in-law of whom she was truly fond. Lady Grantley looked at her earnestly.

'Flora, words cannot express the shame I feel. I simply do not know what to say. A beautiful young woman deserves more on her wedding day. I mean . . . ' she hesitated, 'I would not blame you if you wished to dissolve the marriage.'

'I don't believe that is what Flora wants,' said Lord Thomas. 'Is it, my dear?' he asked quietly, hoping in the back of his mind that she would have a change of heart before it was too late.

'No, Father, but I cannot help Edwin on my own,' said Flora, throwing her father a sideways glance, 'and besides, Lady Grantley,' she went on, 'you should know that my father is ill and his health will suffer with all this. I must stay with him and I would have done, whatever had happened. So maybe God has taken some sort of hand in our lives.'

'Oh dear, it seems troubles come not singly. I sometimes wonder why such things happen when we all love God as we do?' said Lady Grantley despondently, looking towards Lord Thomas.

'Lady Grantley,' Lord Thomas broke in, a tremor of emotion in his voice, 'had things been otherwise, I can assure you that I would have not encouraged Flora to do anything but serve her husband as was befitting. We may love God, but it does not necessarily mean He loves us.'

'Until yesterday,' Flora said in a soft voice, 'I loved your son, Lady Grantley. I hope I may find the strength to find that love again.'

'Well, this is our plan,' said Lord Thomas briskly. 'Edwin will have to remain at Catherine's Court under strict supervision. He will have to undertake this willingly. I am, as Flora has told you, suffering from the coughing sickness, and my steward will be in charge; he is a man of high moral character and I would trust him with my life.'

Prophetically he fell into a violent coughing fit. He slumped forward, white and exhausted, which added to the women's misery.

'Now let me go on,' he wheezed when he had sipped a little wine. 'If I should die, Flora is Ralph's guardian and part of our understanding is that she and her husband will continue to live at Catherine's Court until Ralph comes of age. There are trustees, as Flora knows, and Flora will inherit the gardens and arboretums and a handsome dower house upon my death but as a life tenant so that she may hand her wealth on to her children.'

Lord Thomas looked at Lady Grantley expectantly; he wondered if she had grasped the real meaning of his words. The message was clear; draconian steps had been taken to protect his daughter and they removed any power that Edwin might seek to abuse.

'It is Edwin who will have to agree to this, not I,' said Lady Grantley, nodding slowly. 'Of course I can go on running the estate here as I always have,' she went on hesitantly. 'I planned to move into another house when Edwin decided to give up his position at court . . . but . . . ' Lady Grantley stopped for a moment, nervously twisting the kerchief she held in her dainty fingers, her lips moved faintly as if forming words and then thinking better of them.

'Madam, is there something you are trying to tell me?' asked Lord Thomas beginning to lose patience.

'Yes, there is something I must tell you, I see it now,' stumbled Lady Grantley. 'Edwin has run up horrifying gambling debts. At first I did not know, until he tried to mortgage the estate. My late husband was careful about such things and as long as I am alive the estate is safe. But in truth,' she went on, 'I do not know what is to be done, except that we, that is to say the family, have discussed it. The running of the estate must now be of all our concerns, and frankly Edwin must be made whole again; he must go back to court and make his fortune with the good honest skills he should have inherited from his dear father.'

While Lady Grantley had been talking Lord Thomas had relapsed into a state of resignation; the situation seemed to become worse by the minute, and while the whole horrible story of a rake's progress had unfolded he had sunk into despair. There was an awkward silence while he thought carefully.

'We will have to think what is to be done,' he said, sighing heavily. 'Your son must be made to understand the seriousness of his position. I will undertake to keep him under my roof. But, Lady Grantley, I fear you should know that my power may be short lived. I am a sick man. I must be frank with you, as I have explained. I will do everything possible to protect my family and Edwin will not have the chance to dissipate their fortunes. In the end this may be of some comfort to you, at least.'

'Lord Thomas, I wish from the bottom of my heart that I had known of the true position in which my son had put himself. But the full truth only emerged in the last few days when I had a visit from the family lawyer and by then I did not have the heart to stop the marriage; beside which, I thought Edwin would change and the two seemed so very much in love. He begged me to keep my counsel; he promised me . . . ' She hung her head, unable to continue, and then lifted her chin bravely as someone who must take on a challenge which will require all her fortitude.

'Hmm,' said Lord Thomas ambivalently, crossing his legs impatiently. He knew enough about mothers and sons to realise that the facts may be laid before a mother's heart and however terrible they are she will always seek to make excuses and keep the candle of hope alive in her soul. He knew that Lady Grantley could easily have found out the truth earlier and indeed that she probably had had many warning signs, but she held onto her son's marriage to his beautiful, clever and rich daughter as a life raft that would save him from drowning.

'There will be no more tears, no more backward-looking regrets,' said Lady Grantley hastily, empathetically sensing Lord Thomas's far-seeing perception of the truth. 'We are a family now, and my son will find no quarter here unless he reforms. My heart breaks for Flora, but I want you to know I love her as a daughter; she will come first in all my considerations. I will trust in God to reward her goodness and bring my son to salvation.'

During the exchange between Lady Grantley and her father, Flora had kept silent; her face betrayed little emotion. Rising from her chair, she spoke to them both in a matter of fact way. 'Lady Grantley, we must rest now and return to Catherine's Court at the first opportunity,' she said serenely. 'We have left our family for long enough and must get back.' She had made up her mind that the only way she could survive this appalling calamity was to consider the practical elements without sentiment. She suddenly had an overwhelming desire to return to her home, the home she had always known and loved, to walk in the garden and enjoy the tulips which were at this moment ready to burst on a sunlit world in their crisp, clean beauty, as she had hoped to do as a bride. Flora had discovered an inner strength. From where it came she did not know; in fact she hadn't until now known she had it at all. But other people had seen it and from it gained support and optimism.

'I have learned one thing, Lady Grantley,' she said simply. 'Happiness is not dependent on another person, pleasure is what makes happiness, and that can be found in the small things each day; our garden is at its best now and I hope you will come and see it soon.'

Lady Grantley realised she had already come to love Flora and now she knew that this young woman was the last chance the gods would give her son.

CHAPTER ELEVEN

Catherine's Court, May 1689

The gardens were ablaze with colour. Flora and Edwin walked together down a wide path known as Thomas's Parterre; her dress swished on the laboriously raked gravel and Edwin's arm was about her shoulder.

Lord Thomas watched them from the window of his study. A stranger would have thought them a happy couple, at peace with the world. Their graceful forms seemed to fit perfectly and he saw his daughter laugh at something her husband had said as he dropped his arm to her slim waist and pulled her closer to him. It was then that Lord Thomas realised, with a sense of foreboding, that despite all her fears Flora had become a true wife to Edwin. The body language between them said it all.

Lord Thomas's health had declined at much the same rate as the state of Flora's marriage had improved. Lord Thomas understood, only too well, how the intrinsically optimistic nature of his daughter welcomed the apparent state of calm normality that now pervaded the household.

Edwin was once again the charming person who had at first so impressed him. He had even begun to take an intelligent interest in the gardens, a love of which he now appeared to share with Flora. Lord Thomas knew the healing powers of an understanding of nature and things Arcadian and fondly hoped that, as had happened so many times in his own life, nature in its abundance would heal the man and bind him to a decent life with his daughter. He needed to think this and so he did.

'My Lord, you must return to your bed,' came the no-nonsense voice of Jack, interrupting his reverie.

'There will soon be time enough for rest,' said Lord Thomas, without turning his head; he watched the young couple, and, as if she sensed his eyes upon her, Flora swivelled round and looked towards the house. She knew her father was watching them and her display of affection towards her husband was to some extent in deference to her desire to reassure him.

'Jack,' said Lord Thomas suddenly, 'I have a desire to go into the garden. I need some fresh air while it is still possible.'

Jack agreed at once. He knew exactly what his master meant; the malaise had got a hold on him now, and the household had taken on that queer serenity which waits for the inevitable. He hurried to get a light coat for his master and called through the door for the hall boy to find Hera and Diana.

'Shall I tell Lady Flora that you want to join them?' asked Jack.

'Of course, Jack. You can always read my mind and this seems like a good chance to walk with Lord Edwin and give him another tour of the garden, for I do believe he is beginning to love it as does the Lady Flora. It may not be in his blood as it is in hers, but if he loves her he must also love and care for the things that make her the woman she is.'

Jack nodded in agreement with a gruff noise of equivocal assent. In his heart he had his doubts, many doubts in fact. It was all the talk amongst the servants; Lord Edwin was a reformed character – or was he? The Lady Flora had gone to his bed and lain with him, the master was sick and likely to die, and the young mistress would undertake the running of the estate together with Lord Edwin, whilst the mother, Lady Grantley, would continue to run his own family home; and what of Ralph? It was generally agreed that he had the makings of a fine young man: he would take it all on himself when he came of age, which was only a matter of time. The household's livelihood seemed to be secure, but however much they cared about the Amalie family the future of all who depended on them was understandably Jack's primary concern, and he knew it was chicken and egg. It was the running of the great gardens and the estate that gave them meat on the table and a comfortable roof over their heads.

'My mistress gives too much credence to her husband's motives,' Sarah had confided to Jack the previous day. 'He will never be a man to get his hands dirty,' she had added. 'He plays the dutiful reformed husband, but he does not pull the wool over my eyes.'

'We will be Lady Flora's eyes and ears,' Jack had said darkly. 'He will not bring this place or its people to harm, we will see to that.'

Jack had continued to explain, assuring her that his cousin was manservant to Lionel Wellbeloved, the man who was to be a trustee for the estate. 'His Lordship has left no stone unturned to protect us all.' Jack recalled the conversation as he bumped into Sarah on his way to get a thicker pair of outdoor boots for the master while the boy helped him into his coat.

'Do you see what I see?' asked Sarah, throwing a sideways glance in the direction of the garden.

'I do, Sarah, that I do,' said Jack.

'Behaving like a young lover, the perfect gentleman . . . ' hissed Sarah indignantly.

'Well, you and I know better. Give him enough rope and he will hang himself,' said Jack. 'It's not our place to speak out,' he added quietly, 'but mark my words, the time will come, and life never turns out the way you think. There is enough going on at the moment, pebbles enough have been cast in the pond, let the ripples come to the bank, Sarah.'

Jack's dark twinkly eyes narrowed knowingly, and Sarah felt reassured. The man had a way of speaking in metaphors which fixed in the mind of the listener and Sarah saw an image of a dark pond and a grassy bank where she and her mistress found safety.

*   *   *

Flora smiled happily as her father approached them on the ochre-coloured gravel walk. A fashion imported from Holland, it was set between an avenue of limes, the morning sun dappling through the leaves and filtering a vivid greenish light. Everything about them seemed to move in a symphony of sounds, mingling with the sharp aroma of the delicate lime blossom. Flora could not help feeling optimistic as she thought about Edwin and how his behaviour had changed for the better.

Edwin himself still retained a somewhat embarrassed and sheepish response, to his father-in-law at least. His transgressions had been immense and whereas Flora had been wooed through the eager vulnerability of her young heart and body, he felt that, not surprisingly, the dying man regarded him with both suspicion and a measured dislike, for what he had done to his daughter.

Nevertheless, he had, despite himself, become intrigued by the garden and the extraordinary gift Flora had for botany. He loved the beauty and elegance of the long tree-lined parterres and the impact of compacted planting, with great blocks of colour. It was something he had never seen before and in a curious way it provided a bridge over which he could communicate with both Flora and her father.

'So tell me again, Lord Thomas, how did your mother come to design this wonderful place?' Edwin asked with genuine interest.

The garden and its magical natural order had put him in touch with a part of himself that had for some reason died. Flora had benefited from the apparent metamorphosis, which she attributed to the healing forces of nature. Her youth and optimism led her to the path of least resistance and Edwin could muster charm in abundance when he saw fit and he did so now with disarming effect.

The three settled into an easy pace and Jack held back, pleased to see that both Flora and Edwin took Lord Thomas's arms. He had the gait of a man beyond his years, as if his impending demise weighed him down. The progress of the three was slow and painful for Jack to see, for he remembered the vigorous gait of Lord Thomas in his prime, when for every one long step of his master Jack had been forced to take two to keep up.

'Her bible was a book by John Parkinson,' said Lord Thomas

in answer to Edwin's question. 'He was one of the great botanists. He recorded all the plants that could or should do well here in England and my mother brought with her from Holland the first great tulips England had seen. She soon moved on, with Parkinson's help, to create the lilies you see over the sycamore walk . . . '

They all turned and in the air a heady scent wafted. 'I can smell them already, even though we are at some distance,' marvelled Edwin.

'Well, let us look at them first; they are at their prime today,' said Lord Thomas.

Jack rushed forward with a big shady umbrella that he had brought with him, anticipating the sunshine which would hit them like the opening of a furnace door when they emerged from the shade of the gravel walk into the hot dry soil of the lily gardens.

'Flora, you tell Edwin about these beautiful specimens,' said Lord Thomas. There was nothing he liked more than to hear his daughter's mellifluous voice showing off her exceptional knowledge of every plant in the garden.

'Well, here we have Lilium Cadmium, and that is the white Madonna lily we all know,' said Flora. 'Beside it you will see we have five other forms of what we call Martagons in the garden. Those beautiful deep purple ones and the ones with the different-shaped foliage came from Asia. My father got them himself from the great garden at Moor Park owned by Sir William Temple, who worked with Queen Henrietta Maria,' she said proudly, looking up at her father's stooping figure.

'It is not just the inspiration my mother found in Sir William that drove her – although it was he who brought the more sophisticated element to the very ordered style of the Dutch Garden my mother so expertly transported from Holland. You see over there, through the tulip garden, that we have a wild garden too. It's deceptive, in fact; its construction is carefully planned to clear the eye before you enter the Italian Garden in which my mother built her famous grotto.'

They set off at a leisurely pace and were soon at the spot Flora had so proudly described. Lord Thomas took the opportunity to rest on an ornate iron bench.

'No, Father, you must sit on something, the metal will be hard for you,' said Flora, offering her shawl, which she had had casually draped over her arm. Lord Thomas stood shakily while she laid it on the bench.

'I should like to die in the garden,' he said suddenly.

The remark took the group by surprise and there was an awkward silence, broken by the noisy arrival of Ralph and the two dogs who had strayed from the promenading group to chase the ducks on the lake.

Ralph had heard the remark and his young face clouded. He caught his sister's eye and the telepathy which so often operated between them gave birth to an idea; he knew his sister had thought of it too. They would create something for their father, a great surprise. Ralph indicated to his sister and she responded with a nod and a smile.

Lord Thomas rose unsteadily to his feet, taking Jack's strong arm. 'Now, my family, I will show you the thing of which I am most proud in the garden,' he announced with surprising energy.

He led the way falteringly to the tulip garden. Lord Thomas never failed to be rewarded with a rush of pleasure as he saw the perfect waxy petals supported by sheaths of shining leaves. He often compared them to rows of exquisite Venetian glass vases. There did not seem to be a spot at which one colour was separate from another. There was such a plethora of varied blooms, all at their peak, a melange of dark reds tinted with green, rusty golds shot with fiery scarlet, petals feathery and delicate as lace, and a triangular-shaped bed of blooms which were almost black.

'Let me tell you about the tulip,' said Lord Thomas. 'The Holy Roman empire's ambassador in Constantinople, a man called Busbecq, saw the first tulips in Turkish gardens and sent specimens to Vienna.'

'That was in the 1550s,' added Flora. 'It took ten years for the species to get to England.'

'But no one has what I am about to show you,' said Lord Thomas grandly, spreading his arms expansively. 'This is my great legacy I will leave to the future, together with her namesake.'

Edwin assumed he was to be shown a rare bloom of some kind and suppressed a slight smile at Lord Thomas's predilection for giving his plants a gender.

They passed through the kaleidoscopic ribbons of colour until they came upon a bed of delicate pink, quite different from all the other blooms. The pink was shot with the palest of greens and at the tip of each outer petal was a dash of cyclamen from an inner layer, like the slashed sleeve of a great court lady. The base of the flower was a rich ivory veined with the tiniest of fine lines of a darker cream. Edwin, who until now had never noticed flowers particularly, had to admit that the plant was remarkable. The whispered admiration that issued from the group, including young Ralph, was well deserved. Besides, Edwin said to himself, all this was worth something financially. Men had made fortunes out of tulips. This knowledge of gardens was of some future benefit. He smiled sweetly at Flora and took her arm affectionately.

'This is Flora's Glory,' Lord Thomas said reverently, suddenly retrieving the former resonance of his fine voice. He took off his large hat and handed it to Jack. Leaning down, he snapped off one of the flowers and held it to Flora's pointed chin symbolically. Flora took it and presented it to Edwin. Later Jack observed him tossing it carelessly away in the long grass.

'The King himself will come to see this,' Lord Thomas told them. 'I do not know when but let us pray I will still be here; if not, it is for you my children to show His Majesty.'

CHAPTER TWELVE

Catherine's Court, June 1689

There comes a time in some boys' lives when, like a caddis-fly developing from a larva, they know, for whatever reason, what their chosen path should be, and how they must aim for this end and by single-minded determination achieve their goal, although the path will be rocky and paved with many obstacles. This was about to happen to Ralph.

Since Ralph had come home he had had an admirable tutor who more than fulfilled his duties. Indeed the man, a childless widower who had fallen on hard times, had found Ralph so well grounded in all his subjects that the two explored the scholastic world much as two travellers on an exciting journey. Heracles Prior was a tall skinny man whose kindly face held a shadow of the vaguely handsome man he must have been before life's vicissitudes had chiselled a deep craggy map on his face. But he had a lovely smile; seldom employed, when it appeared it transformed his face and the ghost of the young man he once was shone forth to great effect. He never wore anything but black. He had two suits, one for every day and one for important occasions. He paid particular attention to his white cravats and the mystery of their pristinely white crisp appearance was often discussed by the household servants. He had a habit of removing his small metal glasses and twiddling them idly in front of his face when he wished to emphasise a point. The removal of the glasses always heralded something worth listening to and after he replaced them there would be a reverent silence whilst the information was processed.

It was Mr Heracles Prior who had first identified his pupil's aptitude for botany and encouraged him in his exceptional talent for drawing. They had spent many hours poring over the many rare books on the subject housed in Lord Thomas's library. Heracles was himself a gifted draughtsman and expert in the principles of botanical drawing. He knew that a true knowledge of plants could best be achieved by the rapt attention to detail required by an artist.

Heracles also saw that Ralph was his father's son in more ways than one. The boy had a profound love for the garden his family had created; and Heracles knew that such a legacy was of enormous value financially. Untold wealth had been accrued by the fashionable gardeners of the time with their arboretums and nurseries. He was even more aware of this since Lord Thomas, who had come to trust him as a friend, had confided the arrangements which would come to pass when he died. Ralph was to remain at Catherine's Court under the guardianship of his sister and the watchful eye of the two trustees. Heracles had tactfully enquired about the efficacy of this in view of Flora's marital status and Lord Thomas had explained the situation, which came as no surprise to Heracles since no detail of the family's lives escaped the eagle eye of the servants' hall. Heracles realised that Lord Thomas had left no stone unturned to circumnavigate the law which gave a delinquent husband such power over a woman and he felt a great sense of relief.

For Heracles' part, he did not trust Lord Edwin, and felt it a tragedy that the innocent Flora should be bound to such a fellow. On the other hand, he had formed the most favourable of opinions of the Amalie son and daughter. The two were alike in so many ways, and he had little doubt that for whatever reason their inheritance would survive. But never the less, he foresaw a tangled web and necessary ruthlessness if the eventual outcome was to be satisfactory.

Lord Thomas had set aside a generous remuneration for Heracles, which was to be dispensed by the trustees until such time as Ralph no longer needed his services, and even that eventuality had been catered for. If Ralph felt he needed his services for the running of the estate he was to be retained. All this had enabled Heracles to make plans in his mind for the first time for many years and he had already been promised a small cottage for his retirement. It was as if Lord Thomas had made every conceivable plan to keep his children safe, and the role of Flora's husband was almost redundant. But in the recesses of his mind, Heracles could imagine many dangers lurking, if Edwin were to tire of behaving well. It seemed unlikely that he would be happy to remain quietly at Catherine's Court, letting his mother manage their own family estate. Heracles conjectured that he would soon revert to his old ways once his father-in-law had died. But at least Ralph had decided irrevocably that he would become a significant figure in the new world of garden design. The boy was canny enough to see that he would have a great entree at court when the time came, because the King had a great and almost obsessive love of gardening, as did the Queen. Young men like Ralph Amalie would be in great favour.

All the great houses were beginning to embark on a break from the traditional enclosed Elizabethan gardens which had been the norm for so many years. Epic journeys were embarked upon by men exploring the world for new species and Heracles saw an interesting future for his pupil.

*   *   *

The two were walking through the grounds. They were on their way to see the surprise Ralph and Flora had planned for their father's name day. By some miracle it had been kept from Lord Thomas and none of the servants had been allowed to venture to that part of the gardens, which had been screened off with enormous tarpaulins.

'Today it will be finished,' said Ralph, hardly able to keep his voice steady from the excitement. 'I do not know how the men have managed it in so short a time and without my father having seen a thing,' he went on.

'It has been nothing short of a miracle,' praised Heracles, his wispy grey hair blowing in the balmy breeze, and his white cravat flapping on his face as they walked briskly through the windblown gardens. This was the first fine day for two weeks, which had, of course, all helped the tight secrecy surrounding the construction of Lord Thomas's temple on the exact spot where he had indicated he wanted to spend his last hours.

'It is indeed, Mr Prior,' agreed Ralph. 'It shows how my father is loved. I had thought it would take at least a month but it went up like magic and I think mostly because we had the stone all ready and the windows prepared and the carvings done. Last week they had all the estate workers on it even in the rain. On the one dry day they did all the setting of the stones and got the roof and the pillars up and then they worked in the dry. It is all set without any cement, each stone cut exactly to fit the next. I did not think it was possible but here it is.'

The temple stood in a sheltered corner of the gardens, behind the lime avenue, looking outward over the vista of a wide dipping valley. In the cleft of the hills there was a natural lake. Numerous species of birds and wild fowl swooped and cascaded onto the water, providing an endless source of activity. Above it hung a wide open sky looking towards the west, where the family could watch spectacular sunsets, magnificent gathering storms and still summer nights.

'Yesterday Flora and the house servants finished the interior,' explained Ralph. 'And now Father is to be brought here, almost whatever his condition.'

Heracles saw the boy bite his lip to stay back his emotions, and his hand tremble slightly as he nervously put it to his heart in a gesture of resigned and anticipated grief. Heracles shared this prevailing emotion; the entire household knew as if by osmosis that Lord Thomas would expire within a matter of weeks, if not days. This feeling of anguish was tempered with a natural anxiety about the future and the obvious vulnerability of Flora and Ralph. However much they had all been reassured, a feeling of insecurity still lurked, not helped by the instinctive distrust of Edwin that they all shared.

Heracles had respected the blanket of secrecy surrounding

the magical construction of the temple and nothing in his imagination could have prepared him for the vision that stood before him as they burst through the tarpaulin.

The building was of a light sandstone, built in an octagon with dappled light from all sides, save the eastern aspect where the wall was solid and decorated with arched recesses which matched the graceful curve of the windows. In the recesses hung exquisitely painted panels with all Lord Thomas's most prized blooms tumbling in glorious abundance.

'The paintings: they are truly magnificent,' Heracles gasped in wonderment.

'They are copies of paintings by the Dutch artist Jacob Walscapelle from Amsterdam,' explained Ralph. 'We had them stretched on wooden frames to adapt to the contours of the temple. Actually they were commissioned by Father some time ago, before we had the idea of the temple and in some extraordinary way they came at just the right time, the canvases rolled up. We hid them from Father.'

The two admired the painted bouquets, set on simple stone slabs, the stalks visible in globe-shaped glass vases. In the distance there was just the faintest glimpse of an open window and a beckoning sky through a dark rich background formed of a symphony of flora. At first appearance the composition appeared to be set in careless abandon, but on closer inspection a subtle order emerged such as Heracles had never before seen.

'See the centre of it, the nucleus, is the two luscious cabbage roses, Rosa Centifolia, one red and one white,' said Heracles, taking out his tiny spectacles and peering closely at the sight. 'And then,' he went on, 'the axis of the painting are these two flowers. Do you know what they are, Ralph?' he asked.

'I do, Mr Prior,' replied Ralph, looking closely at the orange blooms, 'they are Hemorcallis Flavia or Cornfield Sword Lilies.'

'Well done, my boy, and they are also known as Gladiolus Segetum,' Heracles applauded.

'But Mr Prior, the crowning glory of the work is the Dragon Tulip at the top and someone has pulled the petals open just a little to reveal the interior; that will be the one that my father will love the most.'

'Oh no, Ralph, the tulip is very fine, but it is the peony on the left, so artfully shaded, with a ladybird resting on the pale pink petals, which says what the artist is trying to tell us about nature. The butterfly, the greenfly and the snail are all part of the grand plan; it all seems so natural, and of course in nature it is, but the artist has brought it to us in such detail we are seeing what we normally take for granted. It is like life under a microscope. I like the way small, humble flowers are peeping through convolvulus, daisies and pansies draped at the base of the vase wild strawberries.

'I think this is how life is, Ralph,' Heracles ruminated thoughtfully. 'The principal blooms are host to all manner of God's things. Flowers, fruit, insects, they are like a good marriage, host to all that matters. It gathers around it a family and they in turn bring their own things to the table. Cut down the marriage and it is like cutting down a tree. You bring down everything in its shade and the creatures which live in its beneficence.'

'My sister does not have such a marriage,' said Ralph suddenly, turning his wide blue gaze upon Heracles.

'Well, I am afraid that not all marriages are made in heaven,' said Heracles quietly, patting the boy on his shoulder.

'My parents had such a marriage. It is that which created this place and all it stands for. It is a thing I hold most dear to me, and I will let nothing damage it; and my sister is part of it, she belongs here, she should not leave it.'

'Now, my boy,' said Heracles soothingly, 'you must not think of this at the moment. We have your father to consider. He is to come here to this beautiful place you have made for him and he will rest on the beautiful silken bed your sister has prepared for him and rest his feet on the woven rugs. Think of all this as the cloths of heaven. He will look towards those hills and the sky and we will all serve him and we will treasure these moments with him, for a life may be quantified by the beauty it gives to the world, both in its living and in its passing. This moment is as precious as any he has given to the world, for you will take this memory with you on your own journey. It will be part of the compass by which you travel.'

Ralph closed his eyes for a moment, not wanting Heracles to see the pooling tears. He knew so much ultimately depended on him and he prayed for strength and courage. The prospect of protecting his sister, their home and all the loyal loving people who were part of their extended family was daunting, but for now he felt a kind of angry impotence because he was still considered a boy and would not be able to take control until he was older.

'I hope I can be what my father would have me be,' he said in a thick voice. He felt Heracles' firm hand on his shoulder and strength came from the warmth of his grip. Ralph said a prayer of thanks that fate had sent him such a source of comfort. He knew something of the man's past, Heracles seemed to carry a great but resigned sadness with him; Ralph knew he had lost his family to scarlet fever, although his tutor seldom spoke of the tragedy. In fact he rather referred to his dear wife and children as if they still accompanied him through his days. Ralph had begun to see that he was a man of great wisdom and who had an intrinsic love of all things. He had once said that God had sent him to Catherine's Court, and Ralph believed that this was most certainly true.

'There is a lot on your shoulders, my boy, but God has judged you capable of the task, just you remember that,' said Heracles.

'Thank you Mr Prior, I will not disappoint you,' Ralph replied steadily.

CHAPTER THIRTEEN

Catherine's Court, June 1689

Flora had carefully planned every detail. Today had been chosen for her father's surprise celebration; it was his fortieth birthday. Some might say a good age for a man, on the cusp of the last phase of his life, but for Flora the number was etched in her mind as the year that his would come to an untimely end. She knew he was gravely ill, even though he made light of his suffering. He still smiled joyfully at the sound of her voice, often he kept his eyes shut when she entered the room and approached the bed. He would stretch out a hand and take hers and place it on his labouring chest and keep it there as she sat on the chair next to him. Recently she had been glad that her father had been unable, that day, to open his eyes. Her sorrow was such that, however hard she tried, she could not control the tears. She would gaze quietly at his fine face and her breath would quicken as she allowed herself to contemplate the awful void which lay before her. She wondered if she would be able to remember his dear voice. How could she imagine the absence of his warm chest as she lay her head upon it and received the considered, loving wisdom which he would give so quietly, the words emollient with soothing, constant, unconditional love. The years ahead without him seemed unbearable. No man could ever replace him, and then she would think of 'little' Ralph, for that is how her father and she would often, through force of habit, refer to the other person they both loved more than anything in the world. How could she protect him in his orphaned state?

Her love for these two men surpassed anything which could be spoken in words and today she knew she must be brave for

Ralph. He needed to feel like a man, to take the mantle his father would leave for him to wear on his young shoulders.

'Dear Father, Ralph and I have a surprise for you as it is your name day,' she murmured close to his gaunt cheek. She could feel his laboured breath on her face. He opened his eyes and she felt her whole countenance bathed in love.

'May I tell you, my dearest child, what I would like most on this beautiful day?' he said.

'Please do, Father,' she replied earnestly, slightly fearful lest it should be something she could not give him.

'I would like to put on my old silk jacket with the embroidery your mother did for me and be taken down to the garden and there rest a while in some quiet corner with you, my dearest children, around me. And then we might savour together the gifts that God has given to us.'

Ralph had joined them and brother and sister's eyes met and she winked knowingly, their father still had not the slightest idea what was in store for him. 'Let us do precisely that,' exclaimed Ralph. 'Jack, see that all is prepared and send for the boy to help you dress his lordship, and we will go before the sun has a chance to change his mind.'

*   *   *

Since dawn it had been like a military campaign, the servants in their best Sunday clothes scurrying to and fro carrying tables, chairs, cloths and hampers of food. There were all Lord Thomas's favourite dishes, Neat's-tongue pies seasoned with cloves and mace and cinnamon, a chine of beef slowly roasted in butter for twelve hours and basted with ginger, cinnamon and sugar. Stewed oysters in beaten emulsified butter, flavoured with onion and pepper. Thistle and asparagus salad, cheese cakes and Lord Thomas's favourite quaking pudding, which was Meg's speciality, a mixture of eggs, sugar, cream and flour boiled in a linen cloth. Jack had produced Morello cherry wine, which he had been distilling since the previous winter and which had now reached its zenith, and there was Flora's recipe, handed down from her mother, of strong cowslip wine. It had been infusing in a good mead for five weeks and this would be the first tasting.

'This is to be a feast fit for a king,' said Jack beaming from ear to ear, as they gathered in the hall waiting for Lord Thomas to be brought down and carried in a sedan chair to the appointed spot.

Flora and Ralph had decided to invite some of the family's closest friends and relatives to the event. All bound to the strictest secrecy. Everyone knew that Lord Thomas was gravely ill, but there was a tangible feeling of happiness in the air. Lady Grantley and two of Edwin's sisters had arrived early and gone for a walk in the gardens where the area of the surprise was cordoned off with scarlet ribbons. Lionel Wellbeloved was the next to arrive with his wife and four eldest children, half a dozen relatives and of course the local squire, and some of the neighbours.

The sick man himself felt a strange surge of energy when he came down the stairs and saw the merry throng all decked out in their summer finery. His tired heart leapt in delight and he felt – however briefly – like a young man. 'This is wonderful,' he exclaimed. 'No use having a party when I am gone. I won't give a tinker's tale for it; I am going to enjoy today.'

A hush fell as he fondly greeted each visitor in turn as they came to him. Lady Grantley was the first to approach. She leant down to him, while, squinting slightly from the light from the open door, he appraised her fine bosom, contoured through a gossamer-thin Brussels lace modesty collar.

'Dear Thomas,' she said affectionately, 'this is a happy occasion, and I pray we may all anticipate a good future for our young; things are going better, I think,' she whispered.

Lord Thomas caught a faint scent of violets and heard the sensuous rustle of her silk skirts and, looking up into her keen blue eyes, he almost felt as if he still had something to offer her. His heart raced a little as he experienced a vague remembrance of the lusty man he had once been. He was happy after all, he comforted himself, all we really have is the present and this was a most excellent present, all of it.

He could hear the excited voices of the young women, the dogs yapping merrily, and the happy mutterings of the servants as the party assembled. The chirping of birds outside in the young summer garden beckoned enticingly; and then to his delight he heard the delicate strains of music.

'Hush everybody,' called Flora in breathless anticipation, and the musicians she had arranged started to play, a viol, flutes and flageolets to accompany them as they made their way to the appointed place, meandering down the gardens to the rhythm of the music, ribbons flying in the breeze, skirts held high to avoid the grass, dainty slippers crunching on the gravel.

Lord Thomas swayed with the movement of the chair borne aloft by two hefty lads and began to feel quite excited, sensing something out of the ordinary. He saw the temple at once as they rounded the corner. He let out a cry of glee and the throng let out a gasp of admiration. The sight of the temple was so astonishing that most people were lost for words, just murmuring in awe.

'Oh my dear,' said Lady Grantley eventually, addressing her daughter-in-law. 'How on earth did you create such a thing in the blink of an eye and why is Edwin not here to share this marvellous occasion?' she looked round anxiously. Until now she had not mentioned the fact that her son had not been there to greet his family, thinking he was perhaps hard at work preparing the wines or something of the sort.

Flora caught Jack's eye. He had heard the question and he shook his head cautioning her to be evasive. She decided to make little of Edwin's absence, determined that nothing would mar her father's day. 'He went riding on his horse and will be back soon I am sure,' she answered convincingly. Edwin had indeed disappeared on his horse, but truthfully he had become resentful of her preoccupation with the festivities and she was glad to have him out of the way. She dismissed the absent Edwin from her mind and Ralph stepped forward in order that they could both help their father into the temple where they had prepared a resting place for him on a high day bed with mounds of cushions.

'We have made for you father, Ralph and I, a sign of our love and gratitude that you are the dearest father in the world,' said Flora. 'We all thank God for our family and friends we are so lucky to be able to share this happiest of days with you. Ralph has written something for you.'

Ralph stepped forward and the musicians struck the first bar of a liquid melody as he began to sing a charming song written especially for his father. At first his voice trembled slightly, and then it became pure and confident. As Lord Thomas heard it he saw that the boy had come of age. The voice was no longer that of a lad but of a young knight. When he had finished there was a silence and many tears were surreptitiously brushed away. Lord Thomas felt a great wave of resolved happiness. For Flora that moment was interrupted by a hand on her arm. Edwin had come back and he stood beside her, smelling slightly of horse and sweat. Lady Grantley saw the arrival and noted with a sinking heart Flora's indifferent response. Edwin sensed it as well and abandoned the idea of feigned domestic harmony, feeling excluded and resentful. Flora was impervious to her husband's temperament and hardly appeared to notice as he melted away, starting to talk to one of his sisters in a loud, intrusive voice.

It is often observed that people find within them a miraculous burst of energy just before they die, as a lamp taking its last drop of oil might do, and so it was with Lord Thomas. Had an observer not known, he might have seemed like a person of robust health and he continued thus for the next few hours, as the sun travelled high in the sky and then began to dip towards the still of late afternoon and finally hovered in the dip of the hills.

There was but one person strangely out of place and of course that was Edwin; he stood back and watched with a kind of ambivalence. He felt completely removed from the emotions that engulfed his young wife and her brother; after all, his own father had not long passed way and there had not been such a flowery orgy of grief. His death had come suddenly, without warning and the man had been a remote figure to his children. Edwin's parents had an exclusive relationship and he could not remember any of the closeness he saw between Flora and her father. His observations of Ralph had sown a seed of resentment and jealousy towards the boy; he had often thought that the children of lovers are orphans and so he had felt from an early age, and he watched his wife's family jealously. There was even a bit of him which felt increasingly impatient with Lord Thomas for prolonging his appointment with death.

The day progressed in languorous pleasure, and Flora determined that she would not stray far from her father's side. Some sort of premonition told her that he would not leave the temple alive. In the middle of the afternoon she took herself the little distance to the lime walk with Ralph and they passed slowly under the sunbeams shining in little circles through the branches. They did not speak, there was no need; they both accepted that they would share a vigil with their father. By the time they returned, the sun had dropped like a purple ball in the sky and the guests were departing. Lord Thomas was sleeping fitfully and they were reluctant to wake him. Everyone knew that it would be a goodbye, and each had their own particular thoughts about the man, all bound in a similar love and respect. But they were without melancholy, because the man had seemed so comfortable with his destiny. It was his children that they all worried about; and most of them looked at the strangely blurred figure of Edwin and foresaw trouble.

Flora returned to the temple quietly; she could hear her father's tortuous breathing, his early burst of energy was now completely spent. She and Ralph sat beside his bed in the golden glow of evening.

Quite suddenly the temperature cooled as the sun began to lose its force. Flora could feel her father becoming cold, as if death were already stealing up on him. She beckoned to Jack. He came at once and she asked for a brazier to be brought, anticipating that the dying man would be happiest where he was.

'I would like to stay here, my dearest children,' her father rasped feebly. 'It will be a full moon tonight, and I can think of no more beautiful place to be.'

'Never fear, Father, we will not leave you,' Flora said, beginning to weep silently. As she looked intently at him she recalled his love for her in every thought, word and deed that had been. Nothing had prepared her for the anguish of this moment; she looked up and saw that Ralph, too, was sobbing silently, anxious that nobody should see.

Their father held out his arms, and they moved onto the bed with him and the three lay quietly. The sun dropped completely as if in a hurry to end the day and soon the moon appeared in the sky, rising magnificently. They watched, each knowing that this would be last night they would share. No words came until the dying man rasped with difficulty some words they could not at first hear. They leant their ears to his lips.

'How I love you both,' he said. 'Don't be sad, the way is bright for you and I will be there at each moment watching over you.'

As the moon became a giant orb over the water in the valley below, they felt him shudder and they knew he was gone. They did not feel the comfort of his last words in the still of the night. The two fell across the bed, holding fast over their father as if to weigh him down and stop him leaving them so alone without the constancy of his protection. There they stayed until Jack and Sarah came creeping down the dewy garden.

'Master Ralph, you are the Lord now and I bring you your coat,' said Jack softly.

'And I, my Lady, let me call the men. We must take his Lordship to the house and we women will look after him,' said Sarah with a catch in her voice.

'Oh Jack, what are we to do?' cried Ralph, responding to the man's spontaneous embrace.

'There, lad, your father has made you the man you are. We will manage,' said Jack gruffly.

The men of the house came and bore Lord Thomas to his rooms. Candles were lit at the four corners of his bed and the priest was hastily summoned. It was the Catholic father who came; Lord Thomas had secretly told Jack that it should be so. He was a man who had known and loved the family all his life, a man who understood the way of the world, a man who did not blame his Lordship for his denial of the faith into which he had been baptised.

'My children,' the man said as he offered his hands for a respectful kiss, noting their obeisance, 'you should know that I came to hear your father's confession two days ago. He knew he was near the end but, so like him, he did not want to spoil your plans for the name day.'

Ralph and Flora knelt down and took the priest's hand and kissed it. 'I am glad you did,' said Flora.

'And I, Father,' said Ralph.

'Now I will say a prayer for the dead from my missal,' said the man.

Jack had remained quietly in the room and Sarah waited with the women from the village to finish the task of preparing their master for his final journey.

'It seems so wrong,' whispered Sarah.

'What is so wrong, woman?' asked Jack sharply.

'Lord Thomas, who has said his confession in the one true faith, now must be buried in the Protestant way when we know it was not what his soul believed.'

'His soul is with God, woman,' Jack rebounded swiftly. 'Do you think God minds? No, He does not. What He cares about is how a man lived his life. All the rest is just talk, and it's gentry talk, that's what it is. His Lordship cared about us common folk. He knew what do which was right for us, and if he hadn't, like as not, we would not have roof over our heads, or even a pig in its stall, or a pot to piss in. So leave it, woman, and do as our master did. God rest his soul.'

The priest made to leave the room the way he had come, that is to say through a secret doorway in Lord Thomas's study. Lord Thomas's father had made it, coming as he did from the turbulent life of the exiled court of Charles II. The comparative religious freedom experienced since the restoration had not seen the need for any subterfuge in a family's chosen faith but the death of Lord Thomas brought such matters back into focus.

Edwin Grantley had been hovering on the edge of the household's grief, harbouring a deepening resentment of his young wife and those who served her. He particularly disliked his young brother-in-law, recognising in him many qualities which he seemed to lack himself.

He had already got wind of the elaborate steps his father-in-law had taken to protect his family from any power he might be able to wield as Flora's husband. What he saw as the smug smile of satisfaction which suffused the face of Lionel Wellbeloved as he emerged from Lord Thomas's study shortly before the man's death had said it all.

He knew he had been disempowered; the control he had hoped to have over his wealthy young wife's fortune and family was not to be. But Edwin was cunning enough to recognise other weapons which might be of use to him, especially as he planned to return to the Protestant court of William and Mary. Amongst other things, he noted the trusted old priest's arrival and departure.

CHAPTER FOURTEEN

Catherine's Court, August 1689

'I am with child,' Flora whispered to Sarah, her cheeks reddening in embarrassment at the woman's shocked face.

'This is a fine thing,' replied Sarah dully. Try as she might she could find little to celebrate at the confirmation of her suspicions. Her mistress had missed her courses for the third time. Two months had elapsed since Lord Thomas's death and the brilliant weather had made way for a damp, cold August. The harvest was not ripening as it should, and the men on the estate were finding it difficult to adjust to the confusion regarding who exactly was their master now. No one had openly discussed Lord Edwin's relapse, but it was plain to Sarah that the master was once again under the influence of powerful and frightening forces, the like of which she had hoped her young mistress would not have to face again.

Mr Lionel had done the best he could to sort out the chain of authority, but each time the Lady Flora had given orders, her husband had contradicted her and so important decisions had been shelved. There was an air of lethargy, as if Catherine's Court was a big unwieldy ship becalmed in the doldrums.

Ralph, of course, although quick and decisive even at his young age, was powerless to intervene and Heracles had confided in Jack that, left to his own devices, the boy could be more than a match for the Lady Flora's feckless husband.

News of a child put a spoke in the many rumbling plans being furtively hatched in the servant's hall.

'We had noticed Lord Edwin might be tiring of the quiet life in the country; will this make him more anxious to remain at your Ladyship's side?' asked Sarah tentatively. Empathising with

Sarah's lack of enthusiasm, Flora burst into tears. She had tried to keep the deterioration in her husband's behaviour towards her a secret, but she knew in her heart of hearts that Sarah was perfectly aware of what was going on behind the bedroom door.

Her eyes moist with tears, Flora began to pull at the kerchief Sarah had given her, pulling it continuously through her hand. 'Oh Sarah,' she cried in desperation, 'what am I to do?'

'What do you mean?' asked Sarah warily.

'I mean just that,' answered Flora, with a trace of irritation. 'This happened before Father died. I believed him when he said how sorry he was, how he would love me and all would be well. I thought he had left all the debauchery behind and become a new person. But I was wrong,' she went on, wringing her hands in desperation. 'It was only once or twice and after Father died not at all,' Flora wailed.

'Leopards do not change their spots,' said Sarah with a touch of, 'I told you so' about it, which caused Flora to look up sharply.

'Yes, I have been a fool,' she said. 'But what else could I do? I wanted Father to die thinking everything would turn out right. He felt responsible, you know, wanting me settled to a man he could trust before he left us. And look what happened,' she added bitterly.

'There is nothing to be done, except make the best of it,' Sarah announced decisively, as if the matter could be settled so easily.

'I did think of something,' said Flora slowly, in a whispered voice. 'The village girls, they have ways of . . . well, you know what I mean,' her words floated on the air like a lost bird.

'Mercy, Lady Flora,' said Sarah coldly. 'If you mean what I think you mean, think again; such things are too dreadful to speak of in your Ladyship's presence. Poor girls driven in desperation to the butcher's knife, pushed into them by the old witch who does it for a few hard-earned pennies, and like as not the poor things die in agony. Some bleed to death, I have seen it with my own eyes. And such a thing done because they see nothing but the choice between that and being cast out to die in the poor house of starvation, they and their puny mite thrown without ceremony into a pauper's grave, without even a decent shroud to cover them, as if what little modesty they had left was denied them even when they met their maker. But you, Madam, you do not have to make such a choice. Why, God knows, you may even love the child,' Sarah finished dramatically, hoping such a graphic response would make way for a sensible plan.

'You make me ashamed, Sarah,' murmured Flora miserably.

'That was not my intention,' Sarah came back gently, drawing up a chair beside her mistress.

'No, I know it wasn't,' replied Flora, meeting the woman's steadfast gaze.

'Does he know?' asked Sarah, thinking a great deal hung on the nature of the reply.

'No, he does not. We rarely converse, and, as I suspect you know, he has started to drink again. I try to avoid him. There is a moment before he becomes insensible when he becomes a beast,' said Flora in a flat voice.

'We will not tell him, my Lady,' shot Sarah. 'He must be got back to London, to the court. There is nothing to be done with him here, and besides he will go willingly, of that I am sure. So let us not put anything before him that might keep him here. Mark me, my Lady, he is not a man to love a child, only what it might bring him, is my guess. Be all sweetness, my Lady,' she advised. 'It is the way to get your way with him. Tell him you will join him when you have settled your affairs. When he has been back there for a few weeks he will have forgotten his young wife in the country. I have seen many such an arrangement with the gentry. Out of sight, out of mind was never truer than in a dead marriage.'

'You are right,' said Flora vehemently, 'it is dead.' She wondered suddenly how she could have been so blind. Even on her father's last day on earth, her husband had not been there to support her. She would no longer bear the hurt and the hidden shame. 'I can never love him now, because he deceived my father in his last days. He pretended he would be a good custodian for me and my brother, for our home, but he never meant it at all.'

Sarah smiled enigmatically and kept silent. She knew perfectly well that poor Lord Thomas in his last days knew his son-in-law was a villain, and that is why he had taken such pains to disarm him.

*   *   *

Later that evening Flora joined her husband for the evening meal. It was just the two of them, Ralph and Heracles having retired early. Edwin dismissed the servants and sloshed some more wine into his glass. His features already glowed an angry red in the firelight. It was a cool evening. The nights were drawing in and already August had given way to a sharp fall in temperature with the arrival of a blustery September. Flora looked pale, a horrible sickness had overtaken her and the evenings were the worst time for her. She looked doubtfully at her husband, and bravely raised the subject of a return to court.

Under the influence of alcohol as always, Edwin was quick to see malice in the topic and his mind raced in a whirl of ferocious paranoia that brought a look of terror into Flora's eyes.

'So, Madam,' the man screamed. 'You want to be rid of me, do you? You want to stay here with your milksop brother, and those impertinent peasants you call servants, do you?' he shouted, crashing his glass to the table where a shard pierced his hand, a thin stain of blood spreading onto the white tablecloth.

'Come here, you witch, come here I tell you,' he yelled.

Flora recoiled in horror as Edwin advanced towards her and seized her by the hair, sending her ivory combs clattering onto the polished floor. 'What is it you want? You disgust me, you are drunk!' she cried.

Flora's heart started to pound, her mouth dried and her throat constricted. She tried to scream but no noise came. Like a crazed animal Edwin grabbed her neck and placed a hand over her mouth and nose. She began to suffocate and lost consciousness. As Edwin felt the weight of her limp body, he removed his hand and, with a sudden realisation of what he had done, all his evil intentions evaporated and a wave of remorse and panic overcame him. He thought for a terrifying moment that he had killed her; he called out her name frantically.

'Flora, my darling wife, what have I done?'

Slowly he lifted her to the divan, rubbing her hands; he saw a faint flutter from her eyelids, noticing, even at this moment, the length of her lashes on her lifeless cheeks. No man is all one thing or another, they are a little bit of each, and at that moment Edwin saw with stark reality the demon within him that he must fight. It was like a revelation. For the first time in many years he prayed. If God could only give him another chance, he would live his life differently.

'Oh Flora,' he wept, cradling her inert head, her hair tumbling in disorder. He clasped her in his arms and felt the reality of love, but contrarily, only just as he might have lost it. He felt her hair slip through his fingers as sand through an hourglass.

It was then that Jack came into the room, followed by the ever-attentive Sarah. They had been hovering outside and had heard Edwin shouting.

'God have mercy on us, what have you done?' shrieked Sarah, rushing to her young mistress and pushing Edwin away. He collapsed onto a chair, his eyes wild and confused. He was a man aware of his own degradation. He closed his eyes, wishing away the moment. If only this were a bad dream, he said to himself, and as if in answer he heard a faint moan from Flora as she slowly opened her eyes.

It was Jack's strong voice that broke the appalled silence. 'My Lord, you had best go from here. Use your eyes and you will see that this is women's business; you have done your worst.'

Edwin followed Jack's gaze and saw a dark red stain on Flora's skirt. Sarah looked down, and Flora put a feeble hand down to feel her sodden skirt.

'Oh Sarah, what is happening?' she cried pitifully, her hand glistening red.

Just then Ralph appeared at the door, followed by Heracles. Ralph shook away Heracles' restraining grip. The boy took in the scene at once and made as if to fall upon Edwin, his fists flying. He was held back by the men.

Flora began to sit up. 'My Lady, it is the baby, you are losing it; we must get you to your chamber for decency's sake,' Sarah whispered.

'Clear the room. Do not worry, Master Ralph, Sarah will see to Lady Flora, she will come to no harm now,' commanded Jack, throwing a venomous look at the uncomprehending Edwin.

'I will send for the midwife,' said Sarah, as Ralph and Heracles took Edwin roughly by the arms and led him from the room.

'If he were a village man he would be flogged within an inch of his life,' Jack called after him in a loud voice that rang in Edwin's ears.

*   *   *

'She will not bear another child,' said the midwife later. Flora lay back on the pillows, white as the sheets in which she lay. Her mind was numb. All she could think of was the relief that the pain was over. She heard the woman's voice, as if it were coming down a long distant tunnel.

Sarah looked at her young mistress and brushed a tear from her own face. She didn't want Flora to see how distressed she was; the girl had enough to contend with.

'How can you know that?' rounded Sarah furiously. 'She is young and strong, she had an accident, nothing more. It was a shock. She lost the child as one of the cattle might throw its calf. They go on to have more, and so will my mistress,' she said confidently, though for the life of her she could not think how such a thing could be contemplated with Edwin, who had as good as murdered his own child.

The midwife was a woman of great experience; she had learned not to ask too many questions, especially where the gentry were concerned. She knew exactly what had happened; word had got out that the new lordship beat his wife and more besides. She above all people knew that men abused their wives in all classes. For all their fine ways, men were the same whether they came from the lowliest peasant or a high-born aristocrat.

'I have seen this before,' she said softly. 'She had a bad time, it took so long. It is just a feeling one gets. But for mercy's sake who with such a husband . . . who would?' The woman stopped herself suddenly, seeing the answering look from Sarah signifying discretion.

'God Himself is the only one who has our lives in His hands,' murmured Sarah. 'My mistress deserves more and the Lord will look out for her. Who knows? Some folk laugh in the face of their good fortune and fate sometimes loses patience with them. Bad men build hostages to fortune, grudges stick to them as flies to glue paper.'

The midwife felt a slight shiver, despite the warmth of the room, for, as was the custom, a large fire had been built up to comfort the mother in her travail. Sarah was a good woman, she could tell that, but her loyalty to her mistress would permit a certain bending of the rules.

'My Lady's husband is on his way to the court in London as we speak,' Sarah said. 'Who knows what is in store for him, but at least his lady is safe with us.'

The midwife nodded and had a brief vision of something she preferred not to see.

Part Two

Part Two

CHAPTER FIFTEEN

Kensington House
(later to become Kensington Palace),
December 1689

'And so, Lord Edwin, Sir Frederick, how think you on our new home?' asked the Queen. Of the King there was not a sign, which must have been a great disappointment to the Queen; he was already confined to his rooms, claiming the wheezing in his lungs had yet again afflicted him.

'Madam, it is so very charming, and already it seems as if Your Majesties have lived here for generations,' lied Edwin with his usual aplomb. He looked around expansively. Reminders of unfinished building works could be seen at every turn, and the noise of hammering and sawing rent the air. He quickly reckoned that the Earl of Nottingham had received a handsome sum; word had it eighteen thousand guineas, way more than he should have expected.

Edwin avoided the eye of his companion Sir Frederick Buckley, knowing the man's ready tendency to mockery. But he could imagine his cadaverous features, wasted as they were by his consistent use of opium and much exasperated by Edwin's attempts to pay lip service to the Queen, whom many of the court blades considered not quite 'à la mode'. The Queen instinctively turned from Sir Frederick and concentrated her attentions upon Edwin. She liked the young man and felt a motherly interest in him. She knew his family and that of his delightful young wife who was regrettably absent from court and supposed the girl was still in mourning for the death of her father.

But the Queen did not like Sir Frederick. There was a faction among the young bloods which troubled her greatly. They still carried with them the whiff of the licentious court that had flourished under her uncle, Charles II It was something that both she and her husband wished to eradicate.

William was a man of strict moral probity and did not suffer fools and fops. Of course, there was one area of his own life to which the Queen turned a blind eye, but in her heart she knew full well that it eroded the clean image that would have made the atmosphere of moral reform so much easier to impose.

The room in which the grand soirée was taking place looked out onto the gardens, the basic plan of which could already be observed. The Queen followed Edwin's eye, pulling her shawl around her as she looked out of the window; there was a light flurry of snow descending delicately from an iron sky.

'I see you looking at the gardens, Lord Edwin,' said the Queen, smiling. 'They are in the Dutch style. You of course are an authority on such things; we plan to visit your family's home in the spring. Your wife's reputation as a gardener gathers apace and as you know it is all things Dutch which so touch my heart,' added the Queen, her eyes inadvertently looking upwards to where her husband the King was. The Queen's remark was loaded with innuendo and confirmed the gossip that her heart was still in the Elysium she had come to love in Holland, with the charming palaces and friendly people who adored her.

'I am hoping to create a more diverse garden here,' said the Queen. 'Whitehall is so cold, standing as it does right on the river, which has already begun to freeze I am told, and Hampton Court is much the same. The King's health will, I hope, improve away from the horrible pall of smoke that gets trapped in the dampness from the river. I miss Holland, you know,' the Queen confided, 'it was so clean and the air so fresh, but here I already feel more at home.'

Edwin had to agree and he nodded enthusiastically; he could see she had begun to recreate these lost pleasures to which she had become accustomed. In an attempt to make herself feel at home she and her husband had amassed a huge collection of art and china. The room looked something like a museum, with the cream of the royal collections inappropriately arrayed on walls that were too small for them. Edwin thought the blue and white china the Queen had made fashionable sat uneasily with some of the elegant paintings. But it was not only material acquisitions that plumped up the Queen's sadly childless life. At her feet frolicked a troop of snub-nosed, fussing pug dogs she had brought from Holland, which were now all the rage amongst the court ladies.

Before Edwin could compliment the Queen on the format of the garden with its tree-lined avenue running from a black and white flagstone terrace and the four parterres dotted with numerous box hedges, miniature trees and shrubs, all of which must have been expensively obtained in a stage of maturity, the Queen's attention was taken by one of the dogs. She leant down and picked the animal up, planting a kiss on its flat black nose. Edwin caught the eye of Sir Frederick who suppressed snigger behind a limp jewelled hand.

The Queen moved on and Frederick nudged Edwin, smirking into his voluminous white ruff. 'I wonder how the prissy Queen likes having the King's whore Betty Villiers installed so close to her domestic bliss?' he whispered. 'The man is such a prig; the King's whore might expect a few baubles at least, or perhaps an honour or two, but she lives in cheap lodgings, and the Queen has a team of disgusting dogs to occupy *her* bed. They say he prefers a pretty boy on the quiet to the lusty demands of a woman. Perhaps the Queen could do with a young stud to liven her up!' Frederick smirked lecherously. 'She likes you, Edwin, what are you waiting for?'

To say that Edwin had been experiencing a moral conflict since his return to court would not be far off the mark. He looked at Frederick steadily when he had finished, and took a moment to work out his feelings. Suddenly he had no doubt: he was disgusted by the man; the Queen was a gentle woman who had shown him courtesy and kindness since his return to court.

She had assumed he was allowing his wife the space she needed to grieve for her father, and she had consulted him on the subject of her beloved gardens with a respect she allocated to him as the son-in-law of one of England's 'great gardeners'.

Until then Edwin had not fully realised the reputation Lord Thomas had enjoyed and had, indeed, been surprised by the whispered expectation that Flora would take up her father's mantle. Gardening was accepted as a seemly occupation for a woman of quality. The Queen had confided in him that she had used the celebrated gardening duo London and Wise for her projects but had sought the advice of Lord Thomas until shortly before his death. Edwin had also begun to appreciate his late father-in-law's modesty; and, supposing that Flora knew of the royal connection, she too had been discreetly reticent on the subject.

'Freddie,' Edwin said, with an emphasis followed by a pause that did not invite interruption. Frederick pulled himself up and threw his magnificent coifed head back superciliously, but uncharacteristically he did not interject. He concluded that whatever Edwin was about to say was clearly of importance.

'I have made up my mind to live differently,' Edwin announced defiantly.

'Differently, dear fellow, what on earth can you mean?' scoffed Frederick with an ill-disguised sneer.

'I do not expect you to understand. I will not attempt to tell you that I have had some kind of moral revelation,' said Edwin, aware that Frederick would not take kindly to this show of independence. 'I will present it to you in language you will understand,' Edwin continued doggedly.

'How kind,' said Frederick sarcastically. 'But do you think this is the time or the place for such revelations?'

'Oh yes, for the things which have influenced me are all around us here,' affirmed Edwin, looking around the room. 'You see, I had no idea of just how much I loved Flora, my wife, until I had lost her. I see now that she is a jewel, and that her family are of great standing here at court. The King and the

Queen both talk of her often and ask why she is not here with me. I lost her because I was a fool. I was beguiled by the most evil thing, the vile devil that you still would have me worship.'

'My dear fellow, you are already beginning to bore me,' said Frederick, flicking some fluff from his waistcoat.

'I have secretly suffered the pains of the dammed to rid myself of it and in so doing have found myself again,' said Edwin.

'Something tells me that I have heard all this before,' said Frederick.

'I am going back to my wife to ask for her forgiveness,' said Edwin in an even voice. 'I will prove to her that she can respect me and trust me again. The Queen wishes to offer her a place at court so that she may advise her on her beloved gardens; there is no more to be said.'

'How very convenient,' sniped Frederick. The one thing he could not bear was the prospect of losing control of one of his acolytes, especially Edwin, and besides he loved Edwin and desired to use him for his own pleasure. Edwin was a few years younger and Frederick had always been the instigator. He was the one who had introduced the younger man to the addictive powers of opium. And he had also found Edwin a lucrative source of income. There were still outstanding gambling debts and, unbeknownst to Edwin, Frederick had a syndicate that pooled the winnings and furthermore had worked out an effective code for cheating at cards. The further Edwin and the other fops had become enmeshed in debt the more they resorted to the release of the drug and at present Frederick was the puppet master to at least half a dozen young men who were bringing their families to ruin. He had a cunning way of putting the debts to one side whilst actually trapping the victims into a downward spiral. The unsuspecting families knew nothing of the full serious-ness until it was too late. Meanwhile Frederick moved further into dangerous areas of corruption, which so far had seemed to be without risk of unravelling

Edwin was about to reply and then excuse himself, there were people he wanted to talk to, but there was a perceptible flurry of activity and all heads turned to the doorway, through which came the Queen's younger sister Anne and her portly husband, Prince George of Denmark. A silence descended as the couple paraded into the room followed by a simpering Sarah Churchill.

'Just watch,' said the indefatigable Frederick, nudging Edwin. 'See the Queen's face, she has prepared the seating; as usual her sister's chair is slightly lower. Really there is no end to this cat fight and the Churchill woman revels in the power she has over both of them.'

Edwin could not avoid joining the communal stare. It was a charade carried out each time the women met, the same ritual performed again and again under the chameleon gaze of the court. The Queen glanced nervously over her shoulder, affecting not to have noticed the arrival of her sister. As the procession moved past, Sarah Churchill spotted Edwin in the crowd and to Frederick's annoyance broke from the group and greeted Edwin in fulsome terms.

'My dear Lord Edwin,' she purred, clacking her fan closed and placing it under her chin coquettishly. 'I had heard you were back at court and have seen you in the distance. So much has happened! You are married – and into the Amalie family,' she paused and glanced around. 'No sign of your new wife,' she gushed. 'Have you left her in the country, perhaps for health reasons which might be a case for congratulations?'

'How kind of you to enquire,' replied Edwin formally, with a little bow. 'The Lady Flora will be joining me soon; she has the gardens to set right and pass to safe hands before she can come to town.'

There was an audible snort of derision from Frederick and he threw his head back, brushing the back of his hand over his forehead before he turned away, pouting angrily. Lady Churchill pointedly ignored him.

'And how goes your husband?' asked Edwin politely.

'Affairs in Ireland do not go well,' replied Lady Churchill, pulling Edwin to one side. He could not help repeatedly glancing at her voluptuous bosom, pushed high in her corsage. At one point he thought it would all fall out. He noted the particularly fine black lace on the edge of the bodice, which contrasted with her ivory white skin. He thought momentarily of Flora, whom he could not imagine in so provocative a costume, and was yet again reminded of her purity and goodness. Lady Churchill's shrill voice intruded on his reverie as she continued, 'His Lordship is, as you know, heavily involved with the campaign in Ireland.' She clicked open her fan and looked at him over the top of the beautifully painted pastoral scene painted on the white silk. 'Fie young man, why are you here at court when your country needs men like you?' she went on. 'You have experience with the horse. I seem to remember your father was a military man. He must have insisted on a spell in the army for his son.'

Edwin felt himself blushing furiously. The woman had perceptively touched his Achilles' heel. He had been thinking that very morning how one way to regain Flora's respect would be to do something unexpectedly dashing and brave.

'Tell me about the campaign in Ireland,' said Edwin promptly.

'Oh my dear, the Irish,' she sighed. 'They are like the poor: always with us. The King is too soft. He wants to try to negotiate with the Jacobites, but now James has arrived in Ireland, having been spurned by everyone else, there is no hope of avoiding bloodshed. The Catholics will have to be stamped on like flies on a dung heap, for that describes the place exactly.' Edwin shuddered slightly as he saw the cold indifference in the eyes of the beautiful Lady Churchill as she described the devotees of the religion she had, when convenient, supported.

'There is a moment,' she said with a serious look, as if reading his thoughts, 'when a man can decide to rethink his philosophies. Just one remark and you see it. There was such a moment when I heard my husband his Lordship comment on the way King James had three hundred and fifty good men executed during the Judge Jeffreys trials and many more, you know, sent into exile. All this because they questioned the despotic beliefs of the Catholic King.'

'And what was the remark, your Ladyship?' asked Edwin.

'He struck the mantle and said, "This marble is not harder than the King's heart." I knew then that should William come to take the crown my husband would support him, and that he did only three years later,' she said with a winning smile. Suddenly Lady Churchill seemed to lose interest in the conversation and drifted back to the Queen's sister Anne and her notoriously dull husband, who was engaging in a sepulchral monologue to which people were no longer even listening.

'Damn fine woman that,' came Frederick's voice loudly, looking in Lady Churchill's direction.

'You think so?' said Edwin equivocally. 'Is there no such thing as principle or loyalty? She was telling me about the moment her husband decided to support our Protestant King.'

'It's the way the mop flops, dear fellow, go with it or be thrown out with the dirty water,' giggled Frederick. 'Haven't you learned that yet?'

'Well yes, is that what you might call pragmatism, the refuge of a coward?' asked Edwin.

'Fine words butter no parsnips,' said Frederick flippantly. 'It was Monmouth's rebellion, that's what it was all about . . . James's brother's bastard son wanted the throne, that is the real truth. It was not about beliefs. It was about power. How else has William stayed the course? He made a calculation and he went over to the Tories.'

One of the court gentlemen had tuned into the conversation and introduced himself.

'Frans Bentinck,' he said with a bow. 'Forgive me for joining you in your discussion, but I do find your English politics so very intriguing. My uncle is, as you know, very close to your King and will be joining him in Ireland.'

'Well, my friend,' answered Frederick with a derisory snort, 'just look at the Queen, always with her uncle Lord Clarendon at her side; he is a clever man as was his father before him who orchestrated the return of the Stewarts. But this one, his son, is responsible for their demise.'

'That is surely unfair,' said Edwin, wearing his newly acquired hat of rectitude. 'He recognised the country's desire for democracy; any monarch who failed to see this would be a fool. He masterminded the Declaration of Rights, which concentrates on the rights and liberties of the English subject and denies the King the right to exact money or maintain an army except through Parliament.'

'But this was a clever move, was it not?' said Bentinck. 'Clarendon is Tory and the old Whig party as I understand it is forever associated with the Jacobite Catholic cause and now the old King is in Ireland with his mercenary army paid by the French King, with his eyes set on a Catholic return to this country.'

'Indeed that is so,' agreed Edwin, seeing that Frederick had wandered away from them with barely disguised boredom. 'As you know,' he went on, 'the King feared that the Whigs, should they remain in power, would lead to a reconstitution of the Old Commonwealth Republic. He knew if he had an election it would create a resounding majority and so by dissolving Parliament and calling the country to decide he had a resounding Tory majority.'

'That, my friend, shows precisely the measure of the man,' said Bentinck. 'And now he has a mandate to go to Ireland and flush out the old King and it is a heroic and necessary cause. Are you an army man?' he asked.

'I am enlisting,' Edwin replied in a steady voice, for reasons he never quite understood. Perhaps it was the sight of Frederick making vacuous conversation across the room or some voice from deep within him, which tapped into the better man he had decided to become. Or was it the grave face of the King who, despite his failing health, was about to cross the Irish Sea and spill the blood of hundreds of men, fathers, husbands and sons who would follow him, blindly confident of his courage and oblivious to the tears of their families. A voice asked him what manner of man he was himself? What life he imagined while others died and he indulged in idle fripperies?

'Then we will be brothers in arms,' said Bentinck, slapping Edwin on the back, 'and may God be with us both.'

CHAPTER SIXTEEN

Catherine's Court, April 1690

Edwin arrived without warning in a flurry of sweaty horse and flying hair. He flung himself from his mount like a madman, throwing the reins of the exhausted animal at the young groom who ran out of the stable, taken by complete surprise, hurriedly pulling off his working apron as was the custom when meeting guests.

'Do not tell your mistress of my arrival,' Edwin ordered.

He found her in the garden; where else would she be on so fair a day? She struck a picture of rustic beauty, wearing a large straw hat tied under her chin with pink satin ribbons. Her sprigged dress was hitched up at her waist, revealing sturdy, much worn and brightly polished leather boots.

She headed a parade of men wearing matching green baize aprons to whom she was talking. They were listening carefully. He had been watching her for some time as she walked slowly between the tulip beds. The air was full of excitement, the blooms still covered by the bright, citron-tinged outer petals, on the cusp of their all too brief but magnificent flowering. His heart in his mouth, he watched her for a few moments, which seemed like eternity. Would she be in the least convinced by his meta-morphosis, he wondered? Sometimes he could not even believe in it himself. There would be plenty of people who would greet it with scepticism, Sarah and Jack for a start.

Somehow he had known she would be in the garden and although Sarah had sped at once through the orchards, her feet sopping in the long grass and her cap spattered with blossom when she heard of his coming, she had not managed to get there before Edwin. She saw him marching down the gravel paths, his hat under his arm and his coat spilling behind him like a sail.

Had she not known the horrible background that caused the separation she might have conceded it made a romantic picture of the tall handsome man approaching her beautiful mistress on a perfect spring morning. But no, her heart felt cold with dread. Life had been so peaceful without him. Old wounds had healed, gentle grieving had been accomplished; the gardens had grown in abundance. Flora had gained a little weight, settled into herself, found fulfilment in them and her increasing fame. Young Ralph had found great contentment with his studies and Heracles Prior had devised a syllabus that included advanced botanical studies, at which the boy was showing great aptitude.

Sarah knew that the arrival of Edwin was about to shatter all this into a thousand pieces. Thoughts flew through her head like trapped butterflies; her mistress had seemed resolute in her rejection of her husband and shown great bravery in the matter. There were many who believed fervently that marriage vows were made to be kept for better or for worse, and that women had to suffer if their husband chose to beat and abuse them. They were a chattel, with no more rights than the family dog. But it was Lord Thomas's foresight which had given Flora the independence to live a life on her own: most women owned nothing from the day of their marriage. The return of Lord Edwin was about to threaten them all once again.

Jack caught up with Sarah as she stood out of breath from her exertions concealed under the trees. They watched helplessly as Edwin, looking as dashing as any woman could wish, swept an astonished Flora off her feet, her skirts rucked up, her hat falling from her head, and her hair descending from its net.

'How dare he do that!' expostulated Sarah under her breath. 'He has a nerve, after all these months, he has no shame.'

'All the same,' muttered Jack warily, 'I don't see the lady struggling to get away, but the man is made from a crooked tree and will never go straight.'

As if sensing their presence, Flora kicked her feet, trying to push Edwin away. He replaced her gently on the ground, giving her a long hungry look, asked the men to leave them alone. The men looked quickly at Flora, who waved a hand in capitulation. Flora and Edwin stood alone in the garden except for Jack and Sarah who remained on guard concealed in the trees.

'I have received your many messages and letters,' said Flora coolly, straightening her dress and carefully replacing her hat. She held her hairpins in her mouth as she methodically wound her hair back under the wide straw brim.

It had been several months since she had felt Edwin's arms around her. Her body seemed to have a life of its own; the smell of his sweat, the brief feel of his beard on her chin and the tightness of his grip around her waist set her tingling. Even after all his wickedness and the things he had done to her, when she felt his lips close to her own, she experienced an overwhelming urge to open her own to taste the sweetness of his tongue, to forget the vile weakness which lurked in his heart. It was beyond reason, and had it not been for the many pairs of eyes which she knew, despite her dismissal, were probably focused in horror on the return of the villain who had so abused their mistress, she might have succumbed.

But suddenly, the still small voice of caution and propriety spoke to her in a whisper which became a shout.

'Sir, to what do I owe the pleasure?' she cried shrilly, backing away from him, aware that the spectacle would be relayed in minute detail to all and sundry.

'Perhaps a word in private, my Lady,' Edwin suggested.

Flora could not help but notice, as her eyes covered the distance now between them, how changed he looked. His face had lost the puffiness that had been the result of his debauchery; his features had sharpened, drawing attention to a strong rugged jaw line. He had lost his former bent swagger and he engaged her with a straight honest look. She could see a pulse in his neck betraying his emotion at seeing her, and it was with a convincing chivalry that he swept her a bow, waiting for her response.

'We will go to the house,' she replied with all the grace she could muster, which belied the confusion she felt.

*   *   *

Together they walked in an awkward silence through the gardens. The retinue had evaporated and Sarah and Jack had hurried to the house, unseen by the two, and had a moment to alert young Ralph. The boy had been at his studies and on hearing the news he jumped from the desk at which he was working and seized his father's sword, of which he had taken delivery on his fifteenth birthday the previous month.

'I will challenge the cad,' he flared. 'I will have satisfaction; he shall not remain here for a single moment.'

Heracles was as puzzled as anyone by what he had seen over Ralph's shoulder. 'No, my boy,' he cautioned, taking the weapon and replacing it in the corner of the room. 'We have all heard accounts of your brother-in-law's reformation of character. Maybe none of us believed it, least of all, I suspect, your dear sister, her Ladyship. But let us look to the scriptures, it is the sinner who gains the love of God as he repents and finds the light, it is for him that the fatted calf is slain. And, besides, your sister is his wife. They are bound by both the rule of God and the laws of man.'

'Do you think he has come back for good?' asked Ralph despondently.

'No, I do not,' Heracles affirmed. 'Word has it that he is trying to recoup his gambling debts and the only way he can do that is by some sort of remunerative position at court.'

'Flora would not be so stupid, would she, Heracles?' Ralph asked.

*   *   *

In the evening they walked together in the darkening garden, Flora wrapped in her mother's old shawl. They talked about the court, the King, of the Irish situation. And then they dined alone in the small parlour, a fire crackling in the hearth. The servants served them silently, with more than an air of hostility. The hall boy spilt the soup on Edwin's shoulder; the lad would never see the man as he was now, only the fallen wretch sunk lower than a sick pig in his father's yard. Oblivious to all this, Edwin wallowed in the sight and proximity of his wife, whom he thought looked more beautiful than all the fine women at court, as she sat in her home surrounded by the immaculate signs of her housewifery: the shining silver, cascades of flowers on the table, sweet-smelling candles she had made in her own lamp room. In their soft light the sight of her sun-burnished skin, her rounded breasts and the softness of her eyes, made his passion for her tear at him.

He was falling hopelessly, passionately in love with his own wife; he had abused this jewel and lost it, the thing which had once been his, and he resolved with all his recovered being to prove to her that he was worthy of her. Whatever it took, he would do it. There was no mention of the past, no mention of anything that might invite an answer as to how and where they would proceed from this moment.

Eventually she rose with a tantalising rustle of silk, as delicate as the sound of a dove's wings. As she leant forward her breast swelled invitingly in her corsage. He felt as a young boy might feel the first tremor of sexual love. This was a novel sensation for Edwin who, with his handsome careless charm, had never had to woo a girl. They had come to him, be it the kitchen maid or even his own cousin, hastily married to a fat old squire with a bevy of children, one of whom looked suspiciously like Edwin.

'I will retire,' said Flora graciously. She left the room, saying nothing about where he should sleep or what he should do. Of course, this was all the more tantalising.

He looked after her as she left in a waft of her perfume, a medley of spring fragrance. He closed his eyes and for the first time in many months prayed.

'My Lord,' came Jack's even voice. Ever the perfect servant, thought Edwin, realising that here in this enchanted place, he must be tainted with an aura of evil. 'Your horse is well rested and cared for. He was tired after his journey,' Jack said blandly omitting to mention his master. Edwin wondered if he were going to be asked to mount the animal and leave.

'Thank you. Warrior is a fine fellow,' he replied, a little discomfited.

'Your saddle bag was unpacked and things prepared in Lord

Thomas's old dressing chamber,' announced Jack, with no flicker on his face that might express his feelings.

Edwin said nothing and with a sturdy step passed through the door and up the oak staircase.

*　　*　　*

Flora had dismissed Sarah and lay in her bed. The shutters were still open and the moon was full, bathing the room in a silver light by which, had she been so inclined, she could have read a book. But she was not so inclined, and instead she lay in suspended animation. Her emotions were in turmoil, and seeing this, Sarah attempted to deliver a warning to her mistress, and was peremptorily silenced by a curt 'Don't say it,' from Flora.

'Shall you bolt the door behind me, my Lady?' asked Sarah as she left the room, her arm covered in linen, which would be miraculously washed, pressed and starched by the next day.

Flora did not reply, but got out of bed and ostentatiously banged the bolt across, only to slide it back as quietly as possible.

It occurred to her, as she lay there, that all her life she had done what was expected of her. She had learned the arts of housekeeping, she played and sang, she was a passable alchemist, she had loved her parents with all her heart and now her dearest brother. She had chosen to marry her childhood sweetheart and then when he betrayed her, after which she had done her father's bidding and made what had seemed an advantageous marriage. She had even gone to court, as her father wished, to find this man and she had begun to love him and then he too had let her down in the foulest of circumstances, squandering that rare second chance at a time when she needed love and support as she grieved for her father. And then he had effectively murdered the child she was carrying.

Despite all this she had recovered herself and found strength and healing in her work in the garden. She had regained the love and trust of her brother and the blind devotion of her friends the servants, who depended on her to show an example of courage and ingenuity. And now she was a woman of independent means, not just because of her father's careful planning but on her own account. People had started coming to her for advice about their garden schemes, and money had begun to change hands. She had ferociously and with difficulty sublimated her natural woman's instincts. She had not allowed her thoughts to enter the rooms in her mind where she longed for a man's touch, longed to lie with his body next to hers as they traversed the secret dreaming world of sleep together. Although the whispered words of the midwife had not been meant for her ears, she had heard them through the fog of her misery and there they were, intruding into the calm acceptance she had worked so hard to achieve: 'After this she will not bear another child.' Over the months, she had been unable to confront this, but in the back of her mind she had a vague feeling that it would not be true.

Underlying all of this was the fact that she was married to a man she had at first loved and then hated. He had become despicable, but the long hours she had had to spend with Edwin's desperate mother Lady Grantley had at least convinced her that he had been traduced by the flotilla of sharks that always circulate around a beneficent institution like the court. There were rich pickings to be had by naïve young men such as Edwin, but first they had to be softened, weakened and disempowered; they were put at the mercy of Satan himself. Flora's initial feelings of hatred towards her husband had changed over the months as she heard various reports of his rehabilitation. When he had appeared today in the garden, she had seen at once that indeed he had changed. He had become a man she had not known. Indeed, she supposed he must be the man his mother, Lady Grantley, tried to describe to her.

The reality was that by law she could not set him aside, she could not even refuse him his conjugal rights. All these things she had put in the back of her mind.

What did common sense yell at her? It told her to be careful; it told her to keep her distance from this man while she had the advantage, to test him out, and to see whether the recovery was genuine, if he could be trusted in all these things. But reason was lost in an overwhelming longing for it all to be true. She could only open her heart to this handsome stranger, bask in his love, and prove the midwife wrong by conceiving a child who would bring laughter and joy to a house that had seen so much loss. It was up to her to make these things happen. Ralph was too young and he in turn deserved happiness and harmony; he had seen too much sorrow, experienced too much loss.

Suddenly Edwin was there. He said nothing; he knew she would not refuse him. He leant over her and pulled the covers back. Her night shift was invitingly open. He tenderly pulled it aside and began to caress his wife in a way he had never done before to any woman. It was as if he had never made love before, just satiated a rough animal need. All his previous experiences had been roughly driven by the monster that had come to live within him. It had eaten his heart and soul, his moral compass, everything of value to a man. Now, in a torrent of love and desire, he made love to his wife and recovered his spirit and the essence of his manhood.

She wept as they broke apart, looking at each other in rapt amazement.

It was this single moment that put the final rivet in the wheel of Edwin's rebirth. But the recovery of a man's soul is the easy part; it is protecting that soul from the vindictive disciples that brought it to ruin which is the continuing challenge.

'Flora, my dearest wife,' Edwin said at last. 'My life has gone headlong, hunted by a fear of myself, but suddenly, in you, I feel I have encountered a friend, a friend and lover.' There was a break in his voice as if he might be suppressing a sob. 'Peace,' he whispered.

Flora turned away from him on the crumpled sheets, dampened by their passion, and wondered even in the joy of discovery and healing if she could truly forget the child they so easily conceived and carelessly lost. She closed her eyes and processed her many confused thoughts. She had realised long ago that a person can choose how to see the world: whether they see storm clouds in the distance or search for the sunlight. She decided to look at the sun.

It was rising in a promising dawn, a rosy light fingering through the window onto their entwined bodies. The dawn chorus began suddenly, without introduction, impossible to ignore; she knew sleep was now impossible, and with a sudden burst of energy she got up from the bed and looked at her husband who held out his arms, inviting her to come back to bed.

'No, Edwin this is a new day,' she said excitedly. 'Come with me and we will walk to the temple; I will send for the priest and we can renew our vows in the sight of God, we need to do this or what has happened has no meaning.'

Edwin knew that the man Flora would send for would be the Catholic Father he had seen taking Lord Thomas's confession. He also sensed that to refuse her this would be to shatter the trust he had regained.

'Flora, I . . . ' he said, putting both hands to his temple, 'I don't know that God is very pleased with me at the moment.'

'There is only one God for us all,' Flora replied emotionally. 'A human soul may find many ways to get to Him and to earn His love. It does not matter which route he takes, as long as the goal is the same.'

'You are right. Let us dress and do as you say,' said Edwin, and although she might have been convinced of his willingness he had many doubts.

Flora went at once to the door and rang a little silver bell. She knew that Sarah would have been up before it was light, as she always was. She came immediately but she did not look inside the room. She knew full well what had happened. She saw the radiant joy in the eyes of her mistress and prayed that her scepticism would be unfounded, that she would be proved wrong about Edwin.

'Send for the Father. My husband and I will meet him at the temple,' whispered Flora.

Sarah knew at once the significance of the request and her mind raced; she had a feeling of dread. Try as she might, she could not believe that this turn of events could bring anything but danger.

CHAPTER SEVENTEEN

Catherine's Court, May 1690

'What is the matter, boy?' asked Heracles. 'I have never seen you so put about.'

Ralph, who normally kept his emotions under control, had thrown a pile of books onto the floor. Now, with his head in his hands, he was grunting like an enraged tiger.

'He has been here for two days and, yes, everything has been going so sweetly,' he hissed between pursed lips. 'But I always said it was too good to be true.'

'Pray tell me, what has happened?' pressed Heracles. 'Compose yourself, Master Ralph. Come and sit quietly at the table in the window where we can hear the fountain in the garden. It will calm you.'

He led the boy to a window seat and pulled aside the thick tapestry curtains. They could hear the patter of water on the lily pads in the pool outside. Heracles reached for the pitcher on the table and poured two glasses of the cordial left each morning to refresh teacher and pupil during their studies.

Ralph pulled himself up and raised his face to look earnestly at the tutor who had become like a father to him. The man's eyes were full of concern, his rather bony hands always stained with ink rung together anxiously and he waited for the boy to tell him what the matter was, although he had quite a good idea, since the only event which could have destabilised the smoothly running household was the return of Edwin.

'I heard them,' said Ralph icily, his voice muffled by the thick material in the curtains.

'Heard what?' enquired Heracles nervously, fearing it might be some intimate detail.

'I know I should not have listened but we all did. I never meant to, but Jack and Sarah had their ears pressed to the door and I joined them. It was for Flora's good, someone needed to know what he was up to,' said Ralph defensively.

'Yes and do you think you should tell me?' asked Heracles hesitantly.

'Of course I do,' Ralph shot back. 'They were talking about plans and he blurted out that he wanted Flora to go back to court with him, he said it was her duty, that it was the only way he could recover his finances.'

'And what did your sister say?' said Heracles.

'She refused,' said Ralph abruptly. 'She said that the King would be coming here to see the tulips, especially the famous Flora's Glory, that preparations were being made for his arrival and that she would never ever go back to court.'

'Of course I knew there had been talk of their Majesties coming here on their tour of spring gardens,' said Heracles slowly. 'It has been kept rather secret as these things must be because there are so many factions about who wish their Majesties harm.'

'Well, Flora went on and told him her life was here and that if he wanted to regain her trust completely he would have to respect what she said, that the gardens were her first love and that as she might have been deprived of the possibility of having children, the garden was her nursery'.

'How brave she is,' sighed Heracles admiringly. 'Few women would speak so independently.'

'What did she mean, never have children?' asked Ralph.

Of course Heracles knew what had happened and was embarrassed that he should have to explain such a thing to his charge.

'Well, dear boy, you know there are some mares in the stable that do not easily carry a foal,' he stammered, hot with embarrassment.

'Heracles, you need not talk to me as if I were a child,' flashed Ralph. 'I know how not to get a child on a woman. Where do you think I go when you think I am cosily tucked up and asleep, and do you think I would risk having a squalling babe dumped on my sister's door?'

Heracles digested this information with alarm. To him Ralph was still a young boy, protected from the sins of the flesh, and now as he looked at him with fresh eyes he saw that the boy probably knew more of women than he would ever know. 'My boy, I hardly know what to say,' he stumbled awkwardly.

'That is not all I have heard,' said Ralph gloomily.

He had no intention of elaborating on the sounds he had heard coming from his sister's chamber on the night when he was furtively stealing back into the house with the connivance of the hall boy, after one of his assignments with Abigail, the buxom young daughter of the estate blacksmith. He recalled the animal cries of his sister being pleasured by her recalcitrant husband, noises that he had just heard himself in the steaming hay in the loft above the stable.

Abigail was his first sexual experience and when he had heard screaming like those of the vixens in the woods he had been appalled, but he had decided that it was only the village women who made such wild abandoned responses. To hear these from his sister shocked him. He had stayed awake most of the night and then as dawn had broken he had had a magic half hour when the whole world glowed. He realised that all men and women are equal. He realised the power of physical love, how it had engulfed all his sister's emotions. It was almost too much for him to cope with, disturbing his equilibrium. He looked at Heracles and thought that even he had once loved a woman. And then he had found compassion and understanding. He understood the power of sex, how Edwin and Flora had their own journey and that he must stand back and let them travel it alone. He didn't feel jealous and excluded anymore, but he knew that one day she would need him and that he would be there.

'Flora is to give Edwin her final answer tonight,' said Ralph. 'Whatever it is I will not judge her.'

Heracles nodded. 'Let us go back to our studies,' he said, 'for it is knowledge and your brain which will control the beast within us all.'

*   *   *

That evening Edwin met Flora in the parlour. There were things he had not told his wife and they were by way of explanation as to the importance of her support at court. These were things about which he was ashamed, the consequences of his delinquent life, from which he was now distanced. But they had profound effects, limiting his choices. Each had things to say; he knew they would go ill with Flora, how could they do otherwise? He was the first to speak.

'I have to explain something to you,' he said evenly, aware of her wide, unflinching gaze. 'While I was not myself I was coerced into gambling. I have incurred terrible debts and as I had no money to speak of I had to use my family estate for security.' He gulped and continued solemnly, almost as if he were talking about somebody else. 'I would have lost it all, every bit of it, the land, the house, the farms, all of it. My mother would have had nothing . . . but for . . . '

'But for what?' interrupted Flora coldly.

'My brothers-in-law have paid off the debts and now they own the estate,' he gulped painfully.

'I see,' said Flora in a low voice, unable to find anything more appropriate to offer. She plunged into a void devoid of hope.

'At least my mother is looked after,' he said sadly.

'Yes, that at least,' said Flora flatly. There was no emotion in her face.

'You see now why I must redeem myself and make my own fortune,' said Edwin. 'I could not fulfil my duty to you, Flora, while I have nothing to offer you. In a sense this is my opportunity for redemption. But surely you see that you are the only person who can support me. I cannot do this on my own. I beg of you, Flora . . . I will get a good position, with your understanding I will be powerful, respected.'

She considered her answer carefully; she could not meet his

gaze when she replied. She could not betray her agony; she had been made a fool of again. 'Surely you know what this place means to me, Edwin, it is my life's work. I cannot leave it; especially now, as you have nothing. I must not let this fall away in the way you have dissipated your own sacred gifts. I am merely a trustee for future generations, for my brother, for my children . . . ' Her voice caught as she said the word children and she saw him flinch.

He saw something different in her now. It was hard, almost cruel. He wanted to say something, but no words came and he knew she intended to dig the knife deeper to make her point.

'The King and Queen are coming here to see the gardens in a few days,' she went on briskly. 'Every day I must go with my men and tend the blooms. You see they . . . *they* are my children. At least you cannot destroy them, can you, Edwin?' Her voice was unflinching and resolute.

Flora made sure her face was a mask. Had he come back for the sole purpose of using her as a means for his recovery or did he genuinely love her? She didn't really know but she did know that she had to fight fire with fire.

Edwin made as if to speak but no words came out of his mouth. She stayed him with her hand. 'You can do this on your own,' she went on, mellowing just a little. 'In fact, you must do it on your own. It is your battle, not mine. I have fought my own battle and I have won. I have silenced my demons; you must do the same. Go back to court and make your fortune. Our ancestors have all done it. And then you will come to the table of our marriage with dignity and spurs which are your own.'

She had thrown down a gauntlet of hope at least and he felt he must be grateful for that. But for now he knew this was the end of the matter. There was nothing to be gained by waiting. He had no choice. Some people might have suggested that he remain for the King and Queen's visit. But no, this he could not do. He would go back to London; he would seek an interview with Sarah Churchill. She would point him in the right direction. If Flora would not come then he might as well use the separation to do what fate had clearly decided for him.

'I will leave today,' he said.

She had turned towards the door; he knew she had things to do; she was always in demand for one reason or another. He suspected she hardly ever had time to think. Her face showed no signs of confusion or distress, and he saw again that she had the makings of a great lady, one for whom he must make himself worthy. After all, he realised he had returned with his new persona, but what did it really mean? The man was the same man; nothing had happened to challenge him on the anvil of life; nothing had yet tested him. He had come back reformed, made love to his wife in her bed, demanded to be let into her life, her future, her dreams – and with her beneficence, her family money, her servants, her brilliance, courage and determination. He had nothing on his own canvas about which he could boast with pride.

'Before you leave the room, Flora, I have something to tell you,' said Edwin. She turned and swept her skirts around her in order to face him. There was no outward sign of the racing of her heart, the despair she felt at his leaving, her feeling that somehow she had been deceived. Her disgust was with herself: perhaps she had been stupid, had let her young girl's heart overcome the ring of iron she had put around herself. She tilted her chin and looked at him with all the appearance of a woman without passion.

'I have decided to enlist in the army; I will be joining the campaign in Ireland,' he announced evenly.

He had already pledged to do this but until now he had not told her, partly because he wanted her forgiveness to come from love and not because of some empty promise of valour on the field of battle.

She said nothing, for the simple reason that she did not know what to say. There was a painful silence.

'You do not need to say anything,' he said eventually. 'I assure you, my beloved wife, I will make you proud of me and my life is in God's hands, where it has always been although I have not seen Him.'

'You are right,' she said quickly. 'May He go with you, Edwin.'

She crossed the space between them and seeing there was a possibility that it might indeed be the last time she ever saw her husband she wished to lock something compassionate and worthy in her memory. They embraced; he closed his eyes, the better to remember the smell of her, the feel of her hair on his cheek and the comforting warmth of her body. She turned and left the room. He summoned the servants to prepare for his departure, and was on the road for London on his faithful Warrior within the hour.

CHAPTER EIGHTEEN

Catherine's Court, May 1690

The night was still, with not even the faintest tremor of breeze; the next day would be fine. All boded well and excitement hung in the pregnant air. Their Majesties were coming and the house was in a high state of alert, but exhaustion had sent most people hurrying to their beds, eager to snatch a few hours sleep. But not Jack; he had a sixth sense that there was danger lurking somewhere, he was like a night animal himself, seeing and hearing all. His mother had always said he had 'the sight', but he kept such things to himself, it didn't do to set yourself apart from other people. All the same, if anything went wrong he felt it would be his fault.

Suddenly he heard a vague rustle outside the shuttered window in the men servants' quarters where he slept. The building abutted directly onto the stable yard and the horses, restive in their stalls, were aware of it too. Soon the yard dogs set up a hue and cry.

Hera and Diana lay sleeping on cushions outside Flora's door but suddenly they leapt up, ears pricked, bodies trembling, sensing danger. Not waiting for an order, they clattered down the polished stairs, waking the hall boy slumbering in his usual place in his leather upholstered seated sentry box by the front door. His head lolled for a moment, heavy with sleep, until he felt a sharp box on the ear followed by Jack's voice.

'Get up, boy; there are intruders in the grounds! Will you sleep there while all our throats are cut?' he boomed. The boy shot up and saw that three other male servants had joined them, their eyes starting with adrenalin.

'Get to it, lads,' hissed Jack. 'We will slip out of the side door and quiet with it; surprise is the best weapon. One of you stay here and make as if you are drawing the bolts on this door to get their attention.' Jack looked at Hera and Diana and recalled their panther-like stalking technique; the breed had mastered the tactic of deadly pursuit. Their lean bodies would home in on the offenders whatever, whoever, they were.

Ralph had joined them in a hastily grabbed jacket and trousers followed by Heracles Prior in his nightcap.

'Mister Prior, keep the women inside,' Jack ordered. 'We won't be long.'

The men sneaked out of the house and the stablemen came out of the lofts and joined the group. The moon was full and a thick mist hung low on the ground from the warmth of the previous day. The group stood still as statues while they listened; there came a swishing and chopping noise from the direction of the gardens. The group moved stealthily in the direction of the tulip garden. The moon had reached its zenith in the sky and the figures cast no shadow. They rounded the corner into the gardens and there were several figures in a frenzy of destruction. There was a strong smell of pulverised resin from the blooms and damp earth where even the bulbs had been wrenched from the ground and pulped.

'At them, lads,' yelled Jack. And men and boys alike fell on the hapless perpetrators, about five in all, three of whom ran into the adjacent woodland with the dogs in frantic pursuit. The estate men and boys outnumbered them two to one and the two stragglers were soon on the ground in a flailing mass of bodies. One of them, a big man, began to put up a spirited fight and Jack saw the flash of a knife, ice blue in the moonlight. He called out.

'Drop your knife, man! You don't stand a chance.'

The man gave a terrifying roar like a caged animal and lunged at Ralph who had stood with his father's sword at the ready.

'Oh, no, you don't,' bellowed the groom and lunged at the man's back view.

'Stand still, fool, and do as the man says, drop your weapon or it will be the worse for you,' Jack shouted again.

In a split second the man turned with brutish force and set about the groom. There was a clash of metal as the man fell forward and staggered to the ground, the dogs slavering at his face. He gave a rasping breath. The groom stood transfixed. He had never killed a man but he had known that it was his own life he had defended. The man rolled over onto his back, clutching his chest, from which came a gushing stream of dark blood.

'Pa, Pa! You have killed my pa!' came the voice of the other captive in a broken adolescent sob. Instinctively, the men released the young man and he fell to the ground, cradling the dying man's head to his chest.

The father recognised his son in his last moments and stretched up a feeble hand to touch the lad's tousled hair. 'Let the boy go, them was only flowers, what's flowers compared to food on the table for six starving babes?' implored the man in a gurgling voice.

'My pa! What is ma going to do without him?' wailed the desperate lad, sobbing uncontrollably.

Jack stepped forward and knelt beside the man. He could smell the sickly odour of blood mixed with earth.

'The lad will come to no harm if you tell us who set you on this hapless task,' he said solemnly.

'A gentleman from London,' gasped the man. 'His man came to the tavern where we men gather to hear tell of work.'

'He brought money, more than we had seen in many a month,' the boy rambled.

A silence descended, broken only by the laboured breaths of the dying man. Each man with his thoughts about the random lottery of life. Each knew that but for the grace of their Lord God they too might have wasted a few plants for the chance of feeding their children.

Jack held the man's hand while the boy cradled his head and then there was silence, Jack placed his hand on the man's rugged, suntanned face and gently closed his eyes. He crossed himself.

'May God bless the poor wretch's soul,' he said quietly.

'My pa was not a poor wretch,' wailed the lad, his recently

broken voice reverting to a boyish shrill. 'He was as fine a man as ever there was. He did this because he lost his job on the farm. They laid off all of them and we lost our home with it, we lost everything, everything, do you hear, and now we have lost him.'

'Take the boy to the house,' said Jack. 'No harm will come to you, boy, but we must find out who led your family to this folly.'

The boy was in shock. He had no boots and had turned ashen white and he was shivering uncontrollably. His face was set in a rigor of terror and Jack could see at once that he was not a lad accustomed to destruction and law breaking. Having been at the side of the father during his last breaths he could see that the man was also a decent fellow who had been driven to desperate actions.

*   *   *

Flora dressed hastily as soon as it was light enough to see the damage. With supreme self-control, she had not allowed herself to imagine just how dreadful the destruction was until she had seen it for herself. The King and Queen were expected in time for the midday meal and preparations for the banquet had gone well. The table was prepared in the long hall and garlands of flowers from the glasshouses were draped on the stiff damask napery, each secured in little phials of water pinned to the cloth. Scented herbs waited in baskets to be strewn on the floors later in the morning and the kitchen fire had been stoked while it was still light. Suckling pigs had been stuffed with rosemary and thyme and basted during the night with honey and mead, and jellies and comfits stood trembling on the cool slate shelves in the larders. Wooden trugs of vegetables and herbs were awaiting preparation and there was the enticing smell of breads coming from the racks outside the ovens, some with almonds and dates and in all manner of shapes, even one twisted in the shape of the royal cipher, which would be served to His Majesty. In the game larder rows of larks and pigeons hung by their feet, ready for plucking since Meg the cook would only make pies from freshly plucked birds.

News of the disaster in the gardens had first begun to filter through to the kitchens when the weeping boy had been brought to the house.

'When the mistress called the priest I knew it would bode ill,' said Meg darkly while she pounded walnuts and dried figs in the giant pestle. This was normally a task undertaken by some of the lowly kitchen hands, but she was angry and the pounding made her feel better. The kitchen always knew when there was trouble and this was a dire moment on a day they had all been anticipating with such excitement. They were to see the King and Queen, to serve them on bended knee, and now it had been spoiled by the actions of these unknown people, and for what possible reason?

'The boy has been sent for,' Meg announced, 'up to Lord Thomas's old study where he will get a good sound whipping that will loosen his tongue. The young Lord Ralph and her ladyship are there and Jack and Mr Prior. Sarah has told me they will get it out of him.'

*　　*　　*

The boy stood with his head hanging in shame, his knees buckling in abject fear. He had heard many a story about the ways men forced the truth: thumb screws or boiling oil on your men's parts; he felt he might be sick. The room was as nothing he had ever seen before and worse still he feared he might open his bowels on the polished floor.

In the event, to his surprise, the ladyship called for a chair. She was as beautiful as an angel but her face was white and sad. There was also a young man about the same age as himself. He had a firmer set. And then there was the man they called Jack, and finally an older man with wispy hair and a fine jacket.

His fear began to subside as they began to ask him questions and he told them everything he knew, which wasn't much. He swore it was the truth on an old Bible they brought to him trailing silken markers. He could hardly find the words for the shaking in his voice, and he could not say the word for he knew it would not go well for him. That was what the man with the money had said. Then another gentleman joined them. They greeted him affectionately, they called him Lionel, and the older gentleman called him Mr Wellbeloved. The man seemed to be the one who was in control, the one they looked to for guidance. He was a fine gentleman, but he had a glint of authority about him. When he spoke, they all listened. They told him what he had said.

'It is clear to me that there are two explanations possible,' Lionel Wellbeloved said in a clear defining voice. 'The most obvious is that this is a vengeful act carried out for religious reasons. There have, as you all know, been incidences of attacks carried out on Catholics. There are many who wish ill to those who still harbour ambivalence to the new order,' he said, crossing himself.

'But the visit of our Protestant King to this house could also be the reason,' interceded Heracles. 'There is also much hostility from local Catholics.'

'It was neither,' blurted the boy. 'The man who came with the money said it was personal, that is what I told you. When I said our Lady I meant this lady,' he said, looking nervously towards Flora.

'The man wished to harm her?' said Lionel Wellbeloved incredulously.

'No, it was her garden. He said if we did what he wanted the woman would learn a lesson, he was very loud about it and then he gave us the money and he said if we did not do the job properly now we had the money he would see to it that we all suffered.'

Jack noticed her beginning to sway and called for Sarah who was waiting outside the door.

'Bring some water for our Lady,' he whispered.

CHAPTER NINETEEN

Catherine's Court, May 1690

'Your Majesties, we welcome you to our home,' said Flora, plunging into a deep curtsey.

'My dear Lady, it is joy for us. The Queen and I are looking forward to this visit and is your namesake, my special bloom, at its peak today?'

The arrival of the royal party was anything but informal. The verdant green of the countryside and the cloudless sky were the perfect backcloth to what seemed to be a symphony of black and white shot with flashes of gold. Magnificent black horses pounded the gravel with white plumed feet; the royal coaches were also black with gold insignia, with the grooms and postilion in the darkest of green with black cockades. But like two actors in the middle of a set piece the King and Queen stood out in luxurious silk, the Queen's broken by an abundance of exquisite white lace trimmings, most apparent in her petticoats, hooked up in swoops with trailing silk bows. Flora thought that although the couple were undeniably elegant there was at the same time a self-consciousness about them, which was somehow at odds with the simple life that Flora had maintained in the country far away from the court. The household had taken a decision not to mention the disaster at once. There was an awkward silence.

Lionel Wellbeloved was concerned that a connection between the royal visit and a Catholic demonstration might prove embarrassing and he was well aware that it would draw attention to the religious ambivalence at Catherine's Court. He had advised the concoction of some story about a freak accident of nature ruining the blooms.

'There is much to see,' said Flora. The Queen came forward

and dismissed Flora's curtsey and in a spontaneous gesture extended both her arms as a mother might do to a daughter.

'My dear, I have not seen you since your dear father joined our own heavenly father.' Her voice quivered with emotion. The matter of fathers was a difficult one for the Queen, since her own father, the old King, had in the eyes of many, including at times her own, been betrayed. And here she was wearing, in effect, her father's crown. But she wore it well, encouraged by her husband's fatalistic view that James, his uncle, had not been worthy of it. He made his wife feel that she was on a crusade to save her country from Popery and all its attendant evils.

The Queen felt Flora's small body tremble as she mentioned her father. The moment passed as Ralph pressed forward to be presented. He had made up his mind to avoid the habit of dissembling, so prevalent in most adult people of the noble class. The destruction of the tulips had happened and now the affair must be explained. The truth should be found and in order to do that the facts must be faced. He had progressed from anger to a resolute determination to flush the real culprit out into the open. All the fingers pointed to the despicable Edwin.

But there was a bit of him that said perhaps that was too simple an explanation. Ralph had good reason to have become a student of human nature in his short life; he knew that things so crudely presented should be regarded with caution.

'Your Majesty,' he said boldly. 'The gardens are at their best, but last night sadly we suffered an intrusion and the famous Flora's Glory was completely destroyed.'

'My Lady, is this true?' said the King in bewilderment.

'Yes, Your Majesty, we have one of the men who did it and we will find out the truth,' said Lionel Wellbeloved hastily, looking furiously at Ralph.

'This is the most distressing news,' said the King, shaking his head and placing his gloved hand on his heart as if grieving for a serious human bereavement. And truthfully he felt the very real pain of loss. He had been excited at the prospect of seeing the tulip he had helped to create. It was the real reason he had come. He had often bewildered and irritated his advisors by digressing from matters of state to visit gardens and works of art.

Despite everything, the party moved into the house where the servants waited excitedly to greet their sovereigns, knowing that this would be an event they would hand down for generations.

*   *   *

When the royal party had refreshed themselves, they set off at a leisurely pace to tour the gardens. Hasty plans had been devised to avoid the ruined tulips but the King was adamant and insisted on seeing for himself.

'This is truly mindless,' he said, his brow furrowed. 'Do we know of anyone who might have some sort of grudge against the family?' he asked probingly. There was something about the systematic destruction that disturbed him greatly. Gardens had been the one consistent and pristine joy of his life. While the world plotted and planned and the seeds of political duplicity scattered around him, his gardens bloomed and regenerated. They were a statement of hope, hope for the world in all its madness. Men died for causes they did not really comprehend but nature paid no heed to it all. And he the King assisted it in its creation of beauty for the civilised man to enjoy. He had been particularly interested in the tulip Lord Thomas had nurtured; it was an example of the summit of horticultural achievement to which he aspired. He had a few of the blooms himself in his magnificent gardens at Het Loo in the Netherlands but he had been unable to return there owing to more pressing matters in England and so had been unable to see them. This act of destruction was to him sacrilegious.

'Lady Flora, Lord Ralph, I will arrange for some specimens to be brought to you from the Netherlands by my special horticultural envoy,' he said later. 'We have many blooms artificially held back and they can be here within days.'

William's rather small beady eyes narrowed. 'We will find out the reason for this,' he said, before moving on to the Italian Garden.

*   *   *

The royal couple returned to court in a sombre mood after their trip. They had seen various gardens in which they had taken an interest, but none had made the same impression as their visit to Catherine's Court.

They had not discussed the disaster with the tulips, but the King had been nonetheless disquieted by it. It was one of the Queen's ladies who mentioned it during the quiet time when Her Majesty and her ladies were sewing their primitive form of crochet called knotting. The ladies had at first been resistant to it, but the Queen's obsessive diligence had made it obligatory and it had now become a fashionable occupation, with ladies even doing it in their coaches. This was one of the times the Queen enjoyed most at Kensington House, her favourite palace, and had it not been for the rumblings in Ireland which pre-occupied the King, and did not bode well for the serenity of their domestic idyll, she would have been content.

The Queen mentioned their recent tour and looked proudly out of the long open windows to the gardens beyond. 'It is in the gardens that the King and I have found the peace and satisfaction that has kept us resolute through these troubled times,' she said wistfully. 'But the real joy comes with a happy marriage,' she added in the rather frank way she had of talking to her women on these occasions. There was a hardly detectable rising of eyebrows among the ladies and their work was nervously rearranged on their silken laps.

'Madam, talking of marriages . . . ' offered the Countess of Dorset, the Queen's lady of the bedchamber. The Queen inclined her head, indicating a continuance of the subject.

'Well,' announced her ladyship dramatically, 'it is said that the handsome Lord Edwin Grantley was responsible for the event which showed such disrespect for Your Majesty's recent visit to his wife's famous gardens.'

'What can you mean?' asked the Queen sharply.

'A lovers' tiff,' suggested Joffer Goldstein, one of the Queen's few Dutch ladies who made no secret of her dislike of the English and all things English.

'No, my dear,' purred Lady Dorset in a patronising tone such as is adopted by someone who has the real and sensational truth at hand.

'Pray, do share this with us,' said the Queen severely, resting her tired eyes for a moment and putting down her work. She disliked gossip, since she knew only too well that her own family and especially her marriage were rich pickings for salacious tongues.

'It is said,' said Lady Dorset, in a confidential way, which was anything but confidential as she well knew, 'that it was out of spite the husband did it because his pretty young wife refused to come to court.' All eyes went to the Queen who displayed no obvious interest at this latest intelligence. 'And what is more,' Lady Dorset went on sensationally 'she refuses to do his bidding, since his Lordship used her so cruelly that she lost the child she was carrying.'

There was a stunned silence amongst the ladies and all waited for the Queen to make some definitive comment. 'If this is true, I shall see to it that Lord Edwin is banished from court,' she said eventually.

'But Madam,' interjected Lady Hoffer reasonably, 'surely if the man has done such a thing he would then return to his wife and make matters even worse?'

'I am told that,' said one of the other ladies, 'the young Lady Grantley is of an independent nature and has become such an authority in the world of gardens that she is in a position to make her own terms, more especially since the young man is rumoured to have gambled away his family estate.'

Lady Dorset sighed, delicately raising her eyebrows.

CHAPTER TWENTY

The Palace of Whitehall, June 1690

To be summoned by the King was a serious matter; Edwin had been notified by one of the King's messengers and his mind raced as he perused what the reason could be, more especially as there was a crisis of alarming proportions occupying both the domestic and the political front. What could be so urgent, he asked himself?

The King's secret service had uncovered a series of Jacobite plots and the perpetrators had been imprisoned at once. Some of them had already been executed without due trial. He was innocent of any involvement, but nevertheless there was something untoward about the situation.

Edwin had chosen his most sombre clothes for the occasion: a dark blue velvet coat with a high-necked shirt and discreet silver buttons bearing the family crest. The coat had a deliberately military flavour, a reflection of his plans. He had spoken with Lady Churchill, who had in turn delivered a promise that she had discussed a commission for him, and, pending any obstacles, he could be assured of a position as an officer.

The large double doors of the King's private audience room were opened by two young officers in naval uniform instead of the usual young pages, and at once his worries were confirmed.

At a long table sat the King and Lord Nottingham, his closest advisor, two men from the Commissioners to the Admiralty, one of the senior Dutch advisors and Captain Butler, the most senior emissary for Ireland. They wore severe military clothing with short grey wigs neatly gathered behind their heads, with the exception of the King, who wore a massive periwig which hung lose to his face, giving his gaunt, beaky features the appearance of a small but lethal bird of prey.

Edwin's mouth went dry; there was no attempt at cursory politeness. A flunky stepped forward and following Lord Nottingham's beady gaze Edwin handed over his sword. Lord Nottingham nodded towards a place facing the King and his advisors. At once he knew that this was to all intents and purposes a courtroom.

The King's face betrayed nothing; he asked Edwin to be seated as was his custom, in order to render his diminutive height less apparent in the company of so many tall men. In front of the King was a pile of documents, some of which bore a seal. Edwin stared at them nervously. 'This is not a court room, Lord Edwin,' Lord Nottingham began ominously, with what Edwin detected was a note of irony. 'But you are here to answer some serious questions; much depends on your answers.'

Edwin said nothing and Lord Nottingham turned deferentially towards the King.

'Lord Edwin,' the King began in his slightly guttural accent. 'I feel it necessary to tell you that, had it not been for the intervention of the Queen, you would not have been given this opportunity to speak for yourself. My Lord, there are serious things which concern us and I repeat, it is Her Majesty who has saved you . . . for the moment. You should be in the Gate House of the Tower, imprisoned with a dozen other gentlemen.'

'Your Majesty, I do not understand what transgression can have brought me to this position,' protested Edwin, his face paling, beads of sweat starting to appear on his forehead. He reached for a kerchief and patted his brow. His accusers noted these signs of anxiety and Lord Nottingham caught the King's eye.

'Mr Pepys said much the same when he sat in that very chair together with his friend Sir Anthony Deane, but there it is,' the King said laconically, spreading his hands to indicate resignation concerning an event about which he cared little. There was a communal smirk around the table as if the pack was drawing in for the kill. 'But maybe you can do more to reassure us,' the King went on, crossing his bony fingers and leaning forward on his elbows. He gave Edwin a look of unnerving intensity; there was silence in the room and Edwin moved his chair nervously on the polished wood floor. The grinding of wood made a noise like the shutting of a creaky door and Edwin shivered momentarily, trying to collect himself, anxious not to betray the fearful anxiety which had begun to engulf him.

'I will invite Lord Nottingham to inform you of the basis of the shameful tale of events,' invited the King eventually, aware of the power of silence.

'Firstly, Lord Edwin, I must ask you some questions to clarify matters,' his Lordship commenced slowly. 'Are you aware of the corruption within the naval suppliers who have weakened the security of our country and the state of which the King is the head? These crimes are therefore crimes which amount to treason and summary execution.'

'I know nothing about these matters,' Edwin protested vigorously.

'These matters, as you call them,' said the King coolly, 'these matters cannot be dismissed so lightly. They are a catastrophe. Elaborate please, Captain Butler,' he finished, inclining the periwig towards the officer.

'Willingly, Your Majesty,' said Captain Butler. 'Sailors, Lord Edwin, ordinary men, sons, husbands, fathers unable to fight, Sir; their guts poisoned by rotten meat, biscuits crawling with weevils, watered ale. And their ships built from unseasoned wood, which springs a leak within hours; sails lost through substandard rope that would not hold a girl's braids. And, as we have just seen, men drown, unable to defend their ship with cannonballs which do not fit the guns.' Captain Butler was in full flow. The King signed for him to continue. 'This scandal has been going on for years, and we are going to root this out once and for all . . . Do you hear, Sir? All these scoundrels who have defrauded the navy under the noses of fighting men who put their trust in them have lined their pockets for long enough.'

The King's eyes narrowed. He watched Edwin carefully; in fact he had a sense that Edwin kept bad company by default. He was a good judge of character and he had decided that Lord

Edwin was most probably guilty of stupidity more than anything else. But he would undoubtedly be able to lead them to the architect of this massive corruption. The more he discovered about the state of the country he now ruled, the more he felt almost messianic. He had a duty to deliver his subjects from the shambolic rule of the Stewarts. He knew the young man had been promised a commission and he was in need of promising young blood beside him, especially as he was about to embark on the Irish Campaign.

He had long ago worked out that fear was a deadly weapon and he had no hesitation in using it. He did not need to be loved. This was in his opinion the first rule of leadership; to be mindlessly loved achieved nothing, it eroded the possibility of decisive decisions made without deference to the ignorant masses. No, he was a man who, as history would prove, did the unexpected; he kept people guessing, even his wife, and he preserved the mystery of Kingship. This meeting would flush out some snakes in the grass and test a young man's loyalty. It was a risk, but William liked risks, his whole life had been a risk. He had come to take the crown on a risk and had won the hearts of the people. But there lurked a greater threat to his rule than this corruption. It was the thing that drove it: the Church of Rome. And he was convinced that what they would discover was not unconnected with the Catholics who still lurked dangerously in high places.

'As God is my witness,' said Edwin desperately. 'I have kept bad company but not anymore, I know nothing of such calumny. I would not be party to such things.'

'It is said that we should keep our friends close but our enemies closer,' the King remarked slowly. 'You, my Lord Edwin, should know your enemies. I would suggest that you have enemies, personal ones perhaps, who are also enemies of the state and it is your duty to think carefully on this. It will do you no good shielding these people.'

Edwin nodded cautiously; he could not quite think where this was leading.

'The Queen has brought a matter to our attention,' the King continued chillingly. 'And it is therefore of concern to us.'

Of course Edwin knew that the term 'us' referred to His Majesty himself. He fiddled nervously with his stiff white cuffs.

'Your private life does not interest me,' King persevered coldly, an indication of what was to follow, 'unless of course it brings the court into disrepute.' He regarded Edwin with an icy look, and Edwin had the distinct impression that the many-stranded case against him, whatever it was, had been carefully rehearsed.

'If you will permit me, Your Majesty,' interceded Lord Nottingham and the King nodded. 'We have noted that Lord Edwin has not signed the Oath of Allegiance and therefore we cannot regard him as a reliable witness. These crimes we have mentioned are part of a wider and deeper rooted origin and motive, a Catholic conspiracy, and it is everywhere we look where trouble is to be found.'

'Ah, yes,' said the King. 'And we are shocked and surprised to learn that you, Lord Edwin, and Lady Flora renewed your wedding vows before a Catholic priest. Do you have anything to say about all this?'

Edwin shuddered as he thought about the man who stood in judgement over him. This man had ruthlessly pushed his wife into taking her own father's throne, and not content with that she had callously usurped her little half-brother, now living in poverty-stricken exile in France.

'I do, Your Majesty,' said Edwin, thinking quickly. 'I know that James is raising a Catholic Jacobite army in Ireland and that he does so with the support of King Louis of France whose ultimate aim is to return England to the Catholic faith and restore to France the power to invade England. This is why I have asked for a commission to serve in Your Majesty's army. I am no papist, of that I can assure you, but my dearest wife, the Lady Flora, trusted the man who had been her family advisor as a young child. It was not a declaration of loyalty to Catholicism, merely her want of happiness. She needed to affirm with God . . . but . . . ' Edwin faltered. He had a vision of Frederick, of the man's furtive conduct, of the Papal masses he had held in clandestine corners of the City. He saw it all as if a curtain had been lifted; he had been used in his own blind stupidity. Fredrick was much more than a dishonest philanderer, he was in a plot more sinister. William clearly knew more than he was indicating. Edwin saw now how serious this was: a threat to the throne and he Edwin had been part of it, unwittingly supporting Frederick while he infiltrated the innermost sanctum of the throne, the constitution on which England depended for her independence and survival.

Furthermore, Edwin also knew that the Irish would use James and his powerful friends but that they cared not one dot for the English throne. Poor deluded James, he thought, he was no match for this man, and neither was he. He began to feel he was doomed. There was nothing left for it but to share these revelations as they came into his mind like pictures in a dream, which came back firstly fragmented and then with a sharp reality.

'Your Majesty, gentlemen,' he started. 'I must decide wherein lies the greater good. Do I sacrifice the confidence of a blaggard who had used me ill and ruined my family? Should I divulge the name? Am I a Judas to do so?'

'No, my Lord Edwin,' shot Captain Butler. 'This man has forfeited his right to friendship; a man must think of the greater good, that is the very essence of human sacrifice to principle. Without it government is impossible. These are dark days and we must all take this chance. We have to save our nation with His Majesty's help. You also have chance to save yourself. Take it.'

Edwin did not hesitate. He told the story of his own moral decline. He spoke of his epiphany, of his love for Flora. He gave them names, recalled from the dark sink of his shameful past. As he did so, he knew that Frederick was a dead man. He saw the rapt attention of the men who listened. He saw that they understood what all men know in their hearts: that it could have been their own story when they were young and green. It was

Edwin's most critical moment. He fought for his future and it hinged on truth, his own truth.

*   *   *

Later that day, as chance would have it, Lady Grantley, Edwin's mother, arrived in London. She went directly to the court where she had found out that her son was residing in one of the many amorphous lodgings that royal servants occupied when they had no London home. She had been in despair over her son's life and fortunes; if he had not been such a fool he would be at the Amalie London house. She had sent an old steward there the previous week, but the place was shuttered and boarded and an ancient caretaker had looked at the man suspiciously and professed to know nothing of his mistress's plans to return, carefully avoiding any mention of Edwin.

Now, she waited for him in a set of rooms on the far side of the great palace. She was pleasantly surprised by the charm of the place. Everything was scrupulously clean in the small apartment, where a maid brought elderflower wine. There were lilies on a table in front of a tall open window where a curtain billowed and sighed in a breeze, mingling their fragrance with the plants in the garden outside. There was a set of chairs reflected in a polished marquetry floor and books carefully stacked on a side table. Double doors revealed a bedchamber in which brushes and bottles were arranged on a military chest in perfect symmetry. The bedcovers were folded monastically, with no suggestion of the licentious abandon that had previously marked her son's bedchambers. She cast her eyes about looking for signs of Edwin, but nothing in the neatness and order was reminiscent of the man she had known.

She was alone in the room in this huge alien palace and for a minute her courage failed her. She had sent the maid to find lodgings and the stewards were dealing with the old tired horses.

'Mother,' said a voice behind her. She had not heard the door open and she turned at once. She went straight to him; although she had rehearsed the meeting a thousand times in her mind's eye, there was no restraint as she had planned.

Both mother and son were shocked in equal measure by the map of pain on each other's features.

As they embraced, Lady Grantley could feel that her son had lost weight and his face had thinned accordingly. All the puffiness caused by his dissolute living had gone and his features had fined out. She stood back and regarded him searchingly. For the first time he resembled his father and she felt a flush of optimism. For a fleeting moment she thought something had changed.

'I have heard it all, I went to see Flora,' she said bluntly.

'Mother,' he said gravely, stepping back and giving her a little bow. 'This is not the Edwin you have known of late who stands before you, but another man. The old Edwin grievously sinned against you and our family. He walked with evil, but he is no more, and before God, Mother, I had nothing to do with the vile events which have caused my beloved wife such anguish.'

She did not waver, although she wanted to believe that he had indeed experienced some sort of metamorphosis.

'That is all well and good, Edwin,' she replied in a quiet voice. 'But I have come from your family and from your dear wife. I wish to take you home, not to Flora for she will not have you, but to us. Leave this place, no good has come of your dissolute life here. Perhaps you could hide yourself in some religious order and make amends for what you have done. Who knows? In time all may be forgiven. I do not know but I do know that the love of a family knows no bounds and your brother-in-law has restored our home. I have the Dower House, and besides you have nieces and nephews you have never even met.'

'I know, Mother, that I need to repair my life,' he said in a voice as quiet but strong as her own. He saw his mother's eyes flickering as she tried to interpret the meaning of his words. Her breast heaved emotionally as she looked at the boy who had tossed his chances so carelessly aside and laughed in the face of his good fortune in all things. She wanted to believe him, and yet . . .

'I will not hide away like a coward behind the skirts of my

long-suffering family,' he went on vigorously. 'I must cast my bread upon the waters. I have prayed to God for a chance to serve my country and my King, to make you proud of me. Even if I must die in the process, I will be judged by a higher court.'

There was an unbroken silence and Lady Grantley turned, seeking a chair; it had been a long journey and she had undertaken it without the approval of her daughter and son-in-law. She knew she could not return the same day, let alone without her son, and she was tired. She did not know what to believe. As if in answer to her confusion there was a tap at the door.

Edwin opened it and there stood a young officer in uniform extending a document. The young man bowed and waited.

'Oh my God, Edwin, we are lost! You are to be taken, what have you done now?' she cried in anguish.

Edwin took the document and hurriedly broke the seal, fragments of red wax sticking to his cuffs like blood. He unrolled it and read it carefully. His features betrayed nothing.

'Mother, it is my commission,' he said at last in a trembling voice. 'The King has given me a second chance.' He took her in his arms. 'I will lay down my life for him, for you, for Flora. I will make amends.'

Lady Grantley took in the immensity of the news and suffered a mixture of emotions. Her beloved son had found himself and she could see that now; but had she found him only to lose him at once? She did not know, but she looked at his jubilant face which bore the expression he had had as a lad before he had been traduced by the world and she could do nothing but thank God for his deliverance.

CHAPTER TWENTY-ONE

Catherine's Court, June 1690

The speed with which the King had sent word to his most trusted gardener in The Hague was a measure of how keenly he felt for Flora in the situation she found herself. Some of the tulips were still in bud. His men had a technique for staggering the blooms, holding them back in order to make the halcyon tulip season of a longer duration.

Peter Van der Zee was to bring them himself in a special container, a travelling nursery designed by the King. It had been a fortuitously flat sea, which had conveyed the ship swiftly with a favourable wind. And now the coach was rounding the bend into the sleepy English village where this mysterious Lady Flora Grantley was to be surprised by the valuable gift. Peter had a picture of the woman in his mind: he saw her as portly and comfortable, in widow's weeds perhaps. She would resemble his grandmother who lived on a small perfect estate outside The Hague with a troupe of dogs and twelve omnipresent grand-children, of which he was the eldest.

'Nearly there, Sir,' cried the upside-down face of the postilion as they approached an avenue of pleached limes and a small lodge, built in a style both familiar and beautiful to Peter's eye.

That same eye was drawn by the acid-green foliage of the trees to the house beyond, and he felt a wave of pleasure. It was of a perfect Dutch design and he knew immediately that the owners had been his kindred. When at last the coach came to a halt, there was a perfect stillness in the air as if the house and gardens were completely comfortable with the world; he thought how it was uncannily like his grandmother's house in Holland. And as if he was, indeed, in front of the very same house, two dogs leapt from a side courtyard, lolloping up to him, unsure as to whether to greet him as friend or foe.

'Sit, girls, good dogs,' came a young female voice. The dogs obeyed at once. But that was not all which was instantly pleasing, not to say charming, to the visitor.

The owner of the voice was a young girl of about his own age, her face reflecting the sun-kissed glow of one who spends much of their time out of doors. She wore a plain country frock which revealed her lovely curves, but then it struck Peter that this was not a simple country girl as one might have at first thought. She was definitely a young woman of distinguished bearing and gentle upbringing. Peter had enjoyed but one romance in his life, a love so true that he had thought nothing could ever dim the light that still glowed in his heart. Beatrice, his dear love, had died of typhoid fever so suddenly he had not had time to say goodbye and so that place in his heart still remained open and unresolved; as until this moment he had thought it always would. But there is no better cure for an old love than a new love and Cupid's arrow left its bow with piercing accuracy. The girl, whoever she was, came close, peering up disconcertingly into his face. He felt a pain in his chest. He raised his hand to the place and gave a slight bow, still engaged by the fierce blue eyes.

'I am Lady Grantley,' the girl said with a note of enquiry. She glanced at the coach and saw the royal arms with the Dutch emblems. She also saw this handsome stranger, more than a foot taller than her, and she saw something about him that she could not quite identify; it was as if they were connected in a way that would obviate the necessity of the semantics of social identification.

'Baron Peter Van der Zee,' he said, with a smile that could hardly contain his delight at finding the recipient of the gift to be such a captivating young woman, who, he saw quickly, wore no ring on her left hand. 'I come with a gift from His Majesty, your King.'

'Well, how wonderful!' said Flora, clapping her hands enthusiastically like a small child.

She had now been joined by a group of protective servants, two of whom seemed to be on unusually familiar terms with their young mistress.

Flora had by necessity escaped into the world within her garden; she had almost forgotten who she was; by forgetting her identity she could also forget her sorrow. She had made Sarah pack away all her fine dresses and lost any interest in her appearance. Seeing the young man's intense gaze, she became confused. Her whole body had felt as if it had been emptied of femininity but now, as if by magic, she felt as she had been filled with a sharp awareness of the summer day. The impact she had made on the stranger and the way in which he was staring at her made her cheeks glow and it was as if she had wakened from a long sleep.

'Would the baron like our men to help unload the coach?' asked Jack.

'Yes, yes, Jack, what a good idea,' stumbled Flora, trying to smooth her earth-spattered apron and hastily pushing back an escaped tendril of hair.

Sarah watched all this and as usual nothing escaped her eagle eye. 'They stared at each other like they had just discovered the secret of life,' she was to recall later in the kitchen. The men started to unload the container strapped onto the rear of the coach and placed it reverently on the forecourt. All eyes were agog to see what could be concealed inside.

'I will just open a corner and let your Ladyship see the precious gift I bring you all the way across the North Sea,' said Peter, grinning happily.

He carefully lifted a glass lid and a pungent smell of loam and the most delicate of scent wafted out. Flora stepped forward and peered inside. Tightly packed were perfectly protected tulips on the cusp of breaking open. The familiar colours just peeping shyly through their tight outer petals hit her in the eye.

'Oh! I cannot believe it! Flora's Glory – and at least a hundred or so of them, and all about to bloom . . . I don't know what to say,' gasped Flora.

'Now I see you, my Lady, I know why they are so named,' said Peter.

*   *   *

Any relationships Flora had previously had with the opposite sex had depended on words. She thought about this the next day: with her father for example, they had talked continuously, he the teacher, she the eager pupil. She recalled her time with Roderick, to whom she had been betrothed. They had known each other all their lives. They were almost like brother and sister, they laughed, they riled each other, they told each other their secrets. Perhaps, she wondered in retrospect, this was why she had never thought it strange that she had never had the least desire to lie with him as she had done with Edwin. And then there was Ralph, her actual brother. There was never a silence between them; sometimes they finished each other's sentences they were so in tune; and Edwin, what of Edwin? They had met at court where the art of conversation was played to an extreme. Each sentence was delivered with possible double meanings, and subtle innuendo. It had been a kind of extravagant dance and one that had to be perfected. It had been as if any form of silence was regarded with disdain; it was ill mannered. Why, even the taciturn William kept up a low murmur of conversation with his wife at all times. How strange then, that the destruction of the garden should result in the arrival of this extraordinary man! With him it was a glance, a touch, the whisper of breath that sent her heart racing.

They spent the rest of the day planting the tulips. He had brought his gardening clothes and a thick leather apron. They worked together, occasionally their hands brushed. He darted a smile and their eyes held. She caught her breath and she thought she felt his on her hair, sweet and fragrant. When she offered him some of the family ale at the start of their labours, he informed her that he never drank strong drink.

191

The quiet communion between herself and the stranger was something new to her; it woke some deep sense she did not even know was there. Occasionally he made some comment about the soil or the dampness in the loam which she had ordered the men to dig into the beds where the old tulips had once been.

'The soil at Het Loo is damp,' he explained. 'The water table is high, as it is here. I feel at home here,' he said smilingly and she thought everything he said was full of some secret meaning. He in turn noticed the way she threw off her gardening gloves when it came to tenderly placing the blooms in their chosen place, the hole having been made with a silver implement like a pastry cutter which she kept in a pouch in her apron.

'I like to feel them with my skin,' she explained. 'I think plants like to be touched and encouraged,' she went on, blushing fiercely as he caught her eye. She knew what he was thinking, what his eyes said. But whereas a court blade would have responded with some clever remark, so much more powerful was his silence as his eyes strayed to her bosom and then back to her face.

'The tools you have, the beautiful little pruning knives and all with your family's crest and your name, who gave you these things?' he asked suddenly. Of course he expected she might say her husband. He knew she was married now, by things which had been said, but the men's faces had become tight and their expressions dense and unreadable when anything personal had been raised.

Had the man died or had he left her? He could not work it out; he felt stupid not knowing. He wondered if he should have asked for more information before he set out on this mission. He wasn't sure, all he knew was he had to complete the task, set the blooms in the soil and then be on his way. But the way the girl looked at him, with sadness in her eyes, which evaporated when they talked together . . . Sometimes they would both stop work at the same time and look up at the cloudless sky, both of them curiously aware of the storms that were about to break on a moment of tranquillity. It was back-breaking work and even with the help of the men the task was not finished until the sun slanted behind the trees and the shadows lengthened.

'You cannot leave tonight, it is too late, we shall prepare you a bed,' Flora said eventually.

'I would be delighted,' he said with nod.

*   *   *

They ate as a family: Heracles, Ralph, Flora and Peter, in the small family dining room near the kitchens where the warmth from the ovens and the cooking fire mellowed the temperature. There was a ceaseless informal chatter from the servants in the background and Peter noticed the absence of formality. The man of the house was never mentioned at all and the talk in the dining room was mostly about the political situation. Ralph was in his element trying to explain to the newcomer the difference between the Whigs and the Tories.

Peter listened, baffled by the blurred lines between the two parties. After a while, having thought carefully, he volunteered a clear analysis, as he saw it.

'Young Mister Ralph,' he said with a most attractive lilt in his voice to which Flora paid rapt attention, 'it would seem that the Whig party are the men to whom King William would most naturally be attracted, since they were the party in power who invited him to take the throne from the Catholic James, whom they feared would have you all become Catholics . . . but then they felt the King was so obliged to them as to be merely a mouthpiece. They gave him no income or finances to perform what was necessary to run the country. His Majesty complained, I remember, that Parliament treated him like a dog.'

'Yes,' agreed Flora. 'And they were about to restore the Bill of Rights which drew the teeth of the Monarchy before the Civil War. The King is a clever man to forestall the Whigs.'

Heracles, who liked nothing more than a political debate, took a sip of wine and broke in vehemently. 'The issue is complex and the Tories, who at first found it difficult to support William, in view of their firm belief in hereditary Monarchy, had to recall all their nobility from the shires to pack Parliament and assure a Tory government in the election, and now we have it for many years to come.'

'And now, Baron,' chimed Ralph, 'the King will take on the Irish question because his powers have been restored and he will take a great army. There are many notable men among them who now support the King; one Lord Nottingham is a good example.'

'A great man, Lord Nottingham,' agreed Peter, 'and now he is the King's most trusted advisor. You see, William has what is most necessary for any effective ruler and that is diplomacy.'

Sarah watched from where she sat in the kitchen, mending table linen. She had lost interest in the conversation in the dining room; however, she had got the impression that the handsome visitor was no ordinary gardener. He knew too much about the political situation and he had more than a passing fluency when he mentioned the King. No, he was something much else besides. She had noted the gold signet ring embossed with a crest that he wore turned into his palm. It had flashed in the candlelight as a page took round the rose water for washing when they sat down, and there was something high about his bearing. She suspected vaguely that he might be among them for some other reason than replacing the famous tulips.

'I wish the laundry maids would be more careful where they dry these,' she said to Meg obtusely. 'They never look carefully enough at the bushes they choose, and the lace gets snagged,' she looked up sharply as she saw the visitor raise his glass and propose a toast to his hostess, complimenting her on the skill and expertise he had seen in the garden.

'That makes a happy sight as I ever saw. My Lady with a smile on her face and a fine gentleman looking at her as if she was a goddess,' the girl sighed, her eyes misting romantically.

'Stop this, girl. No good comes from the sticky cradle of sentiment,' said Jack, who had just returned from the dining room with the remains of the roast guinea fowls, followed by the dogs. The eagle eyes of the kitchen boys fixed on the rich pickings. 'There you are, lads,' said Jack, setting the dish down on the enormous scrubbed table, 'but wait till we have taken in the pies to the mistress or I will box your ears.'

After the puddings Heracles and Ralph retired to the library where they were engrossed in a map of the great continent of America.

'We will join you later,' said Flora. 'It is not yet dark, nearly midsummer's day,' she added, casting Peter a sideways look. 'I am going to take our guest to see the temple.'

Sarah heard the words and smiled smugly at Jack who rolled his eyes to the heavens.

'Women,' he said, 'always thinking of love.'

CHAPTER TWENTY-TWO

Belfast Lough, Ireland, June 14th, 1690

It was Warrior who concerned Edwin the most. They had set sail in William's fleet on June 11th. There were six men of war under the command of a brave officer called Sir Cloudesley Shovell, who had acquitted himself already in a legendary battle off Bantry Bay on the Irish coast where he had seen off the French. He had raided Jacobite harbours, on one occasion entering the Jacobite stronghold of Belfast harbour and towing away a twenty-gun frigate under the nose of the enemy.

Edwin waited with the rest of the officers to unload the horses until at last he was able to go into the hold. At first his eyes could not focus in the fetid gloom of the bowels of the great ship and the smell of sick horse was overpowering. He knew that horses cannot vomit and therefore the effects of a rough sea are much worse for them than for any man. It had been a bad crossing, with storms and strong winds which tossed the great rolling ships mercilessly, until the weather changed on the third day with brilliant clear skies which illuminated the chaotic scene.

Edwin had been in almost constant attendance upon his horse during the four days of the voyage, and had observed his decline from spirited to compliant, resigned, obedient and suffering.

Warrior's head hung low and despondent and his fine eyes had lost their sparkling brightness.

'There, boy,' Edwin said as the animal raised his head weakly at the sound of his beloved master's voice. 'Come, don't be afraid,' he coaxed, in a soft voice he kept for Warrior.

The horse gave a faint but polite grunt, but the whites of his eyes flared in terror as he heard the slow beat of drums that welcomed the ship from the shore. Not for the first or the last time Edwin had reservations about his decision to take his friend, an unseasoned horse, into battle. The animal had been subjected to a few weeks of training, exposed to all manner of explosions and war cries, but Edwin had begun to wonder how he would fare when subjected to the real thing. He was young, only three years of age, and had never been exposed to the harshness of the real world, where the majority thought of a horse as a thing that served them, a thing that suffered in silence until no longer of use, to be quickly dispatched.

The scene was one of organised chaos; the seventy-five-year-old Duke of Schomberg had been appointed commander in chief the previous summer and had landed at Belfast Lough in August, ten months previously, with thirty thousand men and provision for six months.

But it was not the Jacobites – who controlled of the area and had managed to deplete his force dramatically – but substandard supplies provided by a traitorous Commissary-General and the consequent disease and lack of morale, plus the aging Duke's lack of decisiveness, which had pushed William's decision to get to Ireland and sort it out once and for all.

In the end the old Duke had lost control of his men, and atrocities had been carried out on a population which had greeted the 'Williamites' on bended knee with cries of joy.

*   *   *

William and the royal party met the old Duke at the home of Sir William Franklin, whose wife was the Countess of Donegal. The entourage was impressive and included his brother in law, the portly Prince George, brother of Christian Vth of Denmark.

'I mean to spell out the code of conduct which will now be observed by all my men and officers alike,' announced William coldly to the Duke without preamble.

Edwin felt the collar of his tunic nervously. The day was stifling hot and the room crowded to capacity. The air was charged with a mixture of bravado and anxiety, but Edwin felt no fear at all. This was his mission in life, a chance to do something worthy.

He had tapped into a part of himself which had been submerged for a long time and he listened in rapt attention as the King rallied his officers in the way which marked him out from his adversary and father-in-law James.

William had come here to bring matters to a close as quickly as possible. With his crack troops from so many different countries, he had experience on his side. His earnest hope was that he could avoid being responsible for James's death. His informers had told him of the ragbag of an army James had left to him, who, for all their fine uniforms, were underfed and debilitated. He had also lost the support of the Irish people, even previously staunch Catholic Jacobites, whose farms and homes had been ruined by the retreat, and the scorch and burn policy of James's demoralised men. The Irish people had been reduced to unimaginable poverty and starvation. One of Edwin's fellow officers had described the poor wretches that morning: skeletal figures, living in ditches, foraging in the burned remains of their smallholdings for husks of wheat. And, as the man said, reduced to digging corpses from their graves and boiling the flesh in the maggoty skulls.

'We have a strategic plan,' William explained, in his halting English. 'We are separated from the Jacobite army by the River Boyne. We have to negotiate this to achieve our objective and take the Jacobite stronghold of Dublin. James has two options: to proceed slowly down the banks of the river without engaging with us or to stand and fight.'

There was a murmur among the officers.

'We have to cross the river,' whispered Edwin's neighbour, a young gangly officer with a thin moustache he kept twiddling nervously.

'The enemy is exhausted,' continued William. 'We have many things on our side. There is a neap tide in the next few days and the moon is new. We will advance under cover of darkness at a point called Ouldbridge while the enemy sleeps, and now I will hand you to the Duke who will tell you more.'

The old Duke stepped forward. He was unsmiling and had an

air of resentment about him, for he still nursed the feeling that he had been unfairly criticised by William for not attacking the enemy during the winter. But he was of the opinion that William had no idea of just what the Irish situation was all about; and he maintained this defence with vigour despite his advancing years. He was not a man to shirk a challenge, the Irish were an unknown force and through the Duke's caution, it was James himself who had lost the support of the very people who he had thought would stand by him while he reclaimed the English throne. What the old Duke had seen from the start was that the interest of the so-called Jacobites in Ireland was not in any way connected with a desire to assist James in his fight to win back his crown. The situation was confusing in that in 1660, at the Restoration, Charles, James's brother, had assured the common-wealth settlers, who had streamed into Ireland grabbing Catholic lands, that they would not have those lands taken from them. Likewise, old English Catholic settlers had been promised that their lands would be restored to them. The old Duke recalled wryly the Duke of Ormonde, the previous Lord Lieutenant, remarking that 'a new larger Ireland would have to be created to fulfil the promise'.

It had been decided that the watchword was to be Westminster; the old Duke explained the carefully laid plans for the advance towards the crossing, by which time the moon would be five and a half days old. All the while William, who had taken a seat in a throne-like chair offered by the Countess, the only woman in the room, listened enigmatically.

'Each man will do his duty and Long Live our King,' the old Duke finished and every man raised his cap in the air. The feeling engendered was one of complete, almost foolhardy confidence. Edwin felt for a moment as if he were not quite there. A sensation of unreality swept over him and his mind had strayed a little during the Duke's long tirade.

His mind strayed to many things, not least Flora, and the quiet order of the tulip garden, the destruction of which had landed him in this place where blood was about to be spilled by the gallon. The lush fields that ran down to the river would soon be littered with the bodies of sons, fathers and husbands, each one a lost dream. For a fleeting moment he asked himself whether his mission to acquit himself to Flora could not have been achieved in different way. He thought of gentle Warrior who had been his friend and done his bidding whatever the mission. These thoughts were, however, soon forgotten as the men streamed out of the room, their eyes ablaze with a lust for battle.

CHAPTER TWENTY-THREE

Dundalk on the banks of the Boyne, July 1st, 1690

At last Edwin had sight of the enemy; they were across the river, the air was still and he could hear the men talking in the eerie quiet. Although they had been told that James's army was small by comparison with their own it did not appear so. They made a spectacular sight with the blue and white uniforms with red and white loops in their hats. The horses were resting and the men likewise followed the King's example, casually sitting on the grass, grabbing what little sustenance was available while they had the opportunity.

Frans Bentinck had met up with Edwin on the previous day and by chance they found themselves together. 'The King has more than his superior forces,' said Frans breathlessly. 'He is full of guile, more than a match for his ponderous father-in-law. He has planted informers in the enemy ranks who give the Jacobites false information about our numbers; James thinks we are fifty thousand strong.'

'Perhaps this kind misinformation would serve a dual purpose,' replied Edwin, hacking the coarse soda bread apart with his silver-bladed mess knife.

'You are right, of course,' said Frans vehemently. 'One thing I have learned about the Irish is that they have dispensed with the concept of principle. They are fighting for their very existence and we, that is to say both the Jacobites and the Williamites, are one and the same to them. We have raped their country and their women regardless of whom they appear to support. Take the informant you mention,' Frans went on. 'He would have a vested interest in discouraging James from engaging since it only means more despoiling of their land, their homes, and any future these people might have. They have been brought to rags, and a once beautiful, productive land is destroyed for generations. We mean nothing to them.'

As if to prove his point, a strange commotion was heard from near where the barrels of water were kept; dreadful female screams and soldiers' voices raised in anger. Fearing for the safety of the King and his party, Frans and Edwin and several other officers leapt to their feet and ran to the sight of the furore.

There they found a scene of carnage. A man dressed in ragged clothes lay screaming on the ground. The noise stopped abruptly as Edwin and Frans approached. They were no more than a few yards away but could see clearly the butchered remains of what had once been a man. An arm lay severed, his chest was sliced open and the last final scream would have come before his head had been hacked apart. There was blood everywhere. More than a dozen soldiers stood over the handiwork, their faces contorted in anger. Neither Edwin nor Frans could get through the throng. They were held back by some of the men and nearby another spectacle was playing itself out. A scrawny woman was shrieking for mercy as a thick rope was wound about her emaciated neck. In what seemed like a few seconds the other end was slung over the branch of a graceful willow and the woman was lifted from the ground by the neck with a blood-curdling gurgle. Her unshod feet straightened pathetically as her neck broke and her body hung lifeless.

Edwin had never seen active service before. Whereas the few brief skirmishes and loss of men had shocked him during the last few days, nothing had prepared him for so dreadful a spectacle. His first instinct was to intervene at once, but to his relief a superior officer appeared on his horse not far from where the King was billeted in a ruined farmhouse. The men scattered as the magnificent horse barged through to where the gruesome remains lay in a gory heap.

'What is the meaning of this?' boomed the officer.

'God in His mercy discovered them before they could murder the King,' said one of the men, a big fellow with a strong, honest face.

'Murder the King! What do you mean, man? Such a pathetic specimen and the woman no more than a half-starved trollop. How could they have overcome the King's men? Why, they don't even appear to have been armed?' said the officer furiously.

'Look, here it is, a purse full of poison,' said the man, 'there is enough to do for the regiment and the horses. They were about to put it in the water and we caught them as the woman had her hand on the King's own barrel.'

The officer dismounted, the men stood silent and respectful. He gingerly took the evidence and had no need to examine it closely. The previous day, water had been a substantial issue for the army and its horses. Edwin knew as he surveyed the scene that water above all commodities was the commodity on which an army survives. A man can survive without food for many days, but the need for water drives him to madness. Clean water was something that William, also, regarded as of utmost importance. He had himself refused to burden the luggage train with wine for himself and his officers, giving propriety to water for the men. The idea of poisoning a man's water plumbed the depths of an unwritten code among men. The rough justice handed out to the poisoner and his female accomplice was met with unspoken approval.

'Bury these two villains before they contaminate the air we breathe. Well done, men. The King will be grateful,' said the officer. He remounted his horse and left the group without a backward glance.

The following evening they advanced nearer to the point at which they would cross the river and engage with the enemy. They sat on the grass not far from where the King's party was also resting. The men lit fires and set about preparing what little food they had left. Edwin got up to stretch his legs and looked towards William who was no more than thirty yards away. The King seemed in unusually relaxed spirits and was talking and laughing with Frans's uncle, while the old Duke was still mounted on his horse and was trotting purposefully among the ranks of apprehensive men.

The air was still warm but with a hint of the mist which accompanied a drop in temperature. The river with its tidal surges also brought a miasmic damp which, coming from the ground, got into the men's bones as they tried to sleep. Some had tents, but most wrapped themselves in the meagre blanket they carried in the pack on their backs. The foot soldiers had little energy to carry anything else as they were already encumbered with their muskets, of which the barrels alone were three foot long and weighed eleven pounds two ounces. They had also to carry the cumbersome items necessary for firing a charge of gunpowder: a length of match, a cord boiled in vinegar to keep it slow burning and the shot.

Edwin was watching the meticulous way the men were checking their weapons and was joined by Frans. 'Is it not ridiculous that these poor bastards have to get within a few yards of the enemy? The technique of firing a salvo at the beat of the drum might work at close quarters but what use is it here?'

'It is a terrible waste of men,' agreed Edwin. 'I saw it at Dundirk: the first line kneeling and being replaced by the next until they fell . . . '

'But it is a well-tried technique, it may have served well in the past,' argued Edwin, not believing it himself.

'Well, I, for one, am surprised that our men do not have a bayonet fixed to the muzzle of the musket. All the French have it. How is a man to save himself when the enemy breaks through and his musket cannot be used?' said Frans.

'I agree these men will stand little chance with the Jacobite cavalry,' agreed Edwin, 'but despite all this I know we will win the day, for His Majesty is a hero to his men and I for one have seen his meticulous management. The discipline he has is not built on fear, but on a desire to win and the men are inspired. They all believe they are doing something exceptional and that they are privileged to be here.'

It was obvious to Frans that Edwin was speaking for himself as well as for the men, and he decided to find out more of this man whom he had grown to trust and admire.

'You are a surprising man,' said Frans thoughtfully. 'I will tell you something, my friend, now that we might die together. You have a bad reputation, you know. There were base stories about you at court and you are said to have behaved like a brute to your wife. There is worse; they say you even destroyed her family's beautiful gardens when she threw you out and on the day before the King and Queen were to honour her with a visit. Of course the company you kept did not help. Your friend Frederick is as rotten a fellow as a man could be. He boasts that he won your own family's estates off you in a gambling debt and that your mother now lives off charity.'

'Is there more? It is hard for a man to hear such things,' said Edwin dismally since he had heard it all already from another source.

'I make no apologies for speaking thus,' Frans went on bluntly, in a manner that Edwin had come to expect from the Dutch. It was one of the things he had come to like about them.

'You had best say it all,' said Edwin. 'If you do not I cannot assure you of my innocence and, who knows, our lives may one day depend on our trust of each other.'

'I have come to respect you,' said Frans. 'Is any of it true?' He handed Edwin a slither of the cheese.

'Did you know that the Boyne is a sacred river?' asked Edwin disarmingly.

'I had heard something to that effect. Why? What has that got to do with the things I have just asked you?' said Frans doggedly.

Edwin took a deep breath and loosened the top buttons of his tunic. He could feel the locket he kept about his neck, inside which was some of Flora's hair. 'We are men who this night look into the dark abyss of death,' he said slowly. 'Each one of us must look at the map of our lives and ask what have we left to the world.'

'That is true, maybe that is why I asked you those things,' said Frans directly.

'I will be straight with you,' said Edwin, poking a little at the outer embers of the fire with his boot. 'I was seduced by something I can now see as evil. I did terrible things . . . but I never killed a man, not at least until now. I had nothing to do with what happened to my dearest wife's gardens, they were her father's life's work. She is a truly gifted botanist. She creates beauty where I made darkness. I lost her once through my own folly and then God gave me a second chance and that also I squandered. I looked love in the face and I destroyed it. But the King was a friend of my wife's father; he is a good and wise man and he saw my grief. He saw my Calvary, maybe he has had one himself. All of us – all these men who may die tomorrow – he has given us a feeling of love not just for something small but for his fellow men and his country, freedom for man to worship as he wishes. These, Frans, are ideals. I have seen that there is for every man a time when he must embrace that wide self-sacrificing love which is far beyond any particular person. It is about loving all mankind. I have a premonition of death, my own. I want you to go to my beloved wife and tell her what manner of man I really was; I want you to tell her how much I love her and how I am a different Edwin and that my soul will love her and keep her as my body cannot.'

Frans was deeply moved by his friend's words and stretched out a hand. The two men's flesh met in a brotherly gesture.

'And let me tell you about this river, this sacred place,' said Edwin in a lighter tone.

'I should like to hear,' said Frans, settling back on his elbow.

'A young Irish girl wedded an Irish god Nuada who had lost his hand in battle before it was replaced by one of silver. The young wife was told by him that there was secret well in which she must never look, but she did and the waters rose and overflowed and she ran in its path to Drogheda until she drowned and in her path the river Boyne was formed.'

'Well, it is fitting that we should fight here. Let us hope that the sacred place preserves our King for without him we would not win,' said Frans.

*   *   *

The following morning was to be the final push to the point at which the battle would commence. Using their glasses the men could see the Jacobites clearly on the other side of the river. Many of them expressed concern at the vulnerability of the King who had just consumed a picnic in full view of the enemy. But the King's party rode along the banks as if unconcerned.

The men were quiet, their nerves on edge, when there was a sudden whistling through the trees. Leaves scattered and sleepy birds woke in a cacophony of cries followed by the terrible cries of a horse in agony. Raising his glasses, Edwin saw that a party of forty Jacobite cavalry had galloped down the hill; they had clearly concealed two large field weapons behind a hedge and shot at the King at their leisure.

Edwin and Frans rode forward immediately and saw that the old Duke's horse had been shot from under him and now lay dead with a wound in the neck. The Duke's grief was audible but their attention was caught by a second whistling and shouts of alarm from the King's party.

Along with a dozen or so officers, they ran to the place where the King was sitting on the ground with a wound the size of a man's palm. The piece had bounced along the bank and passed off the King's shoulder with such force that it broke the head off a man's pistol.

'His Majesty has been wounded,' cried the men, but the King shrugged it off in his native Dutch, *'T'houbt niet naeder.'*

At three o'clock on the next morning the King was sufficiently recovered to issue an order. The day had come which would decide the future of England and Ireland. Men, horses, mud, blood. Two thousand cavalry were lead by William in a circling movement towards the projected crossing at Auldridge.

'My God, those Jacobite Irish are drunk,' called Frans through the din.

'Word has it they took half a pint of brandy each.'

Edwin looked across the river whence came a terrifying sight. The Jacobite army charged. The order was given, they were to engage. William, with characteristic bravery, advanced towards the crossing. The tide was low and the path soon became a quagmire of mud. The King's horse became embedded and unable to lift his feet. The King sat helpless in the saddle; he had to dismount and was soon himself unable to walk.

One of the fearless Enniskillens appeared at once, orchestrating a rescue for the horse. The animal was dragged, flailing helplessly, out of the mud and eventually righted himself. The King remounted at once, his boots coated to the thigh with earth and slime.

It was not long before Frans's horse suffered the same fate. Rider and animal soon became a sitting target for the rogue cannons on the other side of the river. A deep series of booms rent the air and as ill luck would have it Frans's horse was fatally shot. The noble beast screamed in agony and plunged to the ground in its death throes. Still in the saddle, Frans was hit in the shoulder.

The two fell into the mud, the horse soon still and silent. Frans made a brief attempt to raise himself but fell back into the mud, which rapidly became stained a dark red. Edwin was close at hand and Warrior showed his full strength. His sturdy legs soon had him on firm ground and Edwin leapt from his back. Warrior stood, ears twitching but ever obedient to his master's command. Other men and horses were suffering a similar fate and the scene made Edwin think of a depiction of Dante's Inferno he had seen as boy; the image had stuck in his mind and came to haunt him now.

Edwin struggled in the mire and reached Frans's limp hand for the man's head was quickly disappearing in the thick brown grease. It was clear that he was insensible to the world and blood poured from the wounds in his arm and shoulder. With all most superhuman power Edwin got hold of him under the shoulder, grateful at least that his friend could not feel the pain this would cause. He dragged the man and somehow found his way to the obedient horse. How he would lift Frans, a big man, onto the horse's back he did not know, and then he remembered how he had once trained the animal to kneel. They were still in range of the cannon and another deafening thud shook the ground. Warrior did not flinch and patiently obeyed the command; Edwin pulled the unconscious man onto the horse's back where he hung like a sack of grain on the saddle.

Edwin told Warrior to right himself and then jumped onto the fearless Warrior's rump. 'Well done, my friend,' shouted Edwin, slapping him on his sweating neck. 'If we survive this day I will truly believe in God,' he cried out loud. A roar of cannon drowned his words. The cries and the half-broken voices of boys who had no business to be there filled the air and Edwin prayed. He saw his own death in slow motion. He hoped at least he would be remembered for his bravery, not for the cowardice that had marked him, which had lost him his chance of happiness.

'It is not happiness that we should want, it is love,' he thought to himself as so many young men passed roughly into the next world and as if in a blinding flash he felt an all-pervading light surround him. It was love, not of himself, but love for everything about him: the dying men, both friend and foe, his friend now helpless in blissful ignorance of the brutal carnage around them, love for the hundreds of helpless children of Ireland who had been betrayed by the greed of the aggressor and the defender. Defender of what, for what, he asked himself? He called to his horse Warrior who suffered for all the other creatures, dead and dying. A vision of Flora appeared before him, and there in the mud of a foreign land he suddenly felt an inexplicable happiness.

CHAPTER TWENTY-FOUR

Journey to Whitehall, July 1690

The last of the late tulips had lost all their petals and stood gaunt and bare.

'The time has come when I must leave you, my dearest new friend,' said Peter.

They were eating the first meal of the day, before Ralph and Heracles were about. The day was sparkling and clear. Peter gazed at Flora across the long table; she smiled at him gently. The look spoke of an intimacy that had evolved between them without their even being aware of it. Their eyes locked and all the world was there reflected in the answering gaze of each of them. She saw herself in his eyes, and she felt beautiful and happy. The previous night they had lain on her bed; neither of them had suggested it, it just happened and they had kissed softly. Peter had never felt an attraction so compelling and with such unspoken inevitably about it. He wanted her, this English bloom who shared a love of so many of the things that had driven him in his life. She blushed as she thought now of what had followed, but she had stopped him before the moment of consummation and the anticipation of it still lay before her like an unconsumed delicacy which she knew she would probably not have had the strength to resist; but now he was going and the moment had passed.

She stood up from the table; there were tears in her eyes. He looked at her steadily, and recalled the passionate encounter of the night before; he had known she would try to stop him. He knew every detail about her husband's sordid conduct, and he felt rising anger and resentment towards the man who had abused this woman he had grown to love in such a short, overwhelming time. It awoke in him a heroic streak and a validation for his pursuance of her. But on a note of caution, he suspected that the man was trying to find some sort of absolution by offering to lay down his life for the King and would almost certainly try to reclaim his jewel of a wife. In the back of his mind, he also held onto the belief that they were all helplessly tossed by the hands of fate. Perhaps the man would not survive, but even if he did and Peter allowed himself to love this extraordinary woman in the way his body craved and commanded, he would have to fight for her. All these thoughts hung in the air; he knew they would be resolved today or not at all.

'Peter, I cannot let you go, surely you can stay a little longer? We could say that we are working on a project together.' His departure had been inevitable but they had allowed the stolen moments to enchant them, Flora because she was hungry for happiness, something which had so far evaded her in her short life, and he because her complete beauty and womanly perfection had caught him unawares.

'Come, it is not as sad as you might think,' he said suddenly. 'We will go to the gardens,' he went on gaily. 'I have a plan to put to you.' He took her hand firmly in his and she obediently followed. The grass was still wet with dew as he made for the temple. The sun was not yet high in the sky and the light danced at their feet as if marking their path.

They went inside. Jack had already opened the doors, as he always did on hot mornings. The temperature was perfect and the room was suffused with the exotic scent of lilies and cascades of summer jasmine.

Before he could say anything he took her in his arms and lowered her onto the large expanse of cushions on the reclining chaise where Flora often sat in the long afternoons when she was tired by her work. It was a place where she dreamed her dreams, where she tried not to think that she had been singled out for the seemingly endless challenges of her life.

They both knew what would happen as the sun warmed them though the open doors. He kissed first her neck and then her bared shoulder as the sleeves of her gown fell down and then her bodice fell open, exposing her breasts. The unrequited sighing of the previous night could no longer be kept fermenting. She closed her eyes in ecstasy.

'Don't move, my love,' he whispered, 'I must close the doors lest we should be discovered.' She could hardly bear to let him go as he left her to secure them and pull across the thick hangings embroidered with birds of paradise, silhouetted by the fierce morning sun from outside. They swayed erotically in a slight breeze from the open windows as they abandoned themselves to the hands of destiny.

*   *   *

'I am going to take you with me,' said Peter. They had dressed and now they sat at a table where Flora often worked on the plans for the garden. Sometimes her work seemed at odds with her own experiences, as if she were not a part of the joys which nature bestowed, but now she felt she was in tune with this great miracle. She shocked herself as she realised she had not a single regret.

'What do you mean?' she said. Did he mean go back with him to Holland, leave her beloved home, and her work? And what about Edwin?

'I mean that the Queen is sending a carriage for me, I will not be going alone,' he said with a slight question, noting the tilt of her head as she took in his meaning. 'There are matters we have to discuss about the royal Gardens at Het Lo; Her Majesty is planning a great addition.'

'But I . . . ' she sought to protest half-heartedly.

'No,' he said, putting his finger on her lips to silence her. 'You can come with me to London, my dearest heart. Besides, it is time you went back to court to refresh your connections. You cannot be a recluse in the country forever. There are things you . . . ' he hesitated, 'that we have to face.'

Many reasons why she should not do this flashed through her brain, like unwelcome messengers, but then she saw his handsome face smiling encouragingly at her and her mind was made up.

'Yes, I will come,' she said vigorously. 'There is no reason why not, and anyway I would like to see the Queen,' she added, pressing his hand. 'I will say thank you to her . . . after all, although she does not know it, she has given me back a bit of me I thought had been destroyed forever. I had prepared myself for a sad embittered old age,' she laughed. 'But now the wheels of life are turning again, who knows where they may lead us, Peter?'

* * *

'My lady, I will have to work through the night, your ladyship has gained a little weight,' said Sarah later, amidst a pile of silken skirts and muslin scarves. At first she had been greatly put out by such a sudden plan, but seeing the joy on her mistress's face she had done complaining and set about the practical matter of preparing for the trip. 'You will need your fine lace gloves, my Lady,' she fussed. 'Just look at your hands; they are brown like a common dairy maid.'

It occurred to Flora that Sarah's remarks were always of an affectionately critical nature, but she would be lost without the woman's down to earth devotion.

'Well, Sarah,' she quipped back, 'it is my hands which have put bread on the table of many of the tenants, it is a man's work that I do.'

'Not all the time, is it, my Lady?' Sarah shot back, alarmed at her own impertinence, but the two women's eyes met.

'My beloved Sarah, you would not begrudge me that, would you?' Flora asked.

'No, my Lady, I would not,' Sarah said at once. 'I have seen your sorrow and your bravery and this is a harsh world. At least if you are a fine lady you can expect the protection of your class and your position and, dare I say it, your servants, who would willingly die for love of you. Take your happiness, my Lady, for it is a fleeting thing and we must guard it.'

CHAPTER TWENTY-FIVE

Whitehall, July 1690

'We are fearful, Sir,' barked the rough fellow at the city gates. 'The French are coming; they will rape our wives and kill our babes. Catholic infidels they are and they eat human flesh; we have heard the tales.' The man crossed himself and shuddered. He was one of the gate keepers, impressively armed with pistols and cudgels which he fingered menacingly, looking at them suspiciously.

The journey to London had been arduous and fraught with unexpected difficulty. One of the horses threw a shoe after the first change and they had had to wait for a replacement at the side of the road with no shade except the shadow of the carriage. The rumours on the way had been alarming, the country was on alert and the situation became more obviously worrying as they approached London.

'What rubbish, man,' Peter came back quickly as he saw Flora's ashen face. 'I am a Dutchman, and our great navy is also at sea with finer men and ships than the King of France,' said Peter lightly, hoping to defuse the situation. 'Where is your courage, man? Remember the English fight a good battle at sea. We have nothing to fear from the French save the pox.' Peter laughed and the man seemed encouraged, but only for a moment. Suddenly they were surrounded by militia wearing the arms of London's sheriff; more of them appeared on the scene and Peter sensed the situation was turning ugly. The men meant business and without ceremony they ordered Peter and Flora from the carriage.

'The city is on alert,' bellowed the one of the men. 'You must identify yourselves and state your business.' He jumped from his horse and stared uncompromisingly at Flora as Peter helped her down from the carriage without argument.

'I am Baron Peter Van der Zee,' said Peter calmly, 'kinsman to your King William and this is the Lady Flora Grantley. We are here to join Her Majesty at Whitehall and here are my papers.'

Peter pulled out the tooled leather pouch he kept on his person at all times and the man, seeing his coat of arms, began to shift uneasily. He had been surly and disrespectful to the travellers and now he examined them more closely he could see that the occupants were indeed people of high quality. The lady looked as if she might faint in the mud. He looked at the papers quickly.

'I am sorry, my Lord, I am only carrying out orders. These are terrible times,' he stammered.

As Flora had often noticed with Peter, he had a knack of defusing situations and leaving friends instead of ruffled feathers. 'My good man, I commend your diligence; your country needs fellows like you. It is our good fortune that we have met you at this time. Would you be so kind as to give us your protection on our way to the Palace and I will commend you for your help?'

'It will be my pleasure and an honour to lead your worships,' said the man, recovering his demeanour. Flora gave him a dazzling smile and he made note to tell his wife how he had saved a great and beautiful lady from the possibility of rapists and robbers and escorted her personally to the Queen.

*   *   *

When they arrived they went directly to the Queen's apartments. 'You are so very welcome, my dear,' she said warmly, her arm on Flora's elbow to raise her from a deep curtsey. Spontaneously she drew Flora to her bosom in a gesture of unmistakable friendship.

Flora smiled happily, but she noted the Queen looked worryingly ill and tired, with puffy eyes and a jaw swollen by toothache – a sight not uncommon in all walks of life. 'Your Majesty,' said Flora. 'I am so pleased to be back at court. It has been very quiet in the country and we are strangely isolated from events.'

'Things are very dire, my dear,' said the Queen, a slight tremor in her voice.

'The first we even knew of the threat of a French invasion,' said Flora, 'was on our journey, and the whole city seems to be in a state of terror.'

The Queen indicated a chair near the window, and they sat, spreading their skirts about the floor at their feet. Two black pugs came scuttling into the room, tapping their carefully manicured feet on the wooden floor like a troupe of tiny Spanish dancers. They nuzzled around the Queen's satin-covered feet and she leant down and gave them sweetmeats from a little gold dish on a side table on which sat a sample of her sewing.

'They are such a consolation to me,' said the Queen. 'These are terrible times; I feel very alone. I have been without the King now for over a month. In his absence I have few people I can trust. My health is not good,' she went on, as if at last she had a friend to whom she could unburden herself. 'I have trouble with my eyes again. I have so many affairs of state to see to and can only write to the King at night, when the light is a problem. I have this wretched toothache; the doctors recommend leaches behind my ears. They do nothing for me except to make my face even more of a sight. But let us talk of other things.'

'Is there any news from Ireland?' asked Flora.

'I am expecting Captain Butler any day,' answered the Queen. 'The weather is good and he will travel swiftly. There was to be a great battle by a river called the Boyne. I am so fearful for my husband and I have so much to decide, it is almost beyond me. I have only God to guide me; it is a great comfort to have you here with me.'

'Of course, the French would choose this time to attack us when His Majesty is in Ireland,' said Flora, shaking her head. 'They think they are dealing with a helpless woman, but Your Majesty is anything but that,' shot Flora boldly, regretting her words at once lest they be thought impertinent. She looked at this hitherto unremarkable woman of twenty-eight, and could only imagine the strain she must feel at the burden left to her, surrounded by so many warring self-interested factions.

'The French are in the Channel with their fleet,' said the Queen, involuntarily wringing her hands in a gesture of despair. 'Our own navy is skulking in the Thames estuary, the Dutch fleet has come to our rescue and I thank God for my husband's people. At the moment I feel a shame for my country. His Majesty is our only hope and I pray that God spares him or we are lost.'

'Oh, Your Majesty, all will be well, I am sure of it. We must all be sure of it,' urged Flora, but she didn't really believe that things could be that simple.

The Queen stretched out her hand, the other going to her eyes to wipe away a tear.

'But there, my dear, you too have a husband in great danger at the King's side. I have already heard good things of him; he has proved to be a fine soldier. You see, there is good and bad warring in all of us. It is largely a question of luck as to who will win.'

A commotion outside interrupted the quiet of the Queen's apartments. She looked towards the door and a faint knocking could be heard; she called for the person to enter and the two guards opened the double doors to Lord Nottingham, the Queen's closest advisor. He bowed his face, flushed with excitement. 'Madam, may I escort you at once to the audience room? Lord Butler is here with joyous news.'

'The King, how does the King?' cried the Queen.

'The King does well, Madam,' said Lord Nottingham. 'He sustained some minor wounds but God has protected him.'

The Queen did not respond at once and then replied in a haughty voice. 'His Lordship has not made any acknowledgement at all towards Lady Flora. My Lord, we will proceed at once,' she looked towards Flora. 'But I fear you have overlooked the presence of the lady whose husband Lord Edwin is with the King. I dare say she might also wish for some good news about her husband,' reproved the Queen. She was used to the patron-ising attitude displayed by the gentlemen of the court towards women, even to herself, an issue she had had to fight with courage, often ignored at her own council meeting when she herself was the head of state.

Nottingham darted a look in Flora's direction and inclined an almost imperceptible bow to which she curtsied with exaggerated politeness. 'Regrettably I have no news of individual officers,' he said with ill-disguised irritation. 'Except to say that our casualties were much fewer than the Jacobites, and that, Your Majesty, is attributable to the King's superb campaigning skills.'

Flora looked at the floor as the Queen gave her arm a little squeeze of encouragement. She felt a flutter of shame because truthfully what she really wanted was to find Peter and share the news of the victory in Ireland rather than deal with the confusing issues of the fate of Edwin.

*   *   *

'They drove the Jacobites before them like sheep,' said the King's envoy Captain Butler, 'and His Majesty marched into Dublin where the Protestants came out of their houses, rejoicing, and then to St Patrick's Cathedral, where the people cheered him as he wore the great Crown of State.'

The room was packed. News of the victory at the Boyne had swept through the court. Gentlemen with wigs askew and the ladies still smoothing down their court dresses jostled to hear the details.

Later the Queen withdrew for a council meeting with her most senior advisors, nine men in all, of whom the most senior was Lord Nottingham, the Secretary of State. She had already identified him as 'devious' but she had begun to trust him and Lord Carmarthen, the Lord President. They had at first tried to exclude her from all decisions but Mary had proved more than a match for these two senior Tories. Recently she had begun to assert herself with great confidence and conviction.

'We are disgusted with the state we find ourselves in at home when the King is away and fighting for the survival of our country as we want it to be,' said Mary. 'I am told that the navy hides in the Thames estuary and is unfit to sail,' she added furiously.

'I would not exactly say that,' stumbled Lord Carmarthen.

'And what exactly would you say, my Lord?' retorted Mary.

'I would say that our commander Lord Torrington is playing a waiting game, Your Majesty. The French fleet is posturing, that is all. And, after all, as Your Majesty knows, in the recent engagement when the French were given a run for their money they retired with substantial losses,' said one of their lordships smugly.

'Posturing, Sir?' thundered the Queen. 'What do you mean? Do you think I am devoid of a brain?' Mary enquired vigorously. 'We all know it was the Dutch who fought bravely, sustaining heavy losses while the English fleet held back in the lee of the land, out of range, deliberately letting their Dutch allies become separated from the English fleet to fight alone. Sir, we have become a nation of cowards.'

There was flustered denial amongst the men, followed by an awkward silence.

'I hope I can depend on you gentleman,' said the Queen gravely. 'We must address this shame with the determination and courage that the King would expect. Posturing indeed; well, let us do more than posture,' she continued. 'I am your Regent and I am issuing an order that our fine Admiral Lord Torrington will bring out our navy to fight or he will be brought to the Tower, and I, my Lords, am not posturing. It is my experience that fortune spreads her gifts on those who are least deserving of them, and are least appreciative of them. My Lord Torrington is just such a person, elevated to the undeserved position of admiral and with a title to boot. He has been showered with honours and sits comfortably in his rotting ill-kept ship in the safety of some balmy cove.'

The men realised that the Queen was unstoppable and they sat transfixed in growing admiration. They nodded, none daring to interrupt her because they knew she was putting into words thoughts they had sublimated for weeks.

'Lord Torrington has earned the reputation of an idle drunk whilst my husband fights with the common man, sparing himself no danger,' she continued unabated. 'Three fine Dutch admirals have lost their lives. I will have a full report and if our great navy has been betrayed by this man he will pay the price.'

A silence ensued; each man knew that the Queen meant what she said and that, buoyed up by her husband's triumph, she would not let her country flounder.

'It is true, Your Majesty,' Captain Butler volunteered. 'We have begun to uncover a scandalous rout in as much as the victuals supplied to the men have been of such a poor standard that they are now seriously debilitated. Some of them have scurvy and others various complaints associated with malnutrition.'

'This is beyond comprehension,' expostulated Lord Nottingham, feigning surprise, because he had known full well what was going on but was at odds to know how to address the matter.

'Why has this not been discovered before?' demanded the Queen in amazement.

'Because, Your Majesty,' said Captain Butler, 'there is some sort of conspiracy and a great deal of money has been made by these people who have been doing it for years and it has been well concealed.' He hesitated, darting a look at Lord Nottingham who gave the briefest of nods. 'We think Lord Torrington himself may be part of it, and certainly there is one person at court who is the mastermind and he is, we think, quite close to Your Majesty.'

'Is there no end to the Catholic perfidy?' lamented the Queen. 'It is only a papist follower of my father who could wish to poison the navy. Are we all to stand by whilst we are deceived in this way?'

'Your Majesty, we are seeking to discover the name of the person and in order to do so we are proceeding with utmost caution,' offered Lord Nottingham.

'Once again, gentlemen, I see that you have been concealing things from me and operating behind my back,' the Queen responded coldly.

All nine of the Queen's advisors shifted in their chairs and just as they were all formulating their own defence she pre-empted them and stood up. Leaning forward just as a man might do, she hit the table with two clenched fists. The wine flagons jumped in their coasters and the men started back in their seats.

In the loud and beautifully articulated tone for which she was known, she addressed them with unquestionable authority. 'This will not do! The fleet will be out in the channel within twenty-four hours. Torrington will be relieved of his command and brought to me to offer some explanation, if indeed there be any. Some among you will make it their business to flush this skul-duggery out. I will not have such conduct right under my nose. You gentlemen will put your house in order!'

With that the Queen swept from the room with magisterial command. The air was still. Lord Nottingham paused for a moment and then followed her as fast as he could. He knew as well as any of them that the Queen appeared to have grown in stature overnight. He would assure her of their loyalty or he feared heads would roll and he did not intend that one of them should be his.

He heard her calling to one of her ladies as they ran beside her, keeping up with her long determined steps. They were the steps of a woman in command.

'Tonight we will go to the theatre,' she said loudly. 'To see Mister Dryden's play *The Spanish Friar*. The Queen will be seen by her people and we will have an extra large dining in public and, Nottingham,' she called over her shoulder, 'summon your eight councillors and do not invite Lady Churchill, her husband now his grace the Duke of Marlborough does not please me. I do not like the company he keeps and his wife should learn the concept of loyalty . . . do you not agree?' she quipped.

There was a titter among the ladies; they knew of course the Queen was referring to the newly created duchess's friendship with the Queen's sister who treated the Queen so shamefully.

Flora thought for a moment about loyalty, and how life can

sweep even the best of people, even those who set their moral compass unswerving and true, into dark waters. She thought ruefully that this applied to everyone, even the King and his Queen; even they could flounder, as had the Queen when she took her father's crown. But then she reminded herself that the woman had shown true courage and put her duty as she saw it before the ever-treacherous ties of blood.

CHAPTER TWENTY-SIX

Catherine's Court, August 1690

The three men, Ralph, Heracles and Jack, all had the same endeavour; they would get to the bottom of the mystery. Why had someone decided to harm them all by destroying the garden? Local gossip spoke of dark dealings, popish plots and treason, and for some reason none of them believed now that Edwin was part of it. They had all watched Flora, the object of their protective instincts, as she navigated the challenges of her life. They knew that apart from the fact they all loved her in their different ways, their futures were balanced on her slim but capable shoulders.

Ralph recognised increasingly how clever his sister had been. She had achieved something remarkable, practically unheard of among the women of the gentry, who had neither the skills, nor the physical attributes to take on the world. She had forged a livelihood for those who depended on her. Ralph, although he was rapidly developing the knowledge and obsessive interest which had made his sister so successful, was still thought of as a boy.

But that is not how Heracles had begun to see him. He saw a fine young man with the same gritty determination which marked his sister out. He knew that the father had been ambitious for his clever daughter. He had also worked out that Ralph had had rather less effective input from the father. The boy often spoke of his early years at school where the legendary Ignatius Kettle had ruled with uncompromising brutality, before his father brought him back to live with the family. It was in this evidently horrific place that he had been given the basic grounding that made him such a delight to teach.

As Ralph had less time to bond with his father than his sister, it was Heracles who had assumed the paternal mantle, willingly since he had no children of his own. Heracles was devoted to the lad and in turn had a great respect for Jack, who, Heracles realised, was far more worldly than he was, for the servant had seen the gentry live out the rich fabric of their lives at close quarters.

From Jack's perspective, he believed he had seen their folly and their stupidity, and sometimes their strengths, and mostly he had operated a policy of quiet damage limitation, so subtle that it was seldom, if ever, observed or recognised. The thing he found most curious about his masters was their inability to compartmentalise their physical needs. Lives would be tipped into turmoil because someone had indulged a desire in a brief moment of lust. Where Jack came from, if a man's eye was taken, after the event there were no questions asked. Jack had had his way with a handful of women, some of them married, and nobody mentioned the fact that Josiah Crump, the blacksmith's boy, was a miniature Jack. Everyone was proud of him and his parents were too. Jack had watched the wretched business of Flora's love life and observed the confusion she felt. He agreed that the fine Lord Edwin was a blaggard, but the man had joined the army, he had accompanied the King and was obviously prepared to lay down his life; and, besides, Jack had been keeping a secret which might now have a bearing on events.

The time had come when Jack felt the need to share something with Ralph and Heracles, and an opportunity had come. Ralph had called them all together in his father's old study, which still retained the feel of Lord Thomas: his desk still laid out as it had been when he died, the timepiece on the mantle still wound and a fire lit each evening as the departed master would have wished. Diana and Hera removed themselves to this room each evening and curled up together on the rug in front of the fender and it had become as much for them as for the memory of their master that these rites were observed. The room consequently had the faint aroma of dog mixed with old books and logs.

Ralph stood in front of the fire with the dogs at his feet and Jack was struck by the easy way the boy had begun to assume the role of head of house.

'I have called you here together because I have decided that we are going to London,' Ralph announced, swaying a little, with his hands in the pockets of his breeches. 'We will stay in the family house in Paternoster Row, and Jack, you must send word to the stewards there that we will be arriving in a few days' time.'

'Master Ralph, there is something I feel I should tell you and I would be grateful if you, Mr Prior, could hear me out and give me your opinion,' said Jack suddenly. 'It has a bearing on your plan.'

'Of course, Jack,' Ralph came back quickly. 'I have no secrets from Mr Prior.'

'I have been sworn to secrecy and I gave my word upon the Bible that I would not speak of this. But things have happened which I see now are connected with this secret and I must divulge it so that we may all find out the truth of the matter,' said Jack cautiously.

'Well, man, you must be sure, a man's word on the Holy Book must not be given lightly or broken without dire reason,' warned Heracles.

'It is necessary,' confirmed Jack without hesitation. 'A man's honour is at stake and also the future of the Lady Flora. God will understand,' said Jack.

'Well, man, go ahead,' said Heracles.

'It was after Lord Edwin came back,' Jack began. 'My Lady was out in the grounds, she had a big plan for the arboretum and she was to be gone for some time. Lord Edwin was a happy man, they had come to an understanding, or so it seemed. I did think the man was changed and had decided to renounce his old ways. But then there was a visitor,' continued Jack, his face darkening.

'A visitor, what kind of visitor?' asked Ralph.

'It was a gentleman, if you can call him that,' Jack hesitated, 'a gentleman from the court I think.'

'What was his name?' enquired Heracles, beginning to take a considerable interest.

'I can never forget his name, he was called Sir Frederick Buckley,' replied Jack, disgustedly; the very thought of the man was painful to him.

'I have never heard of him; what was his business?' asked Ralph sharply.

'He had business with Lord Edwin and when I announced the man's arrival his Lordship went quite white and asked me at once how long the Lady Flora would be absent, as if he wanted to get rid of the man as soon as possible. I sensed danger,' said Jack. 'There was something evil about the man. He was a dandy but a bad-looking fellow. I decided when I had shown the man into the solar where Lord Edwin was waiting, that I would not go far from the door. I knew as I often do that it was my duty to . . . ' Jack hesitated, with a conspiratorial smile.

'Oh, you mean you decided to listen at the door, did you?' said Ralph with a laugh.

'I did, young Master, I did,' affirmed Jack, his wise old face set with a ring of unshakable confidence.

'There are so many occasions when I have been grateful for your attention to polishing door locks and such! Thank God for you, Jack, that is all I have to say to that,' said Ralph.

'Well, the man started making remarks to Lord Edwin, sarcastic they were, asking him how long it would be before he tired of life with the Lady Flora and saying the gambling tables were waiting for him and then the man as good as asked Lord Edwin to find money to keep him quiet about his former ways and the bad company he had kept, or he would tell Lady Flora and ruin whatever chance Lord Edwin had to keep his wife's good opinion.'

'This is horrible, it is blackmail,' said Heracles vigorously.

'That it was,' said Jack. 'And the man came out with a goodly tale of Lord Edwin's debauchery, such as I cannot repeat, things as would keep a decent woman from him, I would say,' said Jack gravely.

'What did Lord Edwin do?' asked Ralph.

'He drew his sword, sir,' said Jack simply. 'I heard it as the blade left the scabbard.'

'Oh God, you are not going to tell us he killed the man?' demanded Ralph in horror.

'No he did not,' said Jack hastily. 'But I went in then; I didn't want blood on her ladyship's fine rug, did I?' he said. 'But Lord Edwin had the blade to the swine's throat and I have never seen a man so angry. He bellowed at the man, he told him he could have no hold over him since he had told her Ladyship everything and that Satan had no chance with him now that he loved his young beautiful wife and that he would never let her down again. He would go to the ends of the earth for her and the man should go back to his foul life, and that if he ever darkened their doors again he would never leave alive,' Jack stopped for a moment and shuddered. 'And then I took Lord Edwin's arm and pulled it back. The man leapt up and he gave Lord Edwin such a look of hate as I have not seen since they ducked the old witch Kate in the village in my grandma's time. She put a curse on them that testified against her and everyman who heard it shivered . . . '

Jack paused as he took a breath, about to recall the incident in detail.

'Man, you are getting off the point,' said Heracles irritably. 'We can hear about that another time, what did the man say to Lord Edwin?'

'He said he would go but that he would never let Lord Edwin have any peace since they had made a pact with the devil. He did not think he could lead a decent Christian life and that he . . . the man . . . would destroy him. He would do it in a way that could never be proved . . . but the deed would finish him with the . . . ' Jack hesitated again as if the words were too painful for him to repeat. 'He called the Lady Flora a word one cannot say. He said he would destroy them both.'

'We must find this man,' blurted Ralph. 'This cannot be left as it is. Why did you not tell us this before?'

'Lord Edwin went for the man again and as near as throttled him. I had to pull him off again and Lord Edwin told the man if he ever hurt Lady Flora or went near her he would kill him with his bare hands and there you have it. The man left like the cur, the scurrilous villain, he was and Lord Edwin made me swear not to disturb Lady Flora by telling her, that it would cloud her happiness.'

'You see what this means,' said Ralph. 'It was he who destroyed the garden.'

'Hmm,' said Heracles. 'I would not be so hasty in your assumptions, Master Ralph.'

'Well, all the more reason for us to go to London and find out the truth,' said Ralph.

'I agree, young Master, but firstly,' said Jack slowly, 'I think I need to find a witness to this and I now have a mind to pay a few visits if the young Master gives me permission. There are some favours I can call in and I think there are stranger things than your garden. There are tales I have heard and before we go to London I may have news which will interest the highest in the land.'

'Do you need money?' asked Ralph. 'My father always said a few coins loosened tongues.'

'No, Sir, I do not; we have other ways and best you do not ask any questions.'

Heracles shivered slightly and thought how blurred the lines were between right and wrong. They had all been affected by the arrival of the handsome Dutchman who had, it appeared, lifted Flora out of the resigned half-life she was leading. But Heracles knew that while Flora's husband lived she could not find happiness with another man and then he thought about the question of adultery, one of the deadly sins, and blanched inwardly when he faced the truth that she, the virtuous woman he perceived her to be, had fallen into sin. It was the evil by which her husband had been seduced which had brought her to it. And then he thought of resurrection and how all men and women must have the chance of repentance, even Lord Edwin. But God would decide what was to be, thought Heracles. Edwin was in deadly peril, of that he was sure.

CHAPTER TWENTY-SEVEN

Paternoster Row, August 1690

'I must go to our family house in Paternoster Row,' Flora informed Peter on the day following the visit with the Queen to the theatre. Flora had seen rather too much of court life for the moment. The whole atmosphere was claustrophobic and there was the continual miasma of intrigue and betrayal in the air, not to mention the malodorous domestic arrangements, which, although the King had tried to improve them, coming as he did from the hygienic courts of Holland, were almost insupportable.

'I am not surprised you want a change of scene,' said Peter. 'The disgraceful behaviour towards the Queen last night sickened me to the stomach.'

'I felt for her so terribly but she handled it with great dignity while everyone stared at her,' said Flora.

'Well, she did the only thing she could do and that was to leave,' replied Peter. 'The offending line was said so quickly I did not quite catch it,' he added.

'"Very good she usurps the throne, keeps the old King in prison, at the same time praying for a blessing on the army,"' quoted Flora.

'When the King hears about this I do not fancy Mr Dryden's chances for a successful future,' scoffed Peter.

'Enough of that; it makes me so angry,' said Flora. 'I am leaving before the midday meal in the banqueting hall. The stewards have had a few days to prepare the house, which has not been visited since my father's death. I have been too immersed in my life in the country and in the expanding of my work. Now for some reason I have the urge to take affairs in hand. The house belongs to me, you know, because Ralph had a larger portion of Catherine's Court, and besides I have enjoyed the Queen's hospitality for long enough.'

Peter made no comment, wondering if Flora's father had made the same clever plans to protect his daughter's property from the clutches of a husband; and then he could not help his thoughts straying to the fate of Flora's husband. Nobody had been able so far to get any news of Edwin and there were many others in the same boat. It surprised Peter to see the insouciant way the court displayed such little interest in the affairs of its army and navy who were fighting off such a very real threat from the French. In his mind he compared it to Rome before its fall. And as for the Queen's hospitality, he had never seen so many scroungers and scoundrels as supped at the Queen's table and seemed to doss down anywhere in the vast maze of unmapped rooms at the Palace at Whitehall.

'I think I should accompany you,' he volunteered.

'I think it best you do not,' said Flora rather too quickly.

'You know a plot has been discovered to kill the King and Queen. London is not a safe place for a woman to travel alone, even surrounded by her servants. These are dangerous times,' cut in Peter sharply.

'It was only a tramp in the park who overheard it,' said Flora calmly.

'The man gave a very detailed account of the plans, and two men have been questioned and confessed and now a network has been discovered which leads to the very men at the heart of the Queen's entourage,' corrected Peter.

'How do you know this?' asked Flora.

'Because, my dear,' said Peter, 'there are some things you do not know. A gardener can wear many different aprons, so it is with me. It is my job to know such things and my loyalty to His Majesty is absolute. I am close to both their Majesties.'

Flora looked at him in astonishment. They were in the room she had been allotted by the court for her stay. Sarah was in a small adjoining chamber where she was packing Flora's things and had just brought in a tray of coffee, the new rage in London society. She had been unable to ignore the conversation between her mistress and her young lover. She had of course suspected for a while that there was more about the young baron than he cared to reveal. She ostentatiously closed the door whilst reaching for a glass which she quietly put to it in order to listen whilst her Ladyship conversed without inhibition.

Flora glanced towards the door and motioned Peter to sit down. There was a pair of matching high-backed chairs whose arms were caked in the grease of many hands and she flinched slightly and wiped them daintily on a kerchief from her sleeve. On this bright summer morning the fabric of the old palace looked shabby and ill kempt and Flora empathised with the Queen's desire to spend more time in the well-run smaller palace at Kensington. The grubby room did not lift her spirits and, still reeling from the remark Peter had just made, she was temporarily at a loss for words. She regarded him intently and his answering gaze did not flinch.

'Are you saying that you are some sort of spy, that you have slept with me and enjoyed my friendship for some sort of clandestine operation?' she asked slowly, her breast beginning to heave.

'I did not mean to fall in love with you,' he answered evenly, his clear blue eyes now assuming a very different aspect to Flora than those she had succumbed to with such reckless passion.

'Get out!' she screamed, suddenly rising to her feet and sending the coffee pot and dainty cups smashing to the floor. She fell to him, pummelling his chest with her fists. She was sobbing and her words came in a torrent. 'All round me I find nothing but deception! You as well, you have abused me, Sir. I never want to set eyes on you again, do you hear me?'

He put out his arms and pulled her to him, pinning her flailing fists and stifling her sobs in the velvet of his doublet. She could smell the familiar mixture of skin and the pomade he used after his shave. She could not speak, she could only hold her breath, suspended in a no man's land where she hung desperately onto the passion of their lovemaking and the happiness he had brought to her sleeping heart; then came the awful thought which she did not want to believe, that she had been used.

'No, my Lady,' he spoke urgently into her hair. 'I was sent to protect you, to find out the truth. You must listen. The destruction of your garden was but one thing; there is much more. Men's lives have been lost because of it, good men who are fighting for their country. It is in the small things that such big plans are implemented; men have grown rich from these crimes and the weakness of those they get in their power. I was not sent to do you harm and, yes, I am a good gardener. I should not have allowed myself to love you, but how could I resist? You are the most beautiful thing I have ever seen. I am after all, only a man. If God wills it, maybe we are destined to be together and, my love, you were not exactly averse to my advances.'

His mouth sought hers. Of course she did not resist. She swayed against him; let her head rest peacefully on his fine strong chest and she felt her heart beating in unison with his.

*   *   *

Flora agreed Peter was to accompany her with Jack and Sarah to her home after all, but the approach was a foretaste of what was to follow.

They turned into the narrow street and Flora let out a gasp. 'What has happened to the houses either side?' she called up to Jack who was sitting precariously beside the driver.

'It is the same story all over London,' Jack replied gloomily leaning down into the window. When they rebuilt after the fire, they had to use bricks and not wood. It is the law. London is full of scoundrels and they used the "Spanish". It's a foul mess of, begging your pardon, men's effluent, scavengers' sweepings, poultry feathers, sawdust, anything that will bulk it up and after a year it turns to dust, and the houses begin to fall down. And another thing, they build the inside walls without setting them into the grand exterior.'

It was like a bad dream except for the fact that the Amalie

house stood upright and proud beside its neighbours which were clearly unoccupied, windows falling out and floors askew, with chimney pots fallen into the steeply pitched roofs. And all of it covered in a thin layer of black grime. Peter had been told so much about the London house, which, saving its proximity to Newgate prison, was by all accounts a fine residence. Coming from the well-ordered and pristine town houses of Holland he could never acclimatise himself to the squalor of London, and had imagined Flora's home would prove the exception.

'Well, at least your house stands proud in the midst of all this,' he said hopefully. 'I remember you telling me your father used a Dutch architect who used brick and stone and the finest craftsmen.'

'You are right. It was in advance of its time,' said Flora, thinking yet again what clever man her father had been.

*　　*　　*

Sadly, the first glance at the exterior of Amalie house did not prepare Flora for the shock that confronted her as the carriage drew up in the narrow street. She had also forgotten the noise and perpetual din of London. The street was a seething mass of vendors calling their wares, knife grinders, tinkers banging their pots and twanging kettles, and shrieking voices. Musical instruments and the cries of beggars added to the noise of horses' hooves as they clattered on the cobbles.

The coach came to a halt outside the imposing front door topped by a Dutch arched fan light, whose glass, Flora immediately saw, was obscured by thick black grime. The two coachmen jumped down at once, their faces curling in disgust as their boots sank inches deep in the filth that covered the street. The pervasive sickening stench left no doubt as to its content: rotting faeces both animal and human composed the stagnant mire, piles of rotting refuse formed islands around which the greasy sludge moved sluggishly.

Flora looked down in despair and at once the coachman banged the door of the house, which was answered quickly by the old steward. His once fine green uniform now hung off him in shabby folds and Flora felt a pang of guilt. His old face crinkled with pleasure as he saw her and he bent in a deep bow.

'Where is the duck board, man?' ordered the coachman. 'Do you expect my Lady to wade through this filth?'

A boy appeared and boards were put down, over which Flora edged her way, followed by Peter.

Flora saw at once that the beautiful honey-coloured flagstones laid by her father were a uniform dismal brown; her feet stuck as she walked. And the windows above the stairway let in the dreariest of light, filtered as if through a muddy pool.

'My Lady,' the old man said, lowering his head. He had attempted a bow but he knew his old bones would not raise him from a recumbent position.

'You look ill, man,' said Flora. 'I will replace your suit at once. See that this is done, Jack,' said Flora.

'Please forgive us,' said the old man apologetically. 'We have done our best, but it is many months of neglect and most of the women have gone and it is just me, your old Obadiah, and the outside boy. We have done our best, my Lady, and you will find your chamber prepared as best we can. I sent for a new down mattress as the mice had made free with everything they could find.' He shook his head dismally and sighed.

Flora looked about her, as her eyes became accustomed to the gloom and saw that the battle against dust and soot had been lost. Despite the scrapers outside the doors there was nothing to see of the once finely polished oak staircase and shining flags dotted with the bright rugs she remembered. The fireplace in the hall no longer shone and the brass implements were dull. There was a fetid odour of dust and coal and a powerful waft of human effluent.

'I am sorry,' Peter commiserated. 'It is the use of coal which has fouled this city.' He stopped himself from going any further, although there was much he could say about the filthy English.

'I will have none of this,' Flora announced, calling the coach-man, who was a man of sound reputation. 'Here is a purse,' she said. 'Go to it and find some servants and strong men. We will have this place cleaned and restored to order. Fetch half a dozen sweeps and start with the chimneys, which by the look of it are blocked. Get the soil men; I can smell the pits are full and I don't care if the removal disturbs the neighbours. There are no neighbours anyway except for rats and vagabonds, and I want half a dozen hungry Tom cats.'

'But, my Lady,' said Obadiah. 'We cannot empty in daylight. It has to be done at night when everyone has their windows closed.'

'I don't care,' said Flora. 'I will be answerable, and, Obadiah, we must get the grates polished and the brasses cleaned. And then the windows with vinegar so we can get some light in here, and while we are on it, why have people been burning foul tallow candles here, leaving a smell of rotting animals? I have sent good money for decent wax candles; where has it gone?'

'I am sad to say, my Lady,' the man trembled, 'the under-steward made off with the first lot of money while I was abed with the dropsy.'

Sarah had appeared in the hallway, having explored the kitchens at the rear of the ground floor. Her face was pale and her apron already dirty. 'My Lady,' she said with a grim expression of foreboding, 'I will get your chamber ready for you, but if I might have a word with you privately before we go upstairs.'

'It is the privies,' said Sarah, as they stood aside while the men carried the baggage up the staircase. 'We do not know how such things have happened,' she said awkwardly, 'no one could understand the reason for the stench that came from them. I just got the lad who comes to sweep the cobbles outside to push the effluent into the runnel in the middle of the street and goodness knows how things have become as they are with dead cats and the like . . . '

'Sarah, just what are you trying to say?' asked Flora.

'We need to get the priest,' blurted Sarah.

'The priest? What do you mean?' asked Flora in genuine bewilderment.

'As you know, my Lady, his late Lordship built the thing and much attention it has had. I would say particularly in your absence and, begging your pardon, contents fall straight down the shute into the cellar below, but there was something wrong and we found the source which was in the privy by the kitchens which had blocked. Some poor soul must have got into the house and in a desperate state I would say . . . well,' Sarah continued falteringly, ' . . . we found the body of a babe stuck in there, my Lady. Newly born with the cord still attached.'

Flora recoiled and felt dizzy; she had to sit down for a moment in order to gather her thoughts. Obadiah brought a chair and Sarah had a quick whispered conversation with him. Peter had heard nothing of this and neither did Flora want him to.

'Sarah, on no account call a priest. What have you done with the . . . ?' she gulped, searching for the words.

'We were sick to the stomach. I wrapped the thing in a cloth before the boy could rightly see what it was, but it was only a poor creature, which could never have had a chance in life and was much decayed. I have dealt with it, my Lady, as respectfully as I could. But I thought I had to tell your Ladyship because we are going to do our best to cleanse the house of the reminders of it.'

'Call Obadiah here,' said Flora, recovering herself a little. She was grateful that Peter had heard nothing about this, as he was supervising unloading the bags. 'We will go into the parlour.'

Obadiah came in nervously, fingering his sleeves. He knew that the Lady Flora had much to complain about and he had tears in his eyes. 'I do not know what to say, my Lady,' he faltered. 'I have tried so hard to keep the place as your father had it, but the money has not been there. There were these men, they came to the house, they took the last purse your Ladyship sent for the wages and the candles and lire, and the wax for the floors and the lemon for the brasses and the good coal for the fires to keep the place aired as your Ladyship said. They said you were a married lady now and your husband sent them and if I did not give it, I would be beaten and I am too old to be beaten, your Ladyship, and they gave me a taste, was fearful. The servants left, your Ladyship, save for the boy who was to do the outsides and helped your good woman with her . . . '

He stopped and looked at Sarah. 'Best listen, my Lady, for he has a tale to tell,' said Sarah. Flora nodded.

'Well, with nobody left, I took in this girl. She was a good girl and she had fallen on hard times but it soon seemed she was carrying, by the size of her belly. She still worked as best she could, but the place was so fallen like herself, and then the day came when she started her cries and she left so suddenly . . . No business for a man and I could not find a woman who would bother with it . . . just another poor soul. She went and I never saw her again. But now we know the reason, and that was mercifully only a couple of weeks ago.'

Flora stood up imperiously. 'Sarah, we know nothing of this, and neither do you, Obadiah. We do not want the constables here. The poor wretch of a girl is a victim of the place this world has become. She would be hung and then it is another life gone. No, we will say our own private prayers for the girl's soul and her child. And Obadiah, I take much of the blame for this. I should have come to London and seen what was happening, I have been too much taken with my life in the country and my work. Things will be different from now on, you will see.'

Flora shivered as she thought of the lonely plight of the girl who had given way to her desires, just as Flora herself had done. And what of the unwanted child who had been tossed way so horribly – and her own dead child that was, despite its beginnings, a wanted child? For a moment she felt the hand of retribution. She felt sick and fell to the floor.

She came round in her parents' bed. Peter stood by the open window. The room had been divested of curtains or hangings and now smelled sweetly of lavender and roses. He gave her ale and sweet tea and she soon recovered. At first she could not fathom where she was in the clean bare room. The bed had been moved to the window overlooking the small garden at the back of the house and sun streamed in onto a spotless coverlet.

'Peter, what happened?' she asked feebly.

'You fainted,' he answered, a note of puzzlement in his voice. 'Perhaps you should see the Queen's physician?' he went on. 'But I imagine finding this house in such a state was a terrible shock, and by the way, your maid and I have taken down the hangings. I never understand why the English have such things about their beds. They harbour vermin and stop the air circulating.'

Flora looked at Peter and what she saw was renewal. She felt the air was clean around him. She needed to cleanse herself of the events in the house as well as the perfidy and sluttishness of the court, the squalor of the city outside. Perhaps, she wondered, life would take her to live with this man in the promised land of Holland which the Queen so missed. She thought about these things for the rest of the day, a day of new beginnings when more and more people came to do her bidding and restore Amalie House. She had a mission to regain its position in the decaying street. It gave her sense of purpose and her own place in the scheme of things. She thought of the Queen, a lone woman surrounded by men who tried to diminish her. This woman was a shining example to Flora as she wondered whether she had yet to find her own path in life, outside her small world, a path which she alone could find. The arrival at the house had in some curious way focused her mind on a wider world than the one she clung to.

By evening Peter had returned to the court at Whitehall and Flora was left to survey the transformation. The house as she had remembered it stood there proud and sparkling like a miracle. She asked Sarah to summon Obadiah and the boy plus five new servants who had been hired to help her in the parlour. The room shone, the fine furniture waxed, the floors scrubbed and polished, the rugs beaten, the mirrors cleaned with vinegar. Sarah had brought cakes and ale. Obadiah's uniform was restored and his old face was wreathed in smiles.

Flora remembered her father once telling her that when all around you is in chaos you should focus on the small domestic things. Get them in perfect order and when the time comes the big things will look after themselves. She hoped he was watching.

CHAPTER TWENTY-EIGHT

Suffolk, August 1690

'We will find the truth,' said Jack. 'I have some lads; we are going to the tavern on the marsh where many of the low men gather.'

'Master Ralph must not come with you,' said Heracles.

'And that he will not,' assured Jack, 'for it would curtail my task to have the lad there. I will be back before dawn and I will have the explanation for all of this. Then we will go with all haste to London and join the mistress at Paternoster Row.'

He went on horseback; there had been a storm, and the way was covered in an early drop of leaves. It was still light when he got to the appropriately named Smugglers Arms. The windows were steamed up and tightly closed despite the warmth of the evening, as if all that transpired within would be contained in the secret fetid atmosphere. There was the rough laughter of men in their cups and the occasional high-pitched shriek from one of the barmaids.

Jack had prepared well. The landlord Matthew was a robust fellow who, although a rogue, had a sense of honour among thieves. After all, he flourished because, in his way, he could be trusted in the fraternity of petty crime and 'honest smuggling'. Neither did any serious harm in the scheme of things.

The Amalies had always looked after their people. Many a tenant had been kept in the tied cottage through a long illness or old age, and the landlord's own grandfather had been kept on to build a useless wall round some of the estate when he could no longer till the ground behind the huge pair of cobs. 'Spare a man the ignominy of charity,' was the saying, and the wall was still known by the man's name. It had become a tradition to pay a nodding respect to Old Joseph's Wall when passing on the path to the tavern in the village. Jack had done so from his horse on the way, and he reminded 'Old Joe's' burly son Matthew of this on his arrival.

Hand cradling a mug of ale warmed with the tongs from the fire, which burned every night despite the season or the weather, Jack did not waste time on niceties and came to the point.

'Matthew, there's things afoot which aren't fit, and I think you know when a man has stepped over the mark we country folk respect. There is such a thing as a decent lawbreaker and all the more power to him if it keeps his family from starving . . . ' Jack put his hand to his stubbly chin, which, unusually for him, sported two days' growth. He opened his mouth slightly. It was a gesture known to carry a message and Matthew looked at him nervously. Jack was well respected, and, besides, Matthew owed him many a debt. Everyone knew that a good steward had a quiver of favours to call in if he was worth his salts.

'There are things which bite the hand that feeds us and that doesn't make sense to me, and I know you have things you need to tell me,' said Jack darkly.

Matthew looked up as the thick oak door slammed shut. Two men known to him as friends of Jack's stood in front of it, arms folded. Outside the steamy windows could be seen the shadows of other figures, still and menacing. Jack had not come alone. A silence had descended on the room and the men shifted in their seats, watching Jack.

'Well, lads, I have a little ditty for you,' said Jack portentously, confident that he had the attention of all the men, and of course the two buxom doxies who served at the bar, and much else. 'May the Lord above send down a dove, with wings as sharp as razors to cut the throats of them there blokes that sells bad beer to sailors,' he recited with all the sepulchral grandeur of the pastor at the Sunday sermon.

One of the men tried surreptitiously to slink out of the door into the kitchen, but Jack spotted him at once.

'Silas, just where might you be going?' he bellowed. All eyes turned to the cringing man and with only a nod from Jack, Matthew and two men were upon him. 'Bring him into the room at the back,' said Jack menacingly, 'and leave the door open so that you men may hear what happens to them who as good as murder their own fellow man by their greed.'

'So, Silas, what have you got to tell us?' said Jack quietly when they had dragged the man to a small room beside the bar.

The man was sweating profusely, but his look was not one of capitulation, more of resolute hostility. 'Nowt.' He spat the word, a dribble of saliva remaining on his lower lip which bared to reveal toothless gums.

'My, you are not a pretty fellow,' said Jack with a laugh. 'Seeing as you have no teeth left, us lads will have to find something else to work on, won't we, men?'

'Well, how would you like few changes?' said Matthew in a sinister way, producing a curved knife from his belt. 'Perhaps those ears of yours need a trim?' he went on, looking for agreement among the others, who all sniggered nervously, seeing before them events which might well be a fate in store for them if they broke the comrades' code.

'You know what's been going on round here, ' Jack started, 'and who are the rich bastards you help fatten up, while honest men are kept aboard ship for months at a time being fed on shit you wouldn't give a dog, and rancid watered ale which makes their guts turn to jelly.'

The man met his gaze, his eyes beginning to dart furiously as for the first time he confronted the reality of the actions in which he had been complicit.

Jack spotted the chink in the man's stupid silence. 'You give us names,' he said slowly. Despite his strong stomach he was repulsed by the man's rancid breath, which Jack saw as the stench of the man's rotten soul within. 'Reckon that ear will be the first thing to come off,' he went on.

'Good thinking, Jack, these dogs need a little taster,' growled Matthew, looking towards two large shaggy dogs who seemed to understand what their master said and licked their lips greedily.

'You'll not get nothing from me, it's more than my life's worth, you sons of whores!' screamed the man.

'Well, the truth is your life's not worth much anyway from where I see it,' said Jack, 'but there is always a chance to change, even for scum like you. My brother died on one of the King's ships while they sat in the harbour for two months being poisoned by the victuallers, your so-called friends, who live high on the hog from honest men's blood,' said Matthew.

'You won't get them,' said the man in a quieter tone. 'These are men who ride so high even the King can't nail them . . . can't see what goes on under his dirty Dutch nose . . . like the bitch who grows the fancy flowers, who is no better than the cunny in the village.' Silas sneered and spat again defiantly.

Jack gave Matthew a nod. With a flash of steel he caught the man's greasy hair, pushed his head on one movement and sliced off the ear as if it were no more than a piece of bread. He threw it to the dogs who briefly fought over the trophy, the larger getting the prize and slipping away, crunching it in his jaws. The man let out a long throaty cry as blood covered his face while his arms were held in a vice-like grip. He could do nothing to stem the blood which flowed into his nostrils and mouth, and he choked on his own blood, temporarily losing consciousness. Matthew threw water over him and he came round to hear his tormentor's voice.

'Shall I do the other one? I like to be even handed with my dogs,' said Matthew slyly to the eager crowd of men had gathered in the doorway.

'No, do 'is balls, then there's no more bastards,' called the crowd.

'No! For the love of God, I'll tell you everything,' screamed the man, his voice raised like a girl's.

'Well, maybe those dogs won't get the best bits then. Bring the man some rags. I never could stand the sight of blood,' laughed Jack who, despite his apparent lack of concern about the kind of rough justice of which he had just been part, was a man of conscience. He had long debated in his soul whether this kind of

242

torture was justified, if it would save lives. But when he thought of the many good men betrayed by their own class and then of the fat cats who cared nothing for the working men on whom they built their feckless lives, he had come to his own decisions and squared it with God and the words in the Good Book.

'We never saw the man who gave the orders,' blubbered Silas. 'But I know he is very high, him and some others. They say the men are in with the French King and it's not for the likes of me to think. I only want to feed my children,' added the man by way of a limp defence. 'And the money was good,' he finished as if this final justification would save him.

'No, my good fellow, the money was tainted with blood,' hissed Jack. 'And something tells me you do know a name or two. Now let me see,' he scratched his head thoughtfully and looked at the other men. 'Well, gentlemen, what do you say if we undo this fellow's breeches? We may see what a fine dinner the dogs will have after all.' Even as he said it Jack knew he could never carry out the threat, and so did the landlord. But the men did not know it and just as the men lifted him to the table in the corner of the room he shrieked out the name: 'Sir Frederick Buckley!'

Jack gave the sign, a quick nod of the head, and the men lifted Silas unceremoniously into a chair.

'That is the villain who came to my mistress's house once,' he said thoughtfully. 'He was a friend of Lord Edwin's, if I recall. A debauched devil he was too. I had my suspicions about him but why, man, would he want to harm the gentle Lady Flora and despoil the enterprise that puts food on the table of all the folk who love the Amalie family?'

'It was not about him,' Silas whispered faintly. 'It was the King. Sir Frederick gets favours from the French. He is a Papist, and the Lady Flora's father turned for the Dutch King. For myself I do not care one way or the other,' gasped the man, as Jack gave another nod and two of the men wrenched the man's head back over the chair.

Suddenly Jack saw it all, as if the curtain had been lifted on a dream. He saw the truth, the fact that Lord Edwin had not been responsible for what happened, that the man had indeed reformed and that there were many men who secretly took money from the French to debilitate the navy. They cared not in their avarice that all this would leave the path clear for the French King's ambition to march his armies onto English soil. Jack shuddered as he thought of his own brave country back under the papal rod. The maligned Lord Edwin now offered his life in battle to resist such ignominy but then he reminded himself how once a man has dipped his quill in Satan's ink he is forever stained.

But there was more, more than this low fellow could begin to understand. Armed with the name of Sir Frederick Buckley, Jack left the man to the justice of his neighbours, knowing that the sentence he would receive from them was more of a slow punishment than anything Jack could have devised.

'Make sure the man's children do not suffer. The Lady Flora will be told of all this, send the wife to me tomorrow before I leave for London,' he said in a low voice.

*　　*　　*

'No, Jack,' said Heracles, 'we cannot leave here without the man. We need it straight from his lips, and besides, I do not believe you have got the whole story. There is more we need if these men are to be brought to justice.' He paused for a moment. 'This business has so many dark shadows. This is not confined to a little rancid beer here, weevil infested biscuits there, and broken flowers, it is about a very real threat to our beloved country. There are men involved who are higher than that wretch Buckley.'

'So, are you suggesting we travel with the man to London?' asked Ralph disgustedly.

'Not suggesting, insisting,' said Heracles with a note of authority.

'I for one will not sit with the scoundrel,' said Ralph.

'Sir, I would not let you breath the same air as Silas. He will be brought here and travel with the bags, and God help the man, for I hope you know, Mr Heracles, that when we get him to the city, he will be handed to the King's men and brought to the rack and more, for they will have no mercy on him.'

'Why should we go soft on this creature?' asked Ralph. 'He did not spare a thought for the families of the sailors who died and he has committed heresy. But I worry for my sister. There is something that bothers me. This whole affair is too close for comfort and the trail often leads to my brother-in-law, Lord Edwin. Are we opening a Pandora's box?'

'We must find the truth or we too are guilty, that is all I have to say,' said Heracles. 'And besides, with respect, your sister entrusted you to my care,' he finished with a note which brooked no argument.

'Very well, fetch the man and let us leave as soon as possible,' agreed Ralph.

CHAPTER TWENTY-NINE

Paternoster Row,
beginning of September 1690

'My Lady,' said Sarah, holding up the bath sheet as her mistress emerged from the ornate brass tub in the corner of her dressing chamber. 'I must speak out, my Lady,' she began tentatively. 'It is a matter of some delicacy and your Ladyship has no mother or sister or female person who can speak to you of things which are between women and of things which know no boundaries, where God is the only arbiter as our humble bodies are at His mercy.'

'So what is it that we must speak of as sisters?' replied Flora somewhat coldly, as she put her arms in a beautiful silk robe that Sarah had found in one of her mother's old chests – one of the few things which had escaped the ravages of the mice.

'My Lady, settle yourself on the bed,' Sarah soothed. 'You look tired and I think surely we must both know the reason,' she continued calmly, pulling back the rich coverlet and smoothing down the many cushions on which Flora, in common with all aristocratic ladies, slept, lest death should find them prone and ready to depart this life.

'Restoring the house to order,' said Flora weakly, 'and torturing myself with thoughts of the poor girl who lost her child in this house where she found no comfort. Her sorrow has stolen my sleep from me and then . . . ' She turned into the pillow and began to cry.

'My Lady, of course I understand,' Sarah replied quietly. 'But her plight was not unconnected with the news you carry so secretly. Nothing can be concealed from your servant. I know you have missed your courses three times now and the tightness of your dresses tells me you are with child.'

Flora looked up, her face ashen. 'There you have it, Sarah. I am undone. I am carrying the Baron's child, and I do not know if my husband lives! If he does, what am I to tell him? What am I to tell the world? I cannot live a life with the Baron. He was a dream, he saved me when my soul was starved but I never meant to . . . ' She resumed her sobbing and Sarah pulled her to her, cradling her head on her comforting shoulder.

'The child is not the Baron's,' she whispered. 'You were carrying when you met the Baron, so that at least is a consolation, my Lady. I know you had thought you would not bear another child, and, my Lady, surely you noticed the signs. I thought that was one reason why you gave yourself so freely, if you will pardon the liberty. I did not talk of it because I thought, my Lady, it was your wish.'

'And what do I do? Do I tell the Baron? Tell Lord Edwin the truth, if he comes back a hero and finds his wife has lain with another?' she asked in a broken voice. 'There will be gossip.'

'You tell them nothing,' rounded Sarah. 'The world knows nothing except that the King sent a most trusted gentleman to help you with your garden. Truth, my Lady, can be a double-edged sword. Many lives I have seen wrecked by the truth of such things. The Baron must go back to his own life, he has served his purpose, my Lady, and now you as a great lady must live yours. There are many dependent upon you and there are folk who will talk about you and the Baron but they cannot prove anything. You must never speak of it, for to do so would be to deprive the babe you carry of his heritage. The world must think, as is the case, that you carry your husband's child and no doubt must be upon the thing.'

Flora sat up in the bed and put her hand to her stomach. She held it there for a moment and then a smile suffused her face.

'My dear friend,' she said softly. 'When you speak, it all sounds so simple and already I can feel a joy at the prospect of a new life, a child. I welcome it as the poor girl could not, but I cannot welcome my baby's father.'

'God will tell you what to do, my Lady. You will be surprised. Solutions come where you do not expect them. We will soon have news of Lord Edwin and he has surely acquitted himself well. After all, we are taught from the Good Book that salvation is there for us all. The child will need a father and your heart will tell you that the richness you will gain from forgiveness may well be a gift you have neither sought nor prayed for.'

'I fear you look for too much in my heart, Sarah,' said Flora frankly. 'Lord Edwin ill used me and I cannot forgive him. But I may have to live as many women do, with a marriage in name only and I will devote myself to the good of the public. I have been thinking,' she said slowly. 'I am mindful to buy the houses either side from their absent owners; and rebuild at least one of them as a foundling home for poor girls. At least then I will do something that my father would have been proud of in this wretched world.'

'Truth stumbles in the public square and righteousness cannot enter,' said Sarah suddenly. Flora looked at her sharply.

'Those are fine words,' Flora said. The meaning was clear but they were unexpectedly high for a servant.

'My Lady, I may live my life as a servant and as such I must know my place, but no one owns my soul or my brain and one who is invisible as I must be for much of the time sees more than your Ladyship will ever do. It is the one small consolation for those who serve, whether your master is man or God.'

For the first time Flora felt the chill wind of the divide between them. For all the love and friendship they had both given to their relationship, nothing could ever eliminate the benefits of birth.

'Sarah, you are my friend, I depend on you for your wise counsel, there is no difference between us,' said Flora uncomfortably, knowing in her heart that there was an enormous difference, particularly the fact that her own birth gave her the opportunity for choice amongst many other things.

'My lady Flora, I know what you are trying to say, but let me tell you a fact about servants: you either employ them or you are one, and for the rich the world the poor live in is another country.'

* * *

Not far away, the difference that fate had in store for the rich and the poor was nowhere better illustrated than by the two of the prisoners in the Tower.

Despite the beauty of the perfect summer day, the scene was one of unimaginable horror. The lower floors of the dark formidable building harboured all that was most fetid and vile from the miasma of decay that ran in the mud of the river, on whose edge the building had been built. Even on such a day, the stink of damp filled the air where the sun never penetrated; the ineffective light from the small slit windows did nothing to alleviate the gloom. The men's faces in that foul chamber were only illuminated by the fire that burned continually on a raised platform beside a bench, on which the blood-soaked body of Silas lay stretched. He cried out as the Grand Master continued to ask him the same question to which he received the same answers.

Sir Frederick Buckley sat still in a chair where he had been restrained next to the devil's proceedings, and it was his name that the man kept repeating in his pain and terror. Indeed, it was his face that Silas had identified when a group of court gentlemen were brought to the stinking place.

'Put the torch to the man, just one more time, so that he may take a warning to the others of what lies in store,' incanted the man, who was like the master of Dante's *Inferno*.

Frederick Buckley felt the gorge rising in his throat; he supposed he would be spared the rack as he was a gentleman. But the bleeding man was removed like a hunk of meat and his moans could be heard as his feet dragged across the slimy stone floor of the passage, as, from the dank cells on either side of which, issued forth the cries of despair from the men who all knew there was but one way they would go from this place. Eventually death would be a release.

'Take his fine Lordship to the Palace,' mocked the Grand Master, 'but first throw a bucket of water over him. He has fouled his breeches. And a word in your ear,' said the man in a low sinister tone, leaning very close to Frederick and flicking a piece of something which looked horribly like human flesh from his soiled silk chemise. 'See what lies in store for you if you do not lead your Queen to the men who have rewarded you and his like for their heresy. Better to lose your head in one clean sweep than suffer as this poor fool has done. He will not die with dignity, my friend, but you maybe you can yet save your soul with repentance and the sword of truth.'

The Grand Master's nostrils flared contemptuously, and he gave a brief sign to a lad in the corner of the room who came instantly with a silver bowl full of sweet-smelling water with petals floating on the top. He swished his jewelled fingers in the water and the boy held up a spotless linen towel, as if by performing this ritual the man absolved himself from the evil deeds in the room.

'Your journey may be different from the low fellow you have been watching but your end will be the same,' he said with a snigger.

CHAPTER THIRTY

The Palace of Whitehall, September 1690

'We have news of your husband, my dear,' said the Queen warmly, as Flora raised herself from her curtsey. Flora had known that she had not been widowed for some days now and was bewildered by the maelstrom of feelings which had come to the surface. She knew that she had to send Peter back to Holland but she dreaded the inevitability of their parting.

Her brother Ralph had come with Jack and they seemed to be very preoccupied. Of course it had not taken long for her to hear that the suspects in the wide net of corruption which had weakened the navy and therefore the safety of the country had begun to unravel. The Queen knew it all, and Edwin had been exonerated, although he had been a previous confidant of just one of the villains, Sir Frederick Buckley, who now stood on trial for treason and who would no doubt be beheaded. Furthermore, it appeared that Lord Edwin was a genuinely reformed character, and had gained wide respect for his valour in the face of battle. Peter could not help respecting the man for not playing this card to his wife. The man had not tried to make much of it and had indeed left it to others to communicate details as to his well-being.

'Oh,' said Flora with a lack of enthusiasm and indeed curiosity, which puzzled the Queen. But then, the Queen had to remind herself, there was quite a history in the Grantley marriage. But although the man had behaved like a blaggard, he had been given a second chance to redeem himself by her husband the King, whose judgement she regarded as impeccable. And that confidence had been justified; the man had saved the King's life and then been wounded. He had been in a state of such high fever that he could not even remember his own name. She had been told of the slow recovery aided by an Irish woman, who had set up a field hospital. He had apparently regained his memory and his wits and was valiantly back on his horse at the King's side. These details the Queen imparted to Flora's blank face.

'Now, my dear, we must put the past behind us. There is cause for celebration here. Your husband will be greeted as a hero.' The Queen gave Flora a long searching look. 'There are times when we must think of the greater good,' she finished.

'Of course, Your Majesty,' said Flora with a tilt of her chin. Her husband was now a hero, he was probably destined for great things and she had to admit that given the perfidy in his past he had done the impossible.

'Now we must be seated and I will send for some coffee,' said the Queen. Two footmen came forward at once and stood behind two gold chairs. Coffee was brought and the Queen leant forward and took Flora's hand. 'We will have such a reception,' she said, her face flushing with pleasure, 'and there are many who must receive the King's gratitude. Your servant for example. He uncovered this whole network of corruption in our beloved navy by his brave conduct, by bringing the man to London who could bear witness against Sir Frederick Buckley. Now, don't you see, my dear, had it not been for your garden and the destruction before our royal visit none of this would have been discovered – at least not before more lives had been lost.'

The Queen paused while Flora absorbed the thought, which had never occurred to her. It was as if her father was there in the room and she was transported back to the time before he died when he said that the garden was there to protect her, that the power of nature would be her salvation, and as she considered this she felt the child move like a trembling bird. And while the Queen chattered on, she wished that she could love the father of the child she carried, the grandchild her father had not lived to see. But she could hardly pull the image of Edwin's face out of the book of her past. There were just tiny flashes, but for some reason the dark things were receding fractionally and she suddenly had a great urge to return to Paternoster Row and retreat into the beautiful house it had become, her own creation, where even as she sat in her damask drawing room she could hear the men working on the house next door, where the first women would soon be able to come.

*   *   *

The house smelt sweet, summer flowers adorned the many tables and Flora thought of Catherine's Court. As if in answer to her thoughts, her brother came excitedly into the room. Flora looked up and was cheered to see his happy face; he had grown. He was now probably his full height and his voice had broken. He reminded her so much of their father, her heart stopped for a moment. It was early evening and everything in the house was calm, beautiful and orderly, and inexplicably she felt as if all was well.

'I hope the meal is ready, I am ravenous,' exclaimed Ralph. 'I have been rowing on the river, there are preparations being made for the King's return. There will be such masques and music, the whole city is preparing for the greatest victory parade since King Charles came back from France.'

They went into the dining room where the table was laid for the three of them: Flora at the top and Ralph and Heracles either side. There was a large carver chair opposite Flora that always remained empty, as if waiting for the master of the house who would have taken the traditional role of carving the meat, which instead was performed by one of the house stewards.

Flora waved aside the dish of veal prepared with onions, capers and thyme. The two men devoured it while Sarah came with bowl of calves foot jelly and some dainty wafers for her mistress; she looked frowningly while Flora sipped daintily from her spoon. She knew that her mistress's condition might in the first weeks turn her stomach from her food but now that she was nearing her fourth month she would need her nourishment.

'A little wine, my Lady,' she coaxed quietly in Flora's ear. 'It might recover your appetite.'

'Why not, sister?' cut in Ralph. 'We should all have some since there is so much to talk about, and for once the news is all good.' He looked at Flora commandingly, his eyes dancing with enthusiasm and despite herself she was caught up in the moment, Ralph's moment of ebullient optimism which she had no right to spoil.

'Well, why not?' agreed Flora, signalling to the steward. He went to the kitchen and Jack came in with a bottle.

'Well,' announced Ralph. 'The latest is that Admiral Lord Torrington has been taken to the Tower and replaced by William Russell who has taken command of the navy.'

'I heard as much,' said Heracles. 'Russell is a fine man and I am willing to bet that Torrington will go to the scaffold in the end.'

'Flora,' said Ralph, suddenly emboldened by the effects of the wine. 'May I ask you something which I think we have to discuss?'

'Would you like me to withdraw?' asked Heracles tactfully.

'No, Mr Prior, there are no secrets from you, and yes, I think this is a good time for us all to talk,' replied Flora.

'Your husband, Flora,' said Ralph quietly. 'Will he be returning to the family home?' The question was asked boldly and with no inflection as to the answer. Heracles shifted uneasily in his chair and took a sip of wine. Jack, who had been hovering by the side table, stood frozen to the spot and silence descended on the kitchen as they all waited for an answer.

Flora could not think of one. She looked towards the empty seat at the top of the table and for a moment she wanted to see a husband there, a man who could walk through life with her, a man who would be a good father to their child, a man who would fulfil his obligations to the privileged position he had been born into. Edwin might have proved himself a hero in battle but this new Edwin was a fiction to her, a man she did not know. Was he able to be a hero as a private man, she asked herself? A man who could be hero in the little things of life, the mixed bag of trivia which will compound at the day of judgement. She did not know but Flora could detect a sea change in her brother's heart. After all, he was a young man and his brother-in-law was soon to return and in his extreme youth and enthusiasm he dreamed a dream that all would come right. The boy had suffered enough disillusionment in his life, Flora knew that, and yet she could not find the words her brother wanted to hear.

'I cannot say,' she said quickly.

THIRTY-ONE

The Palace of Whitehall September 1690

Flora went the next morning to Queen Henrietta's chapel at Whitehall, her head filled with the strange dream she had had. It was as if a voice inside her had been telling her what to do. In the dream she had been walking in the tulip garden at Catherine's Court. Edwin was beside her and there were children playing about their feet; at least she thought it was Edwin. However, the man's head always had the sun behind it, obscuring her focus so that it was merely a silhouette surrounded by a golden light. But the feeling she had when she woke with a start, thinking there was someone in the room, was of peace and contentment such as she had rarely experienced. At first she was reluctant to leave the sleeping world, which reveals so much of an inner world, but gradually the dream began to fade, and left her with confusion and bewilderment.

It was many months since she had opened her heart to a man of God with whom she could share her secrets in confidence. The old King James had a confessor who had managed to reach a compromise in his faith, and he now practised a high Anglican worship which sat happily with the court and the present King and Queen. A practical man, Father Daniel was that rare thing, a holy man who stood outside himself and entered the heart of those who sought a path to God without prejudice or bias.

It was early and the building was still cold from a thick early autumn mist. The temperature had dropped in mid-August and there was a feeling that the summer was coming to an end and the languid days of indecision would soon be a thing of the past. Flora felt that now she couldn't go on letting her life meander in the quiet pastures in which she had been planning the domestic routine of Paternoster Row and the creation of the refuge.

Father Daniel was celibate, but all the same he was aware of the beauty of the female form. He thought, as he saw the young woman waiting for him, that her beauty was a thing to celebrate. He enjoyed the moment when he held his hand to her to be kissed, and dispelled any feelings of guilt as he comforted himself by thinking that, after all, to love beauty is to love God.

'My child,' he said, as she raised her eyes to his face. 'Your faithful servant Sarah sent me word that you wished to see me.'

Her lips lingered delightfully on his hand; he did not withdraw it.

'Father, I have sinned,' she whispered in a barely audible voice. A pigeon took flight and flapped its wings outside the high window. He looked away, thinking quickly about what manner of response he should give to those well-tried words which in past times had opened the way to Catholic confession and absolution and forgiveness.

'We have all sinned,' he said softly, putting a steadying hand below her elbow to raise her. He would of course listen to her confession, but his response would not be, could not be, to give her absolution. He would tell her to pray to God to hear her prayers. Looking at her perfect, almost virginal, features as she looked earnestly at him, he could feel the trouble in her soul but doubted that her sin would be a very great one.

He had often noticed the girl, of course. She was close to the Queen and he knew the priest who had confessed the family. He remembered the girl's father because he had been in the room when the old King's young wife had borne the Catholic heir to the throne, the sad young man who now languished in France. He knew the girl's father Lord Thomas had been a brave man, one of the few who had spoken out when the child was claimed to have been a changeling. Now, of course, he could see that God does indeed move in mysterious ways and gives us what is right, although we don't understand how it happens. William was a good man and England seemed the better for an end to the turbulent years of the Stewarts. The old man had decided there was more than one path to God.

Flora raised a tear-stained face and Father Daniel closed his eyes slightly, as if seeking help from a higher power as indeed he was. With his head still lowered, he took her hand. He did not look directly at her; it was the thing he missed most about the confessional box where the confessor sat behind the grid, anonymous, a vehicle to God. But now there would be intensity, the baring of the tormented soul laid bare before him. He had developed a technique of looking either to the sky from which came the deity, or downwards to the ground, but with his eyes slightly closed, but today the radiance of the girl connected with him in a manner which caused him to turn his face, open his eyes and regard her. She returned his gaze with an almost naive frankness. He noticed she was not wearing a wedding ring and that the simplicity of her gown was like that of a noviciate, with no trace of artifice.

'My child, you must unburden yourself to me. What is this great sin?' he asked, continuing to look at her.

'My husband,' she stammered, 'he is now at the King's side and has proved himself to be brave and good, but . . . ' she hesitated awkwardly, 'he was not ever thus. When I married him I did not know it, but he was keeping the devil's company and he indulged in terrible practices . . . ' She stopped, seeing a look of horror on Father Daniel's face.

'Do you mean a perversion in the marriage bed such as we cannot name?' he asked her quietly. 'If it was, that is a sin for which a woman can leave her marriage. It is against God's teachings,' he said darkly, his voice trembling slightly.

'No, Father, it was not that,' she shot back quickly, only half aware of the sodomy he referred to.

'Continue, my daughter, there is nothing that our God will close His ear to,' said Father Daniel, beginning to wonder what the sin could possibly be which had so devastated this girl.

Flora hesitatingly found the words to explain to him about the opiate, how it changed the man's character and then the violence, the degradation, how he had gambled the family home. She told him all of it. At last he held up a staying hand and the papal ring he still wore under the veil of his sleeve caught the light from the high window and reflected on Flora's face.

'And so where is your sin, surely to be sinned against as you have been cannot be of your doing?' he asked.

'He went away,' she said simply. 'He abused me, the child I was carrying died, and then he came back. He was reformed, or at least I believed he was, I wanted so much to believe it. He had cut away from the men who had turned him into the devil. I thought he had changed. I trusted him, but things conspired and . . . ' She left the words hanging in the air.

'You must go on, my child, however painful it is,' urged Father Daniel gently.

'I lay with another man,' Flora blurted. She looked down and began to feel hot and confused. She put her cloak aside and it fell behind her revealing the artfully draped panels of her dress and Father Daniel saw at once that she was with child.

He thought quickly, and assumed that the child she carried was not her husband's. There were many times when Father Daniel had heard such things, and his thoughts had always been for the child. This was not a world where a child does well without a father. He had prayed for his own redemption when he had advised discretion.

'My child,' he began, 'I see that there are more people in this story than it might have seemed. A child needs a father. Your husband, does he know you are with child?' he asked.

'No Father, I have not seen him for four months since he left and joined the King on his campaign. I thought he had committed a terrible crime and I would not believe his innocence and so I found consolation. Oh why are we so frail?' she went on, wringing her hands. 'But I had suffered so much and I had been betrayed so often, Father,' she stammered, 'I have lost my faith in God, in human nature. I cannot be a wife to my husband. I want to believe but I cannot, and besides, how can I live with my own weakness?'

'Firstly,' Father Daniel said slowly, 'we must believe in the possibility of change. It is what our dear Lord Jesus taught us and, remember, it is the man who makes the life and not the life who makes the man. Your husband has proved himself. I know a little of your circumstances, my child. You should put your faith in the path that has been opened for you. There are times when silence is best. If you can find it in your heart to return to your marriage, my advice is that you should be economical with the truth for the sake of the child. After all, you are a strong young woman, you can have many more children and I know,' he said sagely, 'that many people cannot say with any certainty who their father is.'

'Oh no,' Flora reacted quickly. 'The child is my husband's, of that there is no doubt. I was already carrying when he left.'

Father Daniel made some quick calculations, and thought how quickly this pure young woman had given way to the advances of her lover, how soon after the husband had left the marriage bed. Women were strange creatures, he thought, and not for the first time he was glad that he had chosen the celibate life. He examined his heart and concluded this meeting would be the turning point in the girl's life. His relief in finding that the father of the child was in fact the husband was almost palpable. Much as his advice had been pragmatic, he still knew that deception carries a risk, but sometimes that risk is less than the stark truth.

He had often said as much to a man who wanted to reveal all to his wife after some sort of infidelity and indeed he would never trust a man who would tell the world the truth of his private life. But Father Daniel had seen so much of human flesh made raw, he saw little difference in the eyes of God between a man and a woman except that a woman's primary duty was to her children.

'When does your husband return?' he asked eventually.

'On September the seventh, if the winds are favourable,' replied Flora. 'He will be at the King's side and I am to go with the royal party to welcome them.'

'Ask for God's guidance,' said Father Daniel simply. 'You will be sent a sign, of that I am sure, and you will know at the first glance. The man has seen battle, death and suffering. He will be hardened, he will not be the man you knew, but keep your counsel, my child. Your own happiness will not be found through another person, it is within your own gift. If you take him back you must live together; perhaps you should live together but apart, so that you may find your own compass. And of course,' he said half turning to face her directly so that there would be no mistaking his meaning, 'this love you have had outside your marriage . . . God has many ways of working His mysteries, He will not judge you. But now,' he went on, 'you have been given a gift, a child and you must treasure that gift. Ask yourself what is best for that life? You will of course tell your friend the truth that you carry your husband's child. You will both know what you must do.'

Father Daniel made the sign of the cross on her brow. She gathered her cloak about her and she stood to take leave of him, 'Thank you, Father,' she said softly and walked into the sunlight. Sarah waited for her. The bells in the church across the river began to peal for Morning Prayer, the sound rising and falling across the water much as her own confidence did. She still did not know what would happen. There was not that solid unmovable conviction she had hoped for. Her mind raced and she made her way to the Queen's apartments, aware that her servant and friend looked anxiously at her, seeking some indication of a change of heart. But she saw none.

*   *   *

He found her in the gardens near the Queen's apartments; she had sent word and sensing the urgency of her summons he had come at once. He noticed how pale she looked and quickly sat beside her on a white ornamental seat by a fountain; he put his arm about her and he felt her tighten her shoulders. She looked away. He knew her so well that instinctively he could have said the words for her, but she said them anyway and he listened quietly.

'Are you sure?' he said eventually. 'Sure that you carry Edwin's child, because if it were mine I would take you to Holland, of that there can be no question.'

And oh, as she felt the nearness of him, how she wished it were his child; if it were so she would throw caution to the winds and follow her lover to the ends of the earth.

'No, it is not yours, my dear love,' she said dully.

He was not a man of feeble resolve. There was no choice, and he knew the kind of woman Flora was; that was why he loved her so much, this woman who had restored his faith in the prospect of happiness. He would not make things more difficult for her.

'I have business at home,' he said softly. 'I must leave at dawn, but even though we part I leave a part of my heart with you. If you ever need me you have only to send word.'

She could not watch as he left the garden. She did not want him to know the anguish she felt. But she also felt a strange fatalistic kind of resolve born from the sting of fate's sharp arrow.

CHAPTER THIRTY-TWO

Paternoster Row, September 1690

It had been a strange day. The court had heard that the taciturn King had landed two days before and had only just sent word to the Queen. He would be coming to Hampton Court, their favourite palace outside London, where they were to meet; there would be celebrations the following day and a banquet. Flora had returned home as the Queen set off to meet her husband, claiming a desire for privacy in this emotional moment.

But where was Edwin? No word had come, and the household remained suspended. All of them shared a wish for a happy ending, and looked to their mistress as the arbiter of their future, for the word was out that Lady Grantley was expecting a child. There was no speculation amongst the servants as to the father: the Baron had been no more than a protector. There had been a deal of gossip but Lord Edwin had now redeemed himself and stood absolved from any sin, other than his own immaturity and treatment of his wife, who had proved herself to be a great lady, more than able to run her own affairs.

They waited, her family, like people removed on an island waiting for a kind of rescue, and none more so than Ralph who in his young man's mind was now willing to accept his reinvented brother-in-law. He had been proud when people had acknowledged his sister's husband as a trusted officer in the King's victorious army.

There was a bustle in the street outside. Since the King's victory there had been an infectious feeling of excitement, as if a new dawn had come. England was safe, safe from the threat of an invasion; children could sleep easy in their beds and the bloody reign of the Stewarts. The people were in safe hands; the King and Queen were the embodiment of wise parents.

Flora thought about this as she made her way down the staircase to the parlour below. The days had shortened and the evening meal was nearly ready. Sarah had laid out her dress for the evening. She had been too tired to question the grey dove silk shot with pink and green that Sarah had chosen; and not content with organising her mistress's dress, Sarah had been most insistent that she dress her hair in the long flowing manner that most became her mistress. There was something trembling in the air, which Flora could not quite define.

She had received no word from her husband; she supposed he was at Hampton Court. She could not imagine how he would feel after the last four months. The clock on the mantle struck with a tinkling chime in the quiet house and she thought about the time not so very far off when there would be the cry of a baby. She sat down in a chair by the window that opened onto the small garden at the back of the house and she had a longing to be back at Catherine's Court.

Jack came quietly into the room. 'Shall I put a light to the fire, my Lady?' he asked solicitously. Then for some reason the dogs Hera and Diana stood up and began to tremble with all the signs of recognition and pleasure that pre-empted the arrival of a welcome guest. She stilled them and they sat obediently.

'Yes, light the fire, Jack. Do we expect someone?' she asked sadly, wishing for things she could hardly name.

'No, my Lady. Just family,' he said. The flames burst into life and her dress took on a shimmering reflection. She closed her eyes for a moment as in a daydream. All at once she felt a presence in the room. She kept her eyes closed for a moment, for she felt all was well. It was the feeling she used to have when she sat by the fireside with her father, a time she had never revisited. There was a hand on hers.

'My beautiful Lady. My beloved wife,' said a soft voice. She opened her eyes and there before her was the face of a man, it was a man she hardly recognised. He gathered her in his arms, this man. She felt his arms enfold her. She stood and he felt the curve of her body, his hand went to the folds of her dress which hung carefully sculptured to her voluptuous curves.

'I will take care of you, if you will let me,' this new man said. His hand strayed to her cheek, not the soft hand she remembered, but hard and worn, as a true man's.

They stood together until there was a knock on the door. It was Sarah. Without a flicker of surprise she looked at them steadily. She curtsied to Edwin, seeing at once the thing she had begun to hope for.

'The family is waiting for you. The meal is ready, your Lordship, my Lady,' she said, as if it were the most normal thing in the world.

Flora turned as Edwin bowed and she caught sight of their reflection in the mirror above the fireplace. Suddenly the evening sun dipped behind the roofs outside the window, bathing them in a golden light; the green and pink of the dress shot dancing light, like the petals of an exotic flower. They both saw it.

'You see, it is a sign,' he said. 'There you are, the embodiment of Flora's Glory.'

Epilogue

My name is Alice; it is the name my mother gave me. She died as she was giving birth to me. But I am lucky. In spite of this, I had a family, and they were called Grantley. I was born in the Amalie Foundling Home in Paternoster Row in the city of London on April 22nd, the year of our Lord 1699.

I was the first baby to be born there, and the very great Lady who started the home, Lady Flora, was my benefactor. She took me into her own family, and I was given the same privileges as her own children, of which there were seven. Lord Grantley was a fine man and became Lor d Mayor of the city. A more devoted pair it was hard to imagine. The greatest gift that the Grantleys gave me was love, but it was Lady Flora who gave me learning and that is a gift beyond anything. She was the first woman botanist and her exquisite drawings are preserved for posterity in rare collections all over the world. She was admired by men and women alike but she was not afraid to put herself forward in a man's world. She never wavered in her view that anything is possible if you have faith in yourself and that luck comes to a prepared mind. It was her example which has enabled me to become the woman I am and live the life I have had.

I am old now, in my seventieth year, and I look back on my life with such gratitude. I often think of the Lady Flora; she had a quiet wisdom, as if she had suffered, and I am sure she had, for she was born in troubled times. But although she treated me as her own daughter she never spoke of these things. I did not marry; the Foundling Home became my life. When I was no more than twenty I became the warden. Each child that was born there and saved from a horrible death became in a sense my own.

I was with her when she died, ten years after her husband, in the beautiful house in the county of Suffolk. She was surrounded by the many things she loved, her famous garden, her strange thin dogs and her many children and grandchildren, but it was to me that she whispered her last words; for it was ever my fancy, God forgive me, that despite the lack of blood ties, I was always closest to her. It was the faintest of whispers and no one else heard, but I treasure the words. 'We gave them life,' she said. 'But that is not enough, Alice, we have a duty to show them how to live it.'